# WHISKEY LIMA GOLF

# DARIN DANCE

Titles available in the White Rabbit Investigations series
(in reading order):

Whiskey Lima Golf

# WHISKEY LIMA GOLF

## DARIN DANCE

ISBN: 978-0-473-64401-7

ISBN: 978-0-473-64402-4 POD

ISBN: 978-0-473-64403-1 Epub

ISBN: 978-0-473-64404-8 Kindle

Cover Design:    Ted D Hughes

Photography:    Michael Steven Harris Photography

*For all those people with dreams...*

*Go get them!*

*E koekoe te tūi,*

*E ketekete te kākā,*

*E kūkū te kererū.*


*The Tūī chatters,*

*The parrot gabbles,*

*The wood pigeon coos.*


*It takes all kinds of people*

# Contents

Chapter 1 – The Village
Chapter 2 – Reality Sets In
Chapter 3 – Homecoming
Chapter 4 – One Step Forward…
Chapter 5 – Cosmopolitan Caffeine
Chapter 6 – The Veteran Returns
Chapter 7 – Concourse Disputes
Chapter 8 – New Toys
Chapter 9 – Given Notice
Chapter 10 – New Friends
Chapter 11 – The French Connection
Chapter 12 – Mediterranean Tagine
Chapter 13 – Observations and Preparations
Chapter 14 – Miramar Meetings
Chapter 15 – Party With Marty
Chapter 16 – Missing Persons
Chapter 17 – Portside Shenanigans

Characters
Glossary
Dictionaries
Acknowledgements
About the Author

# Chapter One - The Village

*Afghanistan - Summer*

BULLETS THUD RHYTHMICALLY into the building. Crumbling masonry falls onto his helmet and shoulders. Finally he sees his target creep into his telescopic sights, before dropping out of vision again.

Quickly refocusing, he sees the man in black robes at the door of a village hut. He is yelling at the people inside, stepping back, constantly on the move. Transferring his aim, Tom is momentarily frozen, staring in disbelief. The man in black raises his AK-74M and ruthlessly guns down the villagers as they emerge from the doorway. Then the man runs forward, ducking behind a low wall. "Shit," is all Tom says.

"Frickin' bastards," Brett yells as he opens fire on the zone he is covering.

"Tango Delta, this is Whiskey Lima Golf, we need that air support now…" The familiar voice of Tom's leader and best friend Devon, barks into the SINCGARS radio. "…Three…four…nine-a…" his voice is cut off abruptly by the sound of a mortar round exploding to his left. Next comes the whine of a close ricochet to his right, more incoming fire from the approaching black-clad enemy troops.

"They're flanking us, eight x-ray's at 10 o'clock." Trevor calmly relays the information.

"Dammit, we need that air support NOW! Not in five minutes…" Devon demands, before calling to the team, "Hang in there boys, the Yanks are going to be late to the party. Again."

"No surprise there," Brett mutters to his right. Tom hears the distinctive click of a new round being loaded into his M203 grenade launcher.

Tom wipes the sweat from his forehead to prevent any disturbance for his shot. He refocuses on the man who has led the attack on the village, waiting for him to emerge from behind the stone wall.

The familiar rattle of Trevor's FN Minimi light machinegun opens fire in short bursts to his left as his target finally breaks cover, standing to wave on the next assault at their defensive position.

Ignoring the chaotic sounds of battle surrounding him, he releases his breath slowly, feeling the coolness ruffle the hairs on his hand as he squeezes the trigger, and his world suddenly erupts into noise, flames and screaming…

***

When he regains consciousness, Tom almost wishes he hadn't, as a wave of excruciating pain overwhelms him.

"Hang in there, Tom. It's gonna hurt a bit 'til this kicks in," Devon yells as he slams a morphine auto jet into his arm and then proceeds to quickly and efficiently wrap emergency dressings over Tom's leg and hip.

The piercing pain is agonising, a wave of torment almost causing Tom to black out again. Steeling himself, he spits out between his gritted teeth, "Geez-us man! What happened?"

"We got hit by a few mortar rounds before the Yanks

arrived and levelled the village," Devon shakes his head. "Medevac should be here soon, brother. At least we got some of the villagers out before the attack."

Another wave of pain racks his body. Tom waits until it subsides then struggles to sit. "How bad..?"

"Hey, lie down!" Devon commands, "Brett and some of second stick are still down there clearing the village. There could be some more x-rays out there."

"How bad..?"

"You'll live brother. Ah, here's the cavalry."

The distinctive rapid whumph, whumph of a troop of UH-60 Blackhawk helicopters is heard getting closer. Devon's radio squawked. He jabs a second morphine auto jet into Tom's arm and pats him on the shoulder, smiling "Back soon brother. Try and relax." He reaches for the radio, all business again. "Dustoff three ten, come in…"

Tom's awareness drifts as the morphine starts its medicinal magic. He wonders how the pain knows to splinter off in so many different directions, chasing his thoughts, and blurring in his mind.

Time, motion and reality pass erratically under his drug-induced haze. Tom imagines mini whirlwinds of dust turn into towering genies, rising up and tussling amongst themselves, all created by the rotor wash of the Medevac UH-60 helicopter as it descends, the phantasms grudgingly dissolve into each other as the greyish green beast, with its bright red cross splashed on the side, lands.

Brown and khaki clad crew discharge from the beast's belly straddling a stretcher between them, race towards him.

Devon and a flight medic lift him gently onto the stretcher, which glides gracefully into the helicopter. Devon's floating voice follows him, "You take care of my brother… Tom, we will see you soon…"

Another jab in his arm, the flight medic fixes a line into his forearm. "Getting some plasma into you, dude. You've lost a bit of blood."

The engine's pitch turns into a whine as the beast lifts gracefully back into the sky.

Finally feeling safe and able to relax, Tom's mind lets go and he falls gratefully into oblivion.

\*\*\*

*Afghanistan Bagram Airbase Hospital - Next Day*

The light reflects off the cream-panelled walls, his friends awkwardly gather around his hospital bed.

"It's boring as in here," Tom grumbles, fiddling with the intravenous line connecting him to a bag of lifesaving plasma.

"What? With all these pretty nurses?" Devon gestures towards the hard working women in their blue scrubs.

"Yeah man, how many phone numbers have you scored?" Brett asks, eyeing up a blonde nurse tending to another soldier on the opposite side of the ward.

"Not to mention hot food. Trevor points out a half-eaten meal on a tray. "Bloody holiday camp this. Are you going to finish that? No? Good, I'll take it off your hands, now when are you coming back? I can't be doing with breaking in another recruit."

"I dunno Trev, they aren't telling me much." His frustration is clearly evident in his voice.

"George will get some answers brother. He can't be far away, 'cause he told us to meet him here," Devon reassures the team. "So how's the leg and the pain?"

"Well, I was told I was in surgery for five hours while they stitched me back together yesterday and they keep me topped up with local anaesthetic so I can't feel much apart from a dull ache. But enough about me. You haven't told me, what happened back at the village? I mean where did all those x-rays come from? There was nothing about a small Army in Kendrick's briefing."

"Especially bloody mortars," Brett fumes, his hand automatically rubbing the fresh stitches in his face.

"What are you complaining about Brett? Those new beauty marks will improve your chances with the nurses," Trevor playfully punches Brett in the arm.

"Ten-hut! Officer on deck!" a young Marine guard at the wards' entrance bellows.

The American soldiers visiting their friends, quickly stand to attention, as a tall copper-haired well-groomed officer strides into the ward. "At ease for crying out loud. This is a hospital!" The Kiwi accented officer demands.

"SIR! YES SIR! SIR!" the confused young Marine bawls as he goes from attention to at ease and back to attention.

"Oh for Pete's sake!" The officer cries, turns to the marine "Look Private, my men aren't at attention, not because they aren't showing respect, but because we are A in an active zone of conflict and B because we are in a hospital! Just chill out! You are not on a parade ground here Private! At bloody ease!"

The red-faced Marine, drops back into the at-ease stance, wishing that either his relief would arrive quickly or the earth would open up under his feet and swallow him.

Devon stands smiling and acknowledges the officer as he approaches Tom's bed, "Captain Gillies, any news?"

"Gentlemen, Tom. Hell's teeth, where do I start?"

Captain Gillies asks himself, running a hand through his hair, "Okay, knock off the Captain shit Devon. Trevor, acquire a wheelchair as Tom needs to hear this as well but we need some privacy. There's a doctor's office down the hall that Kendrick has commandeered."

"Sure thing George," Trevor purposely walks off stalking his new prey.

"Okay Tom, about your injury," George takes a seat beside Tom's bed and starts to explain, "Mate, the good news is it's not fatal and you get an early ticket home."

"I somehow didn't think I'd be playing any rugby soon," Tom wisecracks, putting on a brave face. "So the bad news…"

"Well, according to these doctors, they managed to get most of the shrapnel out and prevent an amputation, but there's a pile of nerve and tissue damage in your hip and leg." George pauses and grimaces, "Well, there's no easy way to say this, but they reckon that you won't walk unaided again."

His last statement leaves every one of the team speechless.

Trevor bursts back into the ward with a wheelchair, spinning the chair around as he pushes it next to Tom's bed, "Come on, Sunshine, here's your new wheels." Then he notices the silence, "Who's the party pooper?"

Everyone looks at the wheelchair as George's words sink in. Tom realises that if he can't walk, he's out of the troop and probably the Army. He will lose his SAS family. His military career is over. Slowly shaking his head in disbelief. Unbidden tears start at the corner of his eyes. Hurriedly he wipes his eyes.

Seeing the tears, Trevor understands he is missing some important information. Ever the joker he lightens the mood by sniffing the air exaggeratedly. "Did someone drop one? Brett did you let one of your cabbage ones go? God, no wonder everyone is glassy-eyed! New Zealand's own version of weapons of mass destruction! You should be only brought out when we're right in the shit!"

Brett stands up protesting, "Not even ow!"

The team bursts out laughing, the tension eases.

"I'm definitely gonna miss that humour," Tom replies wistfully.

"Come on troops, let's get Tom in that contraption very gently and off to that debrief," George commands.

\*\*\*

"About goddamned time," Kendrick mutters.

Two people occupy the doctor's office as the team enter. General Adams is sitting behind the desk while Kendrick is perched on the edge.

"We had some transport issues, Kendrick," George nods to the other officer, "Afternoon General."

Trevor holds the door open as Devon squeezes the wheelchair through the door frame, Brett making sure the IV line keeps pace with the chair. Tom seeing the occupants, wonders, 'Why is the General here?'

An immaculately dressed General Frank Adams rises from his chair, as Trevor closes the door, "Gentlemen, thank you for coming. I know it's a bit of a squeeze but I'm sure you have been in tighter situations before," he starts attempting some humour. His steely blue gaze rests on Tom, "Son, I trust you are getting the best attention here at the Craig Joint Theatre Hospital."

"Thank you, Sir, there are others far worse off than me here."

"Outstanding. Now straight to business. I don't have much time before the next operation kicks off." General Adams continues, "I've read your preliminary report Captain, but we want your soldier's impressions of Operation Crimson Sky. Kendrick."

"Thank you General, Crimson Sky was particularly successful," Kendrick takes over, looking towards Devon with distaste, "Perhaps we will start with you Sergeant?"

Devon takes his sand-coloured beret off and runs a hand through his unruly hair, "Well, everything went smoothly until we got to the village and then TARFU. I mean the Helo insert went well. Our approach was undetected. We set up cover firing positions and then we approached the contacts' rendezvous spot outside the village."

"Yes, yes, that is all covered in the preliminary report, boy," Kendrick rushes, "Was there anything unusual at all?"

Bristling at the use of the derogatory term, 'boy' his eyes narrow, but staying professional Devon continues, "Our contact seemed very nervous, more so than I expected. I mean we've done plenty of these 'collections' before, where we go in and arrest an insurgent leader and get him back to your mob for ah 'tactical questioning'." The sarcasm dripped off the last word, "and they have gone off without a hitch. The intel on the size of the suspects 'protection' squad was clearly incorrect."

An angry Trevor pipes up, "You said six bodyguards Kendrick, six! Not one hundred and sixty with technicals and bloody mortars!"

The General breaks his silence, "Hmm, what happened there Kendrick?"

Clearly looking uncomfortable, Kendrick replies, "It appears that we had a slight translation error, the contractor assigned wasn't as fluent in Dari as we were led to believe. His Farsi was first class but…"

"Oh for fu…, you used contractors to translate? What about the second translation?" George demands.

"Standard Agency best practise is to only use one translator these days, saves time and money," Kendrick explains, "but we got caught out this time."

"No YOU didn't," Devon interrupts cynically, "WE got caught out."

The General steers the conversation, "Thank you, son for bringing the consequences home to us. Any other impressions any of you had?"

Devon replies, "Yes sir, these combatants were very well trained, their main group attempted fire suppression on our position while using a flanking manoeuvre."

"And their mortar crew only launched two sighting rounds before they had the precise range and accuracy of our position," Brett contributes.

"The numbers and expert training suggests outside influence," George sums up, "as in, I don't believe that this was your average Afghani Taliban unit."

Tom pipes up, "It appeared that the leader and most of his troops were dressed in black. Was this an ISIS group? I thought your lot had taken them out?"

General Adams sighs, "It appears that a militant breakaway group from the Taliban have formed calling themselves Daesh-Khorasan. If you're correct, it seems they are a lot larger than we suspected."

"And they have expanded their active areas from the Pakistani border, where we have been concentrating our green berets efforts," Kendrick admits.

"Their leader was vicious, he gunned down a family in cold blood after ordering them out of their home," Tom reports with a haunted look in his eyes. "He was constantly moving and I couldn't get a bead on him in time…"

Devon gently touches Tom's shoulder. "We do what we can brother," then continuing, "Our contact was clearly under pressure. I suspect the insurgents had his family hostage. My Dari isn't that good, but he knew a little German and he alerted us that the leader was arriving soon with more insurgents. That's when we started evacuating the village."

"That wasn't part of the operation," Kendrick cut in angrily, "you were tasked with capturing the leader."

"General, if I may say so," George speaks up, "this operation was clearly flawed with such poor Intel, that a capture was a remote possibility at best. I have stated in the past unofficially, but now I want it on the record that we Kiwis should have total control of the missions we are assigned, instead of being treated as the hired help."

"And how would you have carried out the mission differently Captain?" General Adams asks.

"I would have inserted a recon team first before the capture team was deployed. The recon team would have assessed the actual situation and would have provided accurate Intel on insurgent numbers. Then they could have given an early warning about the insurgent reinforcements entering the village as well as providing additional fire support." George's voice has risen. "Instead we get half-arsed information and a faulty plan that compromises my men's lives and the mission."

"Now wait just a goddamn minute," Kendrick explodes.

"Gentlemen!" General Adams intervenes, "Kendrick, you can wait for me in my office."

A red-faced Kendrick starts, "I don't take orders…"

"DISMISSED!" The General cuts him off.

Trevor grins and holds the door open clearly enjoying the Agency man's fall from grace.

Kendrick storms from the room. Passing George he hisses, "Kiss your career goodbye Captain, I'll get you yet."

"I know an apology is well-deserved to you and your men, Captain Gillies, and I will kick some ass and get to the bottom of this," General Adams begins, "This theatre of operations is all going to hell and it looks like we will all be recalled soon. In fact, that's one of the reasons I wanted to see you, was to pass these orders on to you."

Standing he hands an envelope to Captain Gillies.

George tears the envelope open and scans the document.

"In short Gentlemen," the General explains, "your government has decided to recall all of its personnel A-sap. I wanted to personally deliver this news and thank you for your outstanding contribution to our operations here." The General continues, "I won't repeat this officially of course, but there is no way our Green Berets would have got out of that last mission without more loss of life."

"Geez Wayne, we're going home!" Brett exclaims.

George walks towards the General, comes to attention and salutes, "It's been an honour sir."

The General returns the salute and extends his hand, locking George's hand in a firm grip, "Likewise Captain, Gentlemen, a C-17 will be ready to transport you all home this evening." Looking at Tom the General adds, "That's including you son, there will be a medical crew on board to make sure you get home in one piece."

"Well men, let's get squared away, Devon will you ensure Tom's personal effects are sorted," George orders.

"Captain, if there is any interference from Kendrick or anyone else, send them to me, understood?"

"Understood General, sir," George salutes.

\*\*\*

## Chapter Two – Reality Sets In

*Auckland - Middlemore Hospital – Early Spring*

*A Week Later*

HOISTING HIMSELF ONTO his bed from the wheelchair causes Tom another wave of pain to shudder through his hip. Through gritted teeth, he swings his right leg up before gently using his left hand to guide his unresponsive left leg onto the bed. After a deep breath, Tom pulls the starched white cotton sheet up to hide his disfigured legs and eases himself back onto the pillows. His breath hisses slightly as he exhales.

He hears a familiar voice in the hall outside his room, "No I won't be long." Devon opens his door and greets him enthusiastically, "Kia ora e hoa! When are you getting out of this dump, eh?"

"Not soon enough, my brother from another mother," Tom grumbles, "They want to keep me here until I'm on crutches and god knows how long that will be."

"Knowing you, about five minutes, brother," Devon grins.

"Hey, it's only about 1400," Tom realises, "you're here early, what's up?"

"I've got all the goss for you. The whole team is breaking up! Okay, where to start?" Devon pauses.

"You're kidding!" Tom exclaims.

"Nah bro, after the Brass medically discharged you, and stuck you in this rat hole," Devon gestures to the peeling paint and thread bare curtains in his room, "the whole team got right fed up and we all started looking at our options."

"Yeah, our public health system sure needs some money spent on it," Tom agrees, "It's got nothing on Craig Joint Hospital in Bagram. Those Yanks have all the shiny new equipment."

"Damned straight there. Okay the news." Devon sounds excited. "First up, good ol' George has been seconded to the SIS and is already in Wellington."

"Wow that sounds cool!" Tom enthuses, momentarily forgetting his pain.

"Brett has resigned and is chasing the big money as a private military contractor. He flies out for orientation in Florida tonight!"

"Far out. Well, he always was reading those old Soldier of Fortune magazines, so I guess it was on the cards."

"Trevor has also quit and bought a big game charter fishing company up in the Bay of Islands."

"Whoa! So that's why he was always penny pinching? Good on him." Tom looks directly at Devon. "So, what about you?"

Devon beams. "I got a job offer from George and I'm off to spooks school."

"You're what?" Tom exclaims, then grins, "Should you even be telling me?"

"No secrets between us, brother." Devon winks. "Besides, you and Koro are my whanau. Officially I've been rotated to some boring Defence Department admin job in Wellington. But my question to you, Tom, is what are you going to do when you get outta here?"

Tom sighs in resignation, "I talked to Koro last night and he said to move back in with him once I'm released. And to have a think about what I really want to do. Maybe go to Vic and get a degree in something."

Devon smiles his trademark wicked grin. "Good, if you're staying at the station with Koro then we can hit the gym together. You never did tell me how he scored that flat, such a sweet location."

"I know right! Wellington Railway station has always been home, but that's Koro's tale to tell."

"And the gym, you up for that?" Devon prompts.

"Sure, why not? I mean that's if you're not off with all those sexy foreign agents," Tom laughs. "It will be great to have a familiar face back home."

***

*Langley, Virginia - Same Day*

"Good morning Kendrick. Close the door behind you and take a seat." The bespectacled overweight man swivels his chair from the expansive view of the trees from his corner office, and faces his visitor. He picks up a piece of paper from his immaculately clean desk. "It appears you had patchy results in Afghanistan. This summary report of yours is obviously incomplete. What I want to know is what you are leaving out and why."

Immediately on the back foot, the normally confident man knows that he must answer in just the right way to keep his job. "Sir, if I may speak frankly," he pauses receiving a nod from his boss, "we had so many leaks over there, I couldn't trust anyone. Not the Intel we were receiving from any of our in-country assets. Our so-called NATO 'partners' were too busy with their own in-fighting to be effective. I'm sure someone was hacking into our intranet, so our online systems were compromised, and we know the Chinese and Russians were monitoring our voice Comms and probably supplying Intel to either Al-Qaeda or IS-Khorasan. Our Afghan allies are a joke, you might as well have invited the Taliban to any briefing we held with them. And you always looked twice at any Afghani policeman to see if they were wearing a bomb vest under their uniform. And those Aussies and Kiwis were so goddamned independent you couldn't trust them to complete a simple job without going all PC, questioning everything and following UN engagement rules. To be honest sir, this was one hell of an assignment."

"I see you haven't lost your sense of humour then," the overweight man smiles briefly, then frowning, continues, "We've taken some flack over Operation Crimson Sky. Too many civilian casualties, and just where did that footage come from that Al Jazeera are using?"

"Over a hundred and fifty terrorists dead, about forty civilians and one injured Kiwi are not bad odds. Besides the Kiwis got twenty or so civilians out before the firefight got out of control," Kendrick summarises. "As for the footage, it wasn't ours. I'd speculate that from the angle it was taken and the lack of focus, it was probably IS-Khorasan from a hilltop hoping to showcase a victory over our Special Forces."

"You know that Washington want a sacrificial lamb for the networks prime-time altar over that footage." The obese man grimaces as he takes his spectacles off and absently cleans them with his handkerchief. "And some voices upstairs are questioning your value."

Kendrick stiffens, awaiting his fate, not sure how to

proceed.

"Kendrick, you saved my neck in Algeria, so I've stuck mine out for you now." He puts his spectacles back on and continues. "You have two options. The first is to retire with a small bonus into your 401(k) retirement plan."

"Thank you, sir, but I'm only 52, I'm too young to stagnate. What's plan B?"

"Did you read the latest Council for Foreign Relations survivability report on mass extinction events?"

"Ah, not yet, sir. Are we talking nuclear war or climate change?" Kendrick is interested despite his predicament.

"Both and anything else they could think of, short of an alien invasion." The stout man grins at his own joke. "The two sensible options are Iceland and one other. Iceland is out, as it's still in the Northern Hemisphere and will probably be affected by nuclear fallout. The other option is already known as a bolthole for the rich and famous and some Tech giants, who have already relocated some of their technical knowhow there. And there has been a proliferation of new embassies and High Commissions opening." He smiles. "Kendrick how would you like a new assignment at the bottom of the world."

"Surely not Antarctica, sir?"

"Almost… Wellington, New Zealand. It's about to become the hottest spot on the planet in the Cold War right now." He breaks into a big grin. "Once you arrive that is."

\*\*\*

# Chapter Three - Homecoming

*Wellington – Summer - Four Months Later – Tuesday*

THE SIGHT OF the familiar red brick building fills Tom with a strange mix of emotions, sadness that he has somehow failed in his chosen career, and happiness that he is coming home to his only surviving family member, his Koro. Tears prick his eyes as the slowing train rounds the final bend passing the familiar blue Kiwi Connection commuter train and he sees the venerable leathery weather-beaten man, his mouth moving while gesturing with his intricately carved Tokotoko enthusiastically. Tom wonders what Tauparapara Koro is chanting while standing at the end of Platform Nine formally greeting the train's arrival.

Tom automatically waves and starts gathering his few possessions into his brown leather shoulder bag, headphones, phone and a battered second-hand paperback that a nurse had given him for the journey. The old Northerner train service from Auckland to Wellington had been recently reinstated to run the opposite direction to the Northern Explorer to provide a consistent same day passenger service between the two cities, a small concession to combating climate change from the previous government coalition. He pulls the straps of his small backpack, containing his few civilian clothes, over his shoulders and grabs his crutches. Edging his way out of his seat into the centre aisle he slowly makes his way towards the nearest exit, the train slowing to a stop. He gauges the gap and swings onto the platform, turns and heads towards his Koro.

He hears the deep gravelly voice chanting a familiar karakia;
"Tukua te wairua kia rere ki ngā taumata
Hai ārahi i ā tātou mahi
Me tā tātou whai i ngā tikanga a rātou mā
Kia mau kia ita
Kia kore ai e ngaro
Kia pupuri
Kia whakamaua
Kia tina! TINA! Hui e! TĀIKI E!"*

*Allow one's spirit to exercise its potential
To guide us in our work as well as in our pursuit of our ancestral traditions
Take hold and preserve it
Ensure it is never lost
Hold fast.
Secure it.
Draw together! Affirm!

"Te hei, mauri ora," Tom responds, tears openly running down his cheeks. "Koro it's so good to see you."

Koro steps closer and puts one hand firmly on Tom's arm. They both lean forward, their foreheads and noses touching slightly as they inhale each other's breath through their nostrils, completing the ancient Māori greeting.

"Ah, come here boy and give your Koro a proper hug," the old man commands.

Tom manages a one-armed hug as he balances his weight on the remaining crutch, nearly toppling them both onto the platform.

As they break their embrace, Koro comments, "Look at the two of us, eh? What a fine pair we make. Hey you're looking good boy."

Wiping the tears from his cheeks with his sleeve, Tom pivots on his crutches and starts the slow shuffle along Platform Nine towards the concourse entrance. "Thanks Koro, hope you've got some good old-fashioned hospitality waiting at home."

Koro feigns a look of mock offence, "You wash your mouth out boy, huh, how dear you question my manaakitanga eh?"

Pushing his luck, Tom smiles, "If you call a soft, stale gingernut and a twice brewed tea bag manaakitanga? Then I guess I'll have to accept it."

"Bloody cheek! You'll keep boy!" Koro exclaims, with a big grin.

"Go on, admit it, you've missed that cheek." Tom laughs, "It's good to be home Koro, I've missed you too."

Once through the entrance onto the concourse, they are intercepted by a waiting black uniformed man with a yellow Hi-Viz vest, sporting a wicked smile, "That was an unsanctioned ceremony on our platform Mr Yelich. I must remind you that you are not permitted to perform such ceremonies without the correct authorisation. I am to inform you that any further breaches of Kiwirail policy will result in your eviction from all Kiwirail property."

"I was welcoming my mokopuna back from…," Koro begins before getting cut off.

"Whatever, just know that I'm watching you, Yelich," the black clad man threatens.

Tom notices the man's footwear and accurately aims his crutches for his next step.

"...any more breaches of Kiwirail policy and I'll have you out of that cushy flat of yours so fast, AARRGGH!"

"Oh, aroha mai mate. Still getting used to these sticks here," Tom mockingly apologies, "You must have forgotten your safety footwear today, I wonder if that's a policy breach?"

"Come on Tom, let's leave Mr Dunkell to his policies and get the kettle on, eh?" Koro laughs.

Limping off towards his office, the man shouts, "I'll get you Yelich, do you hear me? I'll get you!"

***

With the front door to the noisy concourse closed behind them, Koro states, "You are probably better on the stairs than me, you go first and get the kettle on."

In the flat, Tom manoeuvres past the storage boxes and old furniture to head up the stairs to the living area, questioning himself, 'I wonder how big this area actually is? It's always been full of junk.'

Koro is surprised to see Tom rapidly ascend the stairs to the next level. "Pretty fast boy, is that another Army trick?"

"Nah Koro, I just find it way easier going up stairs on my sticks, going down is a whole other story." Tom dodges the old furniture in the living area, peeling his bags off his frame, placing them beside his old armchair before making his way into the kitchenette.

Koro gets to the top of the stairs and puffs, "How long are you going to keep using those sticks?"

"I don't know, the doctors reckon I'll always need

help walking. They were amazed at how fast I got out of the wheelchair. Man, it's good to be home." Tom eyes two relatively clean mugs. He pops a teabag and spoon in one, while the electric jug slowly gets up to temperature. He opens the pantry door and scans the contents, hunting for some treasure.

"They're in the green tin," Koro grunts taking a seat in his armchair. "Never trust those pākehā doctors. They just want to sell you pills. You know, I think I'll have a talk to Sheila. She might have some rongoā that will help."

Tom finds the tin and takes the lid off. Surprised at the contents, he brandishes his prize, waving it towards his grandfather, "Hey, chocolate biscuits. You've been splashing out, old man."

"It's a special occasion," Koro defends himself.

The electric kettle loudly clicks as it reaches its climax. Tom splashes the hot water into both the cups. Quickly removing the tea bag from the first cup he stirs the teabag briskly in the second. He is startled as Koro appears beside him, "Sit down boy, I'll take it from here."

Obediently, Tom slides his arms back into the crutches and makes his way to his designated armchair, turns and gently lowers himself into his seat.

"I could have done without seeing that halfwit in the station," Tom states.

"Oh that jumped up little pen-pusher. He's just trying to make a name for himself."

"He does seem full of himself. What's this eviction nonsense he's talking about?"

Koro puts the tea tray down on the dented wooden coffee table. "You know, I think he's jealous that we have this flat and he wants me out."

"But that's not fair. This is our home. Besides, you

have a perpetual lease from the top dog in Kiwirail, after saving all those people's lives. He can't evict you, can he?"

"You're right, I don't think he can," Koro smiles, recalling, "That was a good move, but I don't think we should annoy him too much, so watch where you put your crutches next time. Now, shall I phone Sheila?"

Safe and content in the familiar surroundings, Tom takes a biscuit from the tray. "Sure, why not. As long as I don't have to drink those foul-tasting teas of hers."

\*\*\*

*Tuesday Evening*

Tom eases himself into the folding chair, letting out a sigh of relief. "You don't appreciate just how many stairs we have here at Koro's until you are using these damn things. Now tell me what spook life is like, bro."

Devon takes a seat next to Tom. "That's why we need to get back to the gym, to get those skinny legs of yours back into shape. I've scoped out a couple that are close by. Les Mills up on Lambton Quay and a small personal trainer running out of the old Tramways building nearby."

"No way! On the corner of Mulgrave and Thorndon?"

"Yeah, I thought we could take a look tomorrow after work."

Tom turns to take in the view from the flat's balcony window. The contrast between concrete and steel offices and apartments and the rolling waves of the deep blue harbour constantly in motion, strikes him as relaxing. This is the home where he grew up, this cosmopolitan city constantly punished by the extremes of wild storms, king tides and driving rain only relieved occasionally by the rare fine day that Wellingtonians are so boastful of. This is his tūrangawaewae, his home, the place where he can recover and stand on his own feet again. A thin train of thought blossoms into hope, maybe, just maybe, he can walk again without these damn sticks. "I reckon that's a great idea Dev," he says, turning back to Devon, "but you can't get out of it so easily. What's work like? Come on, spill the tea."

"Hang on a minute bro, I'll just set this up." Devon takes a small portable speaker out of his bag, then tapping his phone to get some music going, he adjusts the volume with a swipe of his finger.

"Nice beat, who is it?"

"An oldie I heard at the gym. A Kiwi crew, L.A.B." Adjusting the volume until he is satisfied that their conversation will not be listened into, Devon leans towards Tom. "Okay e hoa, well I can't really say too much, but it's kinda like Recon."

"Go on," Tom prompts, then he suddenly grimaces, bends forward and clutches his leg, as a crackling wave of pain surges from his knee up through his hip and into his brain. "Geez-us!"

"Tom, are you okay?"

Leaning back in his chair, Tom releases a deep breath, "Yeah… I get these jolts every now and then."

"Is that, well, normal?"

"The Doc said that the nerve damage is so severe that it will continue for some time. It's frustrating because it's so unpredictable and I can't take anything for it. But enough of me and my injury, tell me more about your role."

"Okay, well there's lots of sitting around in cars, cafés or apartments watching people and seeing who they talk to or what they are up to."

"Exactly like Recon then, so no fancy gadgets or hooking up with drop-dead gorgeous Russian women spies then?"

Devon laughs. "Oh yeah, I forgot to tell you that Sasha and Tatianna will be here soon with the caviar and vodka."

"Now you're talking! We'd better get a couple more chairs then."

Devon takes a bottle wrapped in a brown paper bag and passes it to Tom, "Make yourself useful and open this will you?" He unwraps a couple of tumblers from a tea towel setting them on the side table between them.

A low whistle escapes Tom's lips, "Nice. I might have known you'd bring a single malt, Aerstone eh? Let's see, matured in a warehouse by the sea. Well then, a wee dram brother?" Tom lifts the bottle out of the box, and picks at the black metal seal. Soon it is off and he puts it on the table, before twisting the cork stopper out and pouring golden amber liquid into the waiting tumblers. They both raise their glasses, "Sláinte!"

"Definitely a salty finish," Tom muses, "and…"

"Yeah, and I'm getting a touch of vanilla, nice legs too," Devon considers, noticing the tear drops of scotch rolling down the side of his glass.

The two friends spend the evening getting their whisky nerd on, trading scotch terms back and forth.

\*\*\*

# Chapter Four – One Step Forward…

*Wednesday Evening*

THE SWEET MIXTURE of stale sweat and vanilla hits Tom as Devon pushes the gym door open and holds it for Tom to navigate his way into the reception area.

"You must be Devon and Tom. Come on in," a beaming woman with long chestnut-coloured hair invites. "I'm Taylor Leblanc. Welcome to my little gym. Shall we take a seat over here? I've got a few forms to fill in and some questions, so we can design your training programmes." Taylor opens the door into a small office, and gestures to the chairs surrounding an oval table, on which sits a vase of orchids and two clip boards and pens.

Lowering himself into a chair, Tom gazes around, observing a set of double doors, with round port-hole windows, opposite. He assumes they must lead to the gym and changing rooms. As he turns back to look at the questionnaire, Tom notices Devon is taking a keen interest in Taylor.

With his trademark grin, Devon starts his approach, "We're no strangers to gyms Taylor, but here's a challenge that we're both determined to overcome. We hope you're up for the contest. Tom?"

"Hi Taylor, I'm throwing my cards on the table here. The doctors reckon I won't walk unaided again after my injuries, but I'm determined to prove them wrong. Can you help?"

"I'd be foolish to guarantee anything. Tell me a bit about what we're working with here…"

"What we reveal here must stay between these four walls Taylor," Devon insists. "Are you okay with that?"

"Confidentiality is part of my brand, boys. Now, where do you want to begin?"

Devon starts with their background in the army, keeping Taylor enthralled and slowly revealing their SAS training and deployment. Tom admires his friend's storytelling, watching Taylor's facial expressions range between fascination, wonder and absolute horror. Tom's breathing becomes shallow as Devon begins to retell the village deployment. An anxious feeling rises within his chest as beads of sweat breakout on his forehead. Devon's words fade and are replaced by screams and the sounds of battle, Tom's sweaty hands grip the arms of the chair and he starts to hyperventilate.

Taylor is the first to notice, "Tom? Are you okay?"

Devon leaps from his chair, grabbing Tom's shoulders, his words slowly breaking through Tom's reality. "Tom, what's going on? Tom…"

Taylor jumps up and goes to Tom's side. She grabs a clipboard and waves it rapidly like a fan. "Is this helping?"

Seeing the faraway look in Tom's eyes, Devon repeats, "We're in Wellington, brother you're home…"

Tom takes a shuddering breath, "Oh man, what happened?"

"I dunno bro, you left us," Devon worries.

"It was like I was back there again, you know… in the village, the screams..."

Concern is plainly written on Taylor's face. "Are you

all right now? Can I get you anything Tom?"

"A glass of water would be good thanks."

"I'll be back in a jiffy."

"Brother, you had me worried, there." Devon puts a hand on Tom's shoulder.

"Geez Dev, that was scary. What's happening to me?"

"I dunno, but it's sure good to have you back."

Taylor returns with a carafe of water and some glasses on a tray. "Ah, a quick question Tom, have you seen a psychologist since your injury?"

"No, why?" Tom asks defensively.

"I've seen something like this once before when I was helping a girl who was in a car crash get back on her feet. But if you had a flashback, you could have a serious mental injury as well. I mean, I'm not trained or anything, but surely the army would have offered you both counselling after your time in Afghanistan?"

The boys look at each other and laugh, Devon answers, "The army does provide counselling, but your superiors and colleagues say, excuse the expression, but it's all 'harden up soft cock'. You soon learn to cover up any vulnerability."

"That's so sad and so wrong," Taylor fumes as she pours the water into a glass and hands it to Tom.

"Thanks Taylor," Tom gulps some water down and steady's himself, "Yeah, they do have shrinks and chaplains on staff, but no one uses them."

"Okay, well Tom, I'm prepared to take you on, but only on the condition that you see a professional counsellor or psychologist. I know I can assist with your physical injury, which will help with your mental health, but you will need expert psychological therapy after a combat injury," Taylor explains, a worried look on her face.

"Okay, I guess I'll check out a doctor," Tom concedes, before asking, "So, do you think you can help me walk without my sticks?"

"I'm sure I can," Taylor sees the look of relief on both of their faces, "No, really, look, if I can help people after a car accident, I don't see why I can't after a, what do you call it, a bomb accident?"

A release of laughter breaks the tension, "I've never heard it put quite like that before," Tom smiles, "Okay Taylor, you're on, let's get these forms completed and check out the facilities.

\*\*\*

# Chapter Five – Cosmopolitan Caffeine

*Thursday Morning*

THE BROODING SKY mirrors Tom's dull mood, as he swings his way into the café and heads to the counter to place his order.

"Kia ora sir, what can I get you today?" the bubbly barista enquires.

"Two large flat whites and…" Tom's morose tone a reflection of the inclement weather. He glances at the food display cabinet, "And one of those ham croissants please."

"Find yourself a table and I'll bring those over as soon as they are ready," the barista replies leadenly, catching Tom's gloomy mood.

Tom fumbles for his card, pays for the transaction and weaves his way past the many customers, to an empty table by the front window. He sits in the corner so he can see the whole room and look outside.

Taking his new android phone from his shoulder bag, he checks Devon's text, see you at the French café on the corner of Ballance and Featherston at 9:50. Automatically he opens the web browser to check the news. The negative headlines match his sullen disposition. He forcibly puts his phone down onto the table top resisting the electronic addiction. Re-joining the physical world, Tom takes in the ambience of his surroundings.

Smooth jazz surreptitiously plays over the sound

system, almost unnoticeable over the chatter of the dozens of suited occupants who almost fill the café. Public servants can be easily separated from the business professionals by the multi-coloured lanyards and ID cards hanging from their necks. A few tall pot plants are dotted about to break up the mass of Provencal style furniture. The walls bear the obligatory Parisian scenes and the menu blackboard above the counter is flanked by tricolour flags.

An electric jolt of pain courses through his leg, catching him by surprise. Grabbing his leg with both hands, Tom slowly massages his thigh, breathing deeply and slowly exhaling to centre himself. Gradually the pain releases its grip on Tom's mind and he leans back in his chair, relief evident on his face if anyone cared to notice.

Casually looking around the café, he catches sight of Devon.

Almost nondescript in a black suit Devon carries an overcoat over one arm. He casts about before locking eyes with Tom and purposefully striding his way over.

Devon extends his hand, confidently saying, "Good morning Mr Blake," quickly adding under his breath, "play along for god's sake. We're being watched."

Tom shakes Devon's hand, replying loudly "Take a seat please," then whispers, "What the hell bro?"

As Devon sits, he replies softly, "Two tables over are a couple of state-siders who are watching the table of Israelis a few tables nearer the counter."

"Why didn't you give me a heads up?" Tom asks softly.

"You have an unsecured phone and those Yanks have all the toys to intercept a call or message, so I couldn't risk it. Besides, brother, I only just found out about their surveillance operation. They always keep us in the dark right up until the last minute… and I'm being appraised by my supervisor, who's coming in now." Devon replies.

The barista approaches with his order. "Here you go sir, two large flat whites and a ham croissant."

"Thanks, they look great," Tom sounds a bit brighter.

Devon takes a sip on his coffee. "Mmm, just what I need."

"So this is what you do? Watch the people watching other people?"

"Some of the time, but I'll tell you more later. Right now, I need to see who else is here." Devon is covertly examining the room's occupants. "So, what did you think of Taylor?"

Caught a bit off guard, Tom replies, "Ah, she's nice and I like the gym."

"Nice? She's damned hot and she's your type," Devon grins, then adds, "Ah, just as I thought."

"Mate, no hot girl is gonna want a cripple like me. She's more your type, anyway. What did you think?"

"Don't look too hard, but in the far corner there are three men, with a laptop on their table, which happen to be looking at the two Israelis."

Taking his time, Tom glances over, "Yeah, what about them?"

"That looks like a French team to me. They all look distracted, here, take a photo of me with them in the background," Devon passes his phone over.

"Say whisky," Tom quips as he focuses the camera on the suspected Frenchmen, snapping a few shots.

"Play the long game with Taylor, brother, I thought I saw something in one of the looks she was giving you last night," Devon hints as he looks at the photos. "Good shots Tom. They will be useful." He hands his phone back to Tom, "See if you can get the Yanks and the Israelis in a couple."

Lining the camera up, Tom adjusts the focus and snaps some more photos, "Now what's this BS about Taylor and me. I'm not looking for anyone at the moment. Are you after her?"

Admiring the photos, Devon replies, "You've got a good eye for this, did you do the combat photography course?" Seeing Tom shake his head, "No that's right, it was Trevor from our Troop. I bet he's taking lots of photos of all the big-game fish his punters are landing. Now let's get a selfie together… smile."

"Looks like the Israelis are leaving. So let's get back to the Taylor question, again are you keen?"

Devon's eyes light up with more mischief, "Classic distraction tactic brother, I bet five bucks the Yanks leave next. And a bottle of scotch that you and Taylor have a date within the next two months. Oh, and for the record, she's not my type. Besides, I've got a bit on with this new career. Good ol' George has been promoted. He's still my boss but he's got a wider access to information now."

"Okay, I'm playing the game, I've got five bucks on the French. But you will lose that bottle of scotch, I've got no inclination to ask Taylor out for a sympathy date, because that's what it would be. Now, tell me more about George."

"All in good time brother, now hand over that five bucks 'cause the frogs are ordering another round of lattes," Devon grins wickedly.

"I'll still collect on that scotch," Tom laughs, handing over the bank note.

Devon winks, "Time will tell…"

\*\*\*

*Thursday Midday*

Swinging his way up the short outside steps to enter the Station, Tom shakes his head, wondering if Devon is seeing something he can't. 'I mean she is pretty, with her long hair pulled back into a pony tail, but I'm just another client and she wouldn't, would she?'

A black clad man, emerges from behind one of the large Doric columns that flank the Station's entrance, snidely remarking, "Here comes the so-called 'war hero', too slow not to get shot, eh?"

Wrenched from his thoughts by the cruel comment and completely caught off guard, Tom is rendered speechless. His crutches almost slip on the smooth polished stone floor.

"So how come there is nothing in the newspapers about our wounded homecoming hero, eh? No don't bother to tell me your pathetic excuses, I've worked it out, it's because the army is so embarrassed. You probably got shot running away."

The spiteful words sting, burning their way into Tom's subconscious, doubtful thoughts intrude, 'Is this how other Kiwis see me?'

Walking parallel to Tom, his antagonist fires another salvo, "That's right you dole-bludging cripple. Why don't you keep on running away and get your yellow arse out of my Station so your cowardice doesn't taint the rest of us."

Regaining control of himself, Tom does his best to ignore the malicious words and crosses the Station entrance turning left, he passes beneath the large doorways that guard the concourse.

"Your time here is numbered, cripple. Tell your old

grandpa to start looking for a new place, you hear me?" His assailant finishes stomping off in the opposite direction.

'What's wrong with me? I didn't say anything to defend myself,' Tom thinks as he closes the door to the flat behind him. For a moment he leans against the wall, takes a deep breath and rests, dejectedly gathering himself before attempting the stairs.

An idea struck him as he took in the dusty old furniture and boxes cluttering the space. 'If I could clean this out for Koro, maybe I could have a chair down here to rest on before taking the stairs?'

"Is that you Tom?" Koro's voice calls down the stairwell.

"Hey Koro," Tom replies as he starts up the stairs, "How long are you going to hang on to all this junk down here?"

"What junk? You cheeky bugger, that's all our taonga."

"Treasures? You're joking! I think we should clear some of it out. Maybe donate some stuff to a charity shop? Then we could use the space."

"Hmm, let me think on that one, boy. Now you're here let's have a cuppa."

Tom goes into the kitchenette, flicks the jug on and looks for a couple of cups. "Hey Koro, why has that prick Dunkell got it in for us?"

"Bah, don't mind him. He's all talk and no action, that one. All I know is that he wants us out of our home, but we aren't going anywhere. Now, enough of that, tell me about this gym girlfriend of yours."

"Not you, too. Is this a conspiracy? Bloody Devon was giving me heaps about it at the café. Koro, there's nothing going on. She's a nice compassionate woman who I'm paying to help me get strong enough to walk without these bloody sticks."

"Well, invite her around for some kai so I can meet her and see if she's good enough for you."

"I said there's nothing going on," Tom protests, then slowly looking around the tired, barely sanitary kitchenette, comments, "I may have to have a bit of a tidy up before we have any company."

"Well, do that after our cuppa, eh boy. Sheila is popping in this afternoon with some strong rongoā for you."

"Great, I'm looking forward to it," Tom answers with a touch of sarcasm.

***

*Thursday Afternoon*

His fingers fumble with the white plastic string as he ties the black rubbish bag up. Nodding to himself, Tom looks over the cleaned and tidied kitchenette and lounge, thinking, 'much better, even I could invite someone over.'

The downstairs door rattles and Tom hears laughter below. He puts the electric jug on and grabs the green biscuit tin to prepare for their guest.

"Kia ora Tāmati, come over here and give your Aunty Sheila a kiss," the familiar strong voice commands using the Māori version of his name.

Slipping his arms through the crutches cuffs, Tom steers himself over to their guest, seeing her size him up as he approaches her.

"Hi Sheila, has this old bugger been leading you astray while I've been away?" Tom leans down and kisses her on the cheek.

"Tāmati, you know your Koro has always been an absolute gentleman, more's the pity," Sheila replies with a glint in her eye. "Rangiwahia can you make the tea while I sort young Tāmati out." She casts a critical eye at Tom's stance, "Can you stand without those crutches? Next to the chair so you can balance." She waves.

"Is over here okay?" Tom props his crutches against the wall, turns on his stronger right leg and gently eases the weight onto his left foot. Suddenly pain burns from his ankle up through his left leg into his hip. His leg collapses under him. Flailing his arm he catches the edge of the chair and arrests his fall. Slowly he turns and slides himself into the armchair, "Hell," Tom grimaces, "Sorry Aunty, but that's about all I can manage at the moment."

Sheila approaches Tom, a tear in her eye. She sits next to him, takes his hand and strokes it gently, "Aroha mai boy, but I needed to see just what we are dealing with." She turns his hand over and checks his wrist pulse, "Now tell me what those pākehā doctors told you and what pills they have you on."

While Tom provides this information, Koro carefully lays a small square embroidered table cloth over the folding card table and sets out three sets of cups and saucers, teapot and stand along with a plate laden with biscuits. He turns the teapot three times to the left and once to the right, before pouring the tea into each cup.

"Tēnā rawa atu koe Rangiwahia," Sheila thanks Koro as he passes her the first cup. "Well Tāmati, I think a poultice on your hip for a half hour, after a twice weekly soak in one of my bath brews, will help with that nerve damage and stimulate your body's own healing."

"Phew, so no revolting tasting teas then," Tom teases.

"Tahi rā koe!" Sheila exclaims in mock surprise,

smacking his hand gently, "I see what you've been putting up with Rangiwahia. Such disrespect!"

Koro shakily passes a cup and saucer to Tom, sighing exaggeratedly. "The rangatahi of today have no respect."

Tom laughs and reaches for his cup from Koro, "Oh you two work so well together, thanks Koro."

Sheila takes a sip of her tea. "Mmm, that's a good brew." Then placing the cup and saucer back on the table, she reaches deeply into her bag, withdrawing two brown paper bags. "Now Tāmati, listen closely because your Aunty is too old to be doing this for you. This one," she pulls a broad shaped leaf from the first bag, "is for the poultice, soak about four or five leaves in hot water for about five minutes and place over your hip, leave them on for about a half hour. Here, Tom, look inside the other bag."

He opens it. Inside is an assortment of crushed green and brown leaves, "Looks like one of your famous herbal teas."

Laughing, Sheila replies, "That lot would make a horrible tea. Put four cups of that in a very hot bath, stir it in and have a good soak."

"Thanks Aunty, I'll give it a go." Tom reaches for the plate of biscuits, remembers his manners, and passes the plate to Sheila first, "Chocolate biscuit?"

"Why not? Are you going to join us in a game of cards later?"

Shaking his head, Tom offers the plate to Koro, "I don't want to be a third wheel. Are you guys ever going to get together?"

Koro splutters on his mouthful of tea, "Tom!"

Surprised, Sheila looks at Tom, "Do you mean get together as in the …"

"Hook up, go out, date, even get married. I mean you

two would make such a good couple."

Koro pipes up, "Don't mind him Sheila, he's being hīanga. No doubt because I was teasing him about his new girlfriend."

Looking hurt, Sheila admonishes, "Tāmati, why didn't you tell me you had a girlfriend?"

"I don't. Bloody Devon has been spreading a rumour about the owner of the gym."

"So tell me more, what is she like?" Sheila probes.

"Okay, I'll play the game," Tom answers a bit frustrated, then closing his eyes he recalls, "Her name is Taylor Leblanc, and she has long chestnut hair, light hazel eyes. She has a soft American accent, possibly Canadian, no now I think of it, with that surname more than likely French-Canadian. Well-built and trim, of course she would be owning a gym, ah, switched on and caring. She raced off and got me a glass of water when I had a flashback, that was real scary."

"What's this flashback?" Koro interrupts, concern in his voice.

Embarrassed, Tom replies, "Ah, yeah about that," Tom takes a breath, "While Devon was telling Taylor about the incident where I got blown up, it was like I was right back there again."

"Did you break out in sweat? Or have any physical reaction?" Sheila probes.

Tom looks quizzically at Sheila and Koro, "Yeah I did, short shallow breathing. Devon brought me back out, it felt so real, I could even hear the bullets. Why?"

Koro and Sheila look at each other seriously, Sheila commenting, "We called that 'shell-shock', your great grandfather, Koro's papa had that when he came back from Italy after the war. No one talked about it back then."

"His mates would call me and I used to pick him up from the RSA when he had one of his 'turns'," Koro remembers, "It was scary for everyone because there was nothing we could do and no help from the doctors. They just said to lay off the booze and he said he drank so he couldn't remember."

"Taylor said it might be a mental illness and that I should talk to a psychologist. I don't know how much that will cost," Tom comments.

"Will that Army of yours help?" Sheila asks. "I mean, it happened there, so they should help."

"You know what Sheila, you're right." Tom puts his cup down and grabs his phone out from his bag next to his chair, "I'll call them right now."

"I think that Taylor would like that attitude," Sheila digs, winking at Koro over the top of her tea cup.

\*\*\*

# Chapter Six – The Veteran Returns

*Friday Morning*

GREY CLOUDS SKATE across the sky, pushed by a crisp southerly, only allowing occasional peeks of sunshine to relieve the gloom. One shaft of light strikes the Verdigris horse-riding figure atop the Wellington Cenotaph. Tom admires the monument while he waits for the pedestrian crossing light to allow him to cross Lambton Quay towards it. He remembers the many Dawn Parades he attended with Koro, standing to attention as the light slowly crept into the day.

The metallic buzz of the lamp sounds next to him and he re-joins the world, pushing off with his crutches amongst the many public servants hurrying towards their occupations. He wonders how his upcoming meeting at Veterans Affairs for medical assistance will go, surprised at how quickly he got an appointment.

He swings up onto the footpath by the shrine to the fallen, and is making his way towards Bowen Street, when he hears a loud familiar voice.

"… Decent coffee anywhere here."

Confused, he looks around. Across the road, the man's profile is revealed as he walks towards a café door. Tom pauses in his uphill progress, thinking, 'What the hell is Kendrick doing here?' Instinctively, he pulls his phone out and takes a photo as Kendrick turns side on to comment to his companion before he strides confidently into the café.

His mind blurs, then shaking his head, he continues on his way. 'I wonder what he's doing in Wellington? Of course the CIA will have a presence here, but Kendrick? Maybe Devon will have a better idea.'

Timing his arrival at the next pedestrian crossing perfectly, Tom traverses the crossing and approaches the short set of steps that lead to the entrance of the Reserve Bank building. His destination is on the sixth floor.

He still has ten minutes before his meeting and briefly contemplates, 'should I go back to the café? Nah, I won't have time to get there and back. Besides, what if the bugger recognises me. But then again, nobody really notices me, all they see are the crutches.'

The automatic doors part as he enters the reception. The security guard looks him up and down quickly before dismissing him as any threat. Thinking despondently as he approaches the lifts, 'There you go, see the crutches and not the person.'

A building occupant pushes the up arrow, politely offering, "After you mate," as the elevator doors open.

"Thanks," Tom replies as he props himself in the corner, "Sixth floor please, mate." He pulls his phone from his shoulder bag, and taps a quick message to Devon: heads up Big K in town, attaches the photo and hits the send button.

The elevator slows and lets his fellow passenger out on the third floor before rising to his destination.

He makes his way to the red-and-grey panelled counter, and a young auburn-haired girl says brightly, "Kia ora sir. How can we help you today?"

"Hi," Tom quickly reads the receptionist's name

badge, "… Ceit. I have an appointment to see Megan. I'm Tom Yelich."

"Certainly Mr Yelich, take a seat and I'll let her know you're here," bubbly Ceit taps a message on her computer.

Tom swivels around and heads towards the chairs lined up in orderly fashion against the wall, wondering if he has time to sit before Megan arrives.

"Mr Yelich," a tall dark-haired woman approaches, "I'm Megan Donovan. Call me Megan. Can I call you Tom, or would you prefer Tāmati?" She extends her hand to shake his.

Tom leans on one crutch, slipping his hand from the other cuff and shakes Megan's hand, noting the firm grip, "Hi Megan, yes, Tom is good."

"Great, Tom. I have us set up in the meeting room over here. Come on through." Megan walks to the glass door and holds it open for him.

Tom enters the glass-walled meeting room and takes a seat at the table, lowering himself slowly and then putting his shoulder bag beside him.

Megan takes a seat opposite and pats the thin green folder in front of her, "First of all Tom, I'd like to personally thank you for your service. There aren't many people today who would purposely put themselves in harm's way for our country, so thank you."

A bit taken back, Tom replies, "Thank you Megan. I don't think many Kiwis share your views."

"Not many Kiwi's fathers served in Vietnam and weren't recognized for their service either," a disappointed tone in her voice.

"I take it your father was one of those unsung vets."

"Yes. Secondly, I have to apologise for the fact that no one from VA, contacted you sooner about your rights and access to compensation and medical assistance." Megan pauses, "It seems that your file was mislaid on someone's desk a few months back. That person no longer works here and I only found it last night. I can see why they put it in the 'too hard' basket. There is virtually nothing in your file. That not an excuse, but…"

"I joined the army cadets at seventeen, regular force a year later. I was accepted into the SAS a year after that, so most of my career won't be in my personnel file. It's probably filed under some secret classification elsewhere."

"Yep, that's about all we got and that you were medically discharged about four months ago," Megan replies. "They didn't offer you another position outside of the SAS?"

"They might have, but after the four-day flight back to New Zealand, I was pretty dosed up on painkillers. I ended up in the back end of Middlemore and I remember my troop mates being so upset that most left the service when we got back," Tom recalls.

"Oh my god," Megan has a look of horror which turns to resolve. "That's disgusting! Well, let's see what we can do to help."

"The army referred me to you yesterday arvo when I asked about psychological help, but what's on offer?" Tom asks intrigued.

"Excuse me for saying, but you look seriously injured, so…" Megan pulls out a stapled form from the green file, "If you get your doctor to complete the medical parts of this form and you complete the rest, we can provide you with weekly compensation until you are able to start work again."

"Wow, who knew? My savings are starting to run a bit low."

"I'm not sure if we can backdate it, but I'll try," Megan states, "Now, as for psychological support, again you need to talk with your doctor and be referred to a mental health professional. Once you have that referral, we can step in and help cover costs."

"Geez, it would've been good to hear this from the army." Tom shakes his head.

"I'm sorry, I can't speak for them," Megan apologises, "but, in other words, see a doctor, fill in the form together and get it back to me so I can get this approved."

"Thanks very much, Megan. You've made my day!" Tom smiles back, a little hope blossoming somewhere in the back of his mind.

\*\*\*

*Friday Evening*

Sweat is flowing from his pores, soaking his thin workout T-shirt. Taylor's soft voice encourages him to finish the latest repetition of hip extensions. "Come on, Tom, two more, that's it… seven… one more… eight… good work! Okay, now take a break."

The metallic clink of the Lat Pull Down machine that Devon is working sounds almost like a metronome, with his consistent rhythm.

Glancing at her clipboard, Taylor calls, "Devon, can you please give us a hand to get Tom set up on the next machine?"

"Āe, yes, I'll be right over," Devon replies as he finishes his rep, quickly wiping the equipment down and strolling over.

Regaining his breath, Tom asks with a touch of

sarcasm, "So am I ready for the big boy's machines?"

"When I say so Tom," Taylor's voice is firm. "You may be the client, but I take my role seriously. I want you to get better as fast as possible, but I don't want you to injure yourself further and have a setback." She pauses, letting her words sink in, then continues smiling, "Besides, I can't afford the costs if ACC raise my work levy."

"Sorry Taylor, I'll consider myself told off," Tom apologises sheepishly.

"Devon same as before, if you take the left side, and we will move onto your machine," Taylor instructs.

With Devon supporting Tom under one arm and Taylor the other, Tom hobbles over to the Lat Pull Down machine and sits astride the thin bench. Devon gently pushes him forward, while Taylor guides his knees under the thigh roller pads.

"Do you remember what weight you were pressing last?" Taylor enquires.

"Well I was a bit heavier then, but somewhere between 130 and 150 kilos, eh Devon?"

"Yeah, we had a good competition amongst us in the troop, but you've lost a stack of weight, brother."

"My gym, my rules, I'll have none of that macho BS here, boys," Taylor admonishes. "Tom, I want to see how you go on 80 kilos first," she continues as she resets the machine's lifting weight "Again, two sets of eight and I'll add a bit more for the next set."

"Yes Ma'am. I'm looking forward to this," Tom enthuses as he grabs the bar with two hands and begins his new routine.

Feeling his biceps and forearms flex easily with the weight resistance, Tom effortlessly works through his first two sets.

"Wow, that's better than I thought. Well done." Taylor adjusts the weight again. "Must be all that upper body strength using your crutches. Let's try you on 95 kilos."

Tom powers through the next two sets. "It's a breeze. Too easy."

"Looking good Tom," Devon encourages, "What do you think, Taylor?"

"Okay, let's try 110 today, but that's the limit, I only want four sets then a rest." Tom works through the first two sets with little trouble, but feels his latissimus dorsi muscle across his back starting to tighten in the third, and his forearms and biceps burn as he noticeably slows in his fourth set.

"How does that feel?" Taylor asks.

"That last set was a bit tough," Tom admits.

"Good," she makes a note on her clipboard, "Okay boys I think that's enough for the night. Tom, just rest up there while I get your crutches."

Once Taylor is out of ear shot, Devon advises, "When she comes back would be a good time to ask her out."

"Are you crazy?" Tom whispers, "I'm soaking wet and stink of B.O. No way. Anyway, you haven't told me about what you found out about Kendrick."

"Not here, bro. Let's talk more back at Koro's."

Taylor comes back with the crutches. "Here you go Tom." She hands them over. "You're a lot stronger than I expected, I'm sure we can have you on one crutch soon. Same time tomorrow night, boys? Or are you off to a bar or a club?"

"I don't think I'll be dancing anytime soon, Taylor, so I'll see you tomorrow around 1800. Sorry 6pm," Tom replies.

"Yeah, I can't let my bro down," Devon agrees.

As they walk towards the changing rooms, Taylor asks gently, "How did you get on with a counsellor Tom?"

"I've got an appointment on Monday with a doctor that Veterans Affairs recommended. Evidently I need a referral." Tom thinks to himself, 'God, she's so kind and thoughtful but I don't know if she'll ever be interested more than just professionally.'

"That's good news, okay boys. See you soon." She heads into the women's changing room.

Devon holds the men's door for Tom and winks at him as he passes. "See I told you she's sweet on you."

"I don't see it bro," Tom fires back. "Besides, I reckon she wants you to ask her out to a club."

"Ha, we'll see about that!" Devon laughs.

***

"Flick the lock please Dev," Tom shuffles through the front door, pausing to look at the piles of discarded items still cluttering the downstairs entrance to the flat. He turns to Devon. "How long do you reckon it would take to clear this lot out?"

Devon scans the area sceptically, "Geez brother, maybe a day or two? I could maybe hire a small truck for the afternoon and cart it away. But no offence, I don't think you or Koro will be much help."

"I was thinking if you could help sort it with us, we could get Salvos or Hospice to collect what they want and maybe dump the rest for a donation."

"Sounds like a plan. Have you talked to Koro about it?"

Grinning Tom takes to the stairs enthusiastically, "Just about to, my man. Come on, let's go and break the bad news to him."

Koro, eyes closed, his quiet snoring nodding his head in time with the fresh-faced young TV newsreader droning on about the latest negative headlines, homelessness on the rise, increasing racial violence and another war starting in Africa.

Tom creeps almost silently past his grandfather and is heading for the kitchenette when Koro opens one eye and says, "Put the jug on, boy, I could do with a cuppa."

This makes Tom jump and nearly lose his balance, wobbling before he corrects his stride, "Geez-us! You gave me a fright!"

"That will teach you not to go sneaking around," Koro replies, then patting a seat beside him, he says, "Huh, Devon come here and tell your Koro about your new job."

"Koro, don't be naughty. You know I can't tell you much. I'll give Tom a hand to carry the tray in."

"Tāmati, when are you going to enrol at Vic? Don't you think that would be a good move for him Devon?"

"Oh, lay off Koro, I'll get there soon enough," Tom counters.

"Maybe a job then?" Koro pushes.

"I said lay off Koro, besides, I thought we could tidy up downstairs tomorrow," Tom calls from the kitchenette, changing the subject. "Are you doing anything?"

"Huh, it will take a bit of sorting, but if Devon could help, we have a big storage cupboard in the roof access stairwell."

"It's all go then," Tom asserts, filling the teapot.

Devon takes over, "Sit down, brother, I've got this."

"Huh, I'll call Bert to give us a hand. Now how was the gym, boy?" Koro asks as Tom eases himself into his chair.

"Good thanks, Koro and before you ask," Tom gets in quickly. "I didn't ask her out."

Devon pours the tea. "Tom's doing well, Koro, making real progress. But he's a bit slow on the woman front."

"He's always been shy in that department," Koro comments, then with a trace of bitterness, "Married to the bloody army and look what it did to him?"

"Koro!" A shocked Tom exclaims.

Gently Devon intervenes, "To be fair Koro, it wasn't the army's fault." Taking a big breath, and getting glassy-eyed, he continues, "It was all my fault, no one else's."

Tom whips his head around to look at his friend in askance.

"What are you saying, Devon?" A surprised Koro asks.

"I mean I could have, and bloody well should have, pulled the teams out sooner, but... well... we were all taken by surprise. I should've done more... Oh damn it, Tom, I'm so sorry," Devon puts his head in his hands.

Tom stretches over to put a hand on his friend's arm, "No Dev. You can't take this all on your shoulders. You didn't fire the mortar and you didn't provide the bad Intel, or make the insertion plan."

"Devon, you are like another moko to me, I don't hold you responsible," Koro gently replies. "But it was the bloody army's fault," Koro grumbles determined to pin the blame.

"Sorry Koro, not anyone in the army," Tom is angry, "but I know who it was. Someone I thought I'd never see ever again in this life. Until I saw him this morning... bloody Kendrick."

"Who's this Kendrick bloke, then?" Koro demands loudly, pushing himself up out of his chair, shaking his fist,

"I'll bloody well sort him out! Where is the bastard?"

Devon looks up, wiping his eyes on the back of his hand, "Officially, the bastard doesn't exist." Seeing Koro's look of incomprehension, Devon sighs, "Please sit down Koro and let me explain."

Koro sits reluctantly back in his armchair, "Boys, I think it's about time I heard the whole story. You can stuff your army's secrecy, right up the Prime Minister's arse, I want to know everything."

Tom and Devon look at each other. "I think we all might need a drink to tell this sorry tale, Dev. Go on, you know where the scotch is kept."

Devon gathers the bottle and glasses and deftly gives everyone a freehand standard pour. "Did you want some water with yours Koro?"

"Maybe if we have a second glass," Koro answers in a determined voice, "Now who's starting?"

Devon begins, "What most Kiwis don't know about the SAS, is that most of our deployments are classified 'Top Secret Special' or 'Above Top Secret' depending on who we are working for."

"Above Top Secret? Just what exactly does that mean?" Koro insists.

"In practice, it means that no one, not our army general staff, or the politicians that send us overseas, know what we get assigned to do. Sometimes they don't even know what country we are operating in," Devon explains.

Tom adds, "So we are actually highly-skilled hired guns, contracted out to, normally the US or the UK, but sometimes others, to do their dirty work."

Devon continues, "Our CO, Captain Gillies, was pushing back, trying to get more control of our operations, but he was shut down by the top brass because of pressure from our conservative politicians."

Tom chips in, "Yeah, our government, the colour doesn't matter, has been using us to get back in the Yanks' good books, ever since they kicked us out of the ANZUS alliance years ago."

"More dirty little secrets eh? No surprises there," Koro comments taking a sip of his scotch. "Politicians are crooked bastards, the whole pack of them,"

"Well, you know we were in Afghanistan, but what you don't know is that we were assigned to the CIA, who were running their own operations," Devon pauses to take a drink.

"And Kendrick is the CIA agent who was running the show," Tom adds.

"Go on," Koro urges.

"We were tasked, along with another troop, to infiltrate a village and arrest a suspected Taliban leader," Devon begins. "We had a local contact who was meant to point out where the Taliban leader was. We were told that this leader had six men with him, probably bodyguards who were lightly armed." He pauses for another drink before continuing, "We had a helicopter insertion a few clicks away, sorry kilometres away, then hiked to the village and I set up our troop as cover and led second troop in to meet the contact. Everything went according to plan until we started talking to the contact, then everything went to hell in a handbasket." Devon sits back in his seat, rubbing his forehead with his free hand in an effort to rub some of the horrific memories away.

Tom picks up the story, "From our observation point, I saw a large number of armed men in black emerging from some of the village homes, and in the distance I saw five vehicles approaching flying black flags. I let Devon know on the headset that we had a lot more company than we thought."

"Oh my god. How many of you against how many of them?" Koro's face a mask of horror.

"Eight of us, well nine counting the unarmed contact, who I told to evacuate the village, against about one hundred and sixty. Second troop started to pull back with some of the villagers, when the enemy started shooting," Devon continues, "I sent the villagers one way with the contact, while second troop and I laid down some covering fire for them."

Shaking his head, Koro states, "A hundred and sixty! Holy crap!"

"I managed to take out the driver of the lead vehicle, which crashed and slowed the other vehicles down," Tom adds, "while Brett and Trevor covered Devon and second troop so they could get back to our position."

"Tom, are you okay to carry on?" Devon asks, genuine concern written all over his face.

"Yeah, I'm okay at the moment. It's a bit easier with us both taking turns.

"What happened next?" Koro asks.

"I made it up to the covering position with second troop okay, when they started firing a mortar at us," Devon picks up. "From our elevated position, I saw so many armed figures firing towards us and amongst the remaining villagers, I knew we were up shit creek without a paddle. I called in an airstrike between the mortar rounds."

"Tom, what were you doing?" Koro asks gently.

"As the sniper in the troop, it's my job to take out high value targets. Like the vehicle driver. I got a couple of the gunners on the back of the vehicles, we call them a 'technical'. Then I saw the leader and was lining him up when the mortar round exploded near me."

Tears start flowing down Devon's face, his voice chokes and then he carries on, "I was on the radio when I saw Tom blown over towards me. It didn't look good. I demanded a medevac helicopter and more fire support immediately, then tended to Tom. It was messy."

Tom's face goes white, "I remember seeing that leader shooting some villagers just before the explosion. That was horrific."

Koro's eyes are wet and he is looking pale, "What happened next?"

Devon takes a breath before continuing. "The cavalry arrived in the form of a flight of US F/A-18 Hornets dropping Mark 77 bombs, a modern type of napalm, then the AH-64 Apaches arrived and finished the job."

"Koro, that means they wiped out the village completely," Tom explains, "Fortunately Devon managed to get about twenty villagers out beforehand."

"And then the medevac helicopter arrived and took Tom back to Bagram air base hospital," Devon concludes.

"My boys, my poor boys," tears run down Koro's face, "I can't imagine the horrors that you've witnessed. How do you cope?"

"By being there for your brothers, Koro," Devon answers genuinely.

"Thanks bro," Tom wipes his eyes, "just thanks.

"Just like my Dad and his mates at the RSA," Koro nods.

Silence envelopes the trio, as they sip their scotch, all deep in thought.

"So this CIA man, Kendrick, he's in town?" Koro asks.

"Yeah, I saw him this morning heading into a café

opposite the Beehive. What did you find out Dev?"

"Only that he's not officially here according to George, sorry Koro, that's Captain George Gillies. He's now my boss at SIS," Devon explains, "George and the DG had no idea he was in Wellington and didn't believe me until I showed him your photo Tom."

"Which means what exactly?" Koro asks.

"That he's CIA black op's and we can't lay a hand on him without causing an international incident," Devon continues.

"We'll see about that," Koro states, "show me that photo."

\*\*\*

# Chapter Seven – Concourse Disputes

*Saturday Afternoon*

"JUST WATCH YOUR hand, Bert," Devon advises, "It's a bit of a squeeze."

The two men angle the old bedframe through the door, out onto the Station concourse and position it next to the assorted pile of furniture and boxes against the nearby wall.

"Fortunately, there's nothing on at the Cake Tin, or this place would be full and you guys would be in a spot of bother... oh damn, speak of the devil," Bert replies, as they duck back inside out of sight.

"Ah Koro, you may want to get out there," Devon calls seeing a red-faced official making a beeline towards them.

Koro grabs his tokotoko walking stick and heads towards the front door, to greet his foe, "Tēnā koe i tēnei ahiahi Dunkell."

"I've finally got you now, Yelich," Dunkell spits as he furiously writes on the clipboard, starting to enter the flat, "Gross misconduct, bringing Kiwirail into disrepute."

Koro holds his tokotoko up, barring the on-comer from crossing the threshold, "Unless you have a warrant or an invitation Dunkell, you are not coming into my home. Now let's step outside and you can tell me what this nonsense is all about."

Frustrated, Dunkell backs up continuing to write for a moment then signs at the bottom of the form, "Here you go Yelich, your marching orders, one eviction notice," he triumphantly brandishes the paper trying to hand it to Koro.

Ignoring the offered paper, Koro leans on his walking stick with both hands, eyes narrowed, "Perhaps you'd like to explain this 'misconduct'?"

Devon takes a position behind Koro, "That would be 'alleged' misconduct."

Dunkell bristles, "You have created great big piles of rubbish in the main concourse. That's obstructing Kiwirail clients' freedom of movement for a start and tarnishing our reputation for another, by making the place look like a tip."

"We've stacked everything against the wall and I haven't seen anyone inconvenienced yet," Devon retaliates.

"You keep out of this boy, I'm talking to Yelich," Dunkell snarls.

"I think you need to be taught some manners Mr, just what is your name?" Devon asks, pulling himself to his full height and steeling Dunkell with a look that could kill.

Not noticing his peril, Dunkell barks back, "No boy, what's your name, eh? Are you taking on boarders Yelich? That's another breach of your tenancy. I'll add that too," He puts his paper back on his clipboard, furiously writing.

Tom comes through the Bunny Street entrance doors, flanked by three older men and one woman all wearing purple tops. He points to the pile and the people start carting the stuff away. He swings over towards the gathering at the door to the flat.

"So, I'm giving you until tomorrow to vacate the flat," Dunkell waves the eviction notice in Koro's face.

"And what happens if I stay put Dunkell?" Koro asks.

Dunkell is gleeful. "Please make my day and try to.

I'll have the cops frogmarch you and your tribe down to the police station."

Winking at Tom, Koro continues, "So, let me get this right, because I have an 'alleged' boarder, you can kick me out?"

"You are slow, old man, aren't you? That's just what I said."

"But wouldn't you have to prove that I have an 'alleged' boarder?" Koro asks innocently.

"Well, that's easy, he's here. All you lot live on top of each other, I'll find something," Dunkell replies.

"Hmm, I suppose you might, if it was true, but it isn't," Koro states, then asks, "So then what have you got?"

"Well, then Yelich I've got you on all this rubbish out here, are you really that thick?" Dunkell eyes Koro, his paper filled hand pointing towards the concourse.

"Okay Dunkell, let's take a look at all this 'alleged' rubbish shall we?" Koro invites.

"Are you blind, as well as thick Yelich?" Dunkell asks, turning to look where his hand is pointing at the empty hall, "Over th…"

"Huh, where exactly?" Koro asks.

"What…? Where'd it all go?" Dumbfounded, Dunkell walks over to where the boxes and furniture were, "It was right here."

"You didn't duck out for a quick couple of pints over lunch, did you Dunkell?" Tom asks innocently.

Crestfallen, Dunkell wanders off in a daze towards his office door, muttering, "I had him. How did he do that?"

Bursting into laughter, Koro points over to the Station bar, "Come on you lot, we've all earned a cold one, my treat."

"What's his problem Koro?" Devon asks, as they

cross the concourse.

"Never you mind, moko," Koro stops to answer Devon.

"Don't stop him Dev, he's buying!" Tom laughs "Come on Bert, we couldn't have done all this without your help."

"That was perfect timing, I must say." Bert grins, "What with you arriving with the Hospice volunteers."

"Geez, I thought you were going to take him out, Dev," Tom notes, "I've seen that look in your eyes before. Dunkell has no idea how lucky he was that Koro was blocking the door!"

"Damn straight brother," Devon responds, "he's one rude bastard. Koro how do you put up with his BS racist attitude?"

"You boys have grown up in a very different New Zealand to the one that Bert and I grew up in, eh Bert?"

"Too right, Rangi. Some of us fought the good fight."

"Like the Springbok tour, eh?" Koro laughs, "I remember you decking a couple of those Red Squad Nazi's."

"What's this?" Tom asks.

"Old Rob's Mob, they got a lot of us at Whitmore Street on the march," Bert reminisces.

"They were out for revenge because they had to call the Hamilton game off," Koro explains, "bloody split the country in two that bloody rugby tour did."

"That's right. Back in the early eighties, wasn't it?" Devon asks.

"Yeah, Rob Muldoon was the conservative Prime Minister and he got voted in by promising a rugby test with South Africa," Bert explains, "They had a racist apartheid system and us Kiwis were living under the illusion of living in 'Gods-own' country with the happiest of race relations. The seventies and eighties were full of protests, land marches and occupations."

"And those bloody dawn raids targeting our island brothers," Koro adds.

"Okay, sounds like we need a history lesson here. I mean it happened way before we were born, but what's this about Nazi's and Red squad? And no boring bits please," Tom pleads.

"The Red Squad was the police's first anti-riot squad, and they were brutal!" Bert explains.

"We called them Nazis because they were all big white bastards and racist pricks to boot," Koro chips in, "look at that web thingy on your phone."

"Just doing that Koro," Devon replies, "Geez! Check these images out brother." He hands his phone to Tom.

"I can't believe it!" Tom exclaims, "Why weren't we taught this at school?"

"I don't think any government wants to teach kids that they have the power to change political decisions," Bert answers, "Besides, after the tour I think the whole of New Zealand was so shocked at what happened, that they just wanted to bury those ugly memories."

"But why?" Tom asks.

"You have to remember boys, that Aotearoa is a small country. We know most of our neighbours and we had to go back to work and live in our communities with people who we were physically fighting street battles with. It wasn't easy…" Koro trails off, deep in his memory.

"Muldoon was chucked out at the next election and Labour swept into power, but they found out that Muldoon had bankrupted the country, so the eighties became a decade of asset sales and Rogernomic's, no nukes and getting kicked out of ANZUS, the French bombing the Rainbow Warrior and the '87 stock market crash," Bert continues, "I guess we got a bit distracted. Crazy times eh Rangi?"

Koro stands abruptly, grabs the cold glass jug and tops up everyone's glass. "Sure was Bert, now enough history, or you'll just hear two old-timers going on and on. It's time for another jug."

\*\*\*

# Chapter Eight – New Toys

*Monday Morning*

THE COFFEE MACHINE complains with a screech of protest as the barista aerates the milk, talking over the noise, "Take a seat sir and I'll bring the coffees over shortly."

"Thanks mate, I'll be over there in the corner booth." Tom indicates with a nod of his head.

Clocking each of the patrons as he navigates his way to the table, Tom wonders, 'How many people here are as they appear? What secrets are they hiding? I wonder if Devon is going to use me as cover again?'

As Tom reaches his table, he sees Devon enter the café and gives him a smile as he lowers himself into the chair, "You have impeccable timing, the coffee is on its way."

At the orange booth bench seat, Tom slides himself along and props his crutches up against the white planter box that caps the end of the booth. He winks at his friend, "Private enough bro?"

"Perfect brother, I hadn't heard of this café before," Devon places his overcoat on the end of the shiny white table.

"That's Wellywood for you. We must have more cafés per capita than any other city in the country, maybe even the world." Tom shakes his head, then lowers his voice,

"So who are we watching today? Let me guess, perhaps the couple over by the fire extinguisher?"

Devon laughs, "You chose the café so unless someone of interest wanders in, I have no idea."

Tom looks a little crestfallen. "Oh, of course, you're right."

"Don't worry, I've got something else that will perk you up, no pun intended." Devon puts his briefcase on the end of the table and pats the top of it.

The barista arrives, placing their coffee on the table beside the briefcase, "Two large cappuccinos with cinnamon."

"Awesome design mate." Tom nods appreciatively at the barista's artwork in the frothy milk.

"Smells fantastic," Devon acknowledges.

Once the barista has moved out of earshot, Tom turns back to Devon. "Okay, you've got me. What's in the case?"

"All in good time, brother," Devon takes a sip of his frothy white brew. "Ahh, I needed that. It's been a heck of a morning."

"Go on spill." Tom picks up his cup.

"What would you say if you had a chance to work with me and George again?"

Taken aback, Tom puts his cup carefully down, "Are you serious? I'm a cripple. There's no way I'd pass a fitness test."

Devon smiles. "You take a pretty good photo and you've excellent observation skills. No doubt from our Recon training. You're loyal, already have clearance and can be relied upon. And besides, that's what George wants. So, what do you say?"

"Hang on a minute mate. Just what exactly is on offer here?"

After a quick check to make sure they aren't overheard, Devon explains. "George was mighty impressed that you spotted Kendrick last week and got that great photo which clearly identifies him. We know that he's black ops from our time spent with him in Afghanistan. What we don't know is why he's in Wellington. That's where you come in."

"Go on, I'm listening," Tom replies intrigued.

"George wants to run you 'dark' via me, so that no one at work knows about it," Devon continues.

"Wait a sec," Tom holds up both hands. "So, George has 'plausible deniability' if the shit hits the fan? I dunno Dev, if things go south, where does that leave me?"

"Look around you Tom. We're in Wellington. It's hardly a war zone." Devon grins and pats the briefcase. "Besides, we're talking surveillance and that involves some new toys for you."

"Like...?"

Devon clicks the slide latches and opens the case so that the lid obscures any onlookers' view. Pointing to the items, he reels off, "Here's your new secure phone. It has two numbers in it. The first 'Alpha' is me, always use that one."

"And the second?" Tom asks.

"Only if it's an emergency, then call 'Bravo', that's George." Devon pauses, "If he sees you calling, he knows both of us are screwed and he'll storm in with the cavalry."

"I thought you said this isn't a war zone," Tom comments, "but nice to know that there's some back up."

"Exactly. Now the camera on this phone shoots up to 108 megapixels, so you can zoom in afterwards and not lose too much definition. It also has a modified microphone for high quality sound and voice recording. Much better than the laptop version the French were using last week."

"Sounds impressive. Anything else I should know about this phone?" Tom asks.

"Both George and I have access to the inbuilt GPS tracker. The difference with this one is that it has its own power supply, so if the phone is off, we can still find you. The phone works off the best network signal available, or satellite if you've got no network coverage."

"Very clever. Very Big Brother, but very clever," Tom nods in appreciation.

"Ha, good one," Devon laughs, pulling out a black vest, "now here's your new underwear."

"Fancy, does it come in any other colour than sexy black?" Tom jokes.

"Sorry bro, only black," Devon adds, "This light material is cashmere, deceptive ain't it?"

"Warmer than merino?" Tom asks with mock innocence.

"Ever the joker. Nah man, this is level three body armour. It's even stab proof, which you might need as you're an easy mugging target on those things." Devon points to his crutches.

"Bro, this is serious stuff. Next thing you'll pull out will be a pistol."

"Close, but you're not 007... yet," Devon answers deadpan, "a couple of pepper spray devices, eight-metre range, in a gel not an aerosol so you don't get any blow-back in the Wellington winds, and it's got a UV marker dye."

Tom lets out a low whistle. "Man, this is too much."

"I know right," Devon grins. "Gotta look after my bro. Of course, George wants his arse covered, so you've got a couple of papers to sign."

"Of course, he has." Tom pauses, "So, what's in it for me?"

"What more do you need than the satisfaction that you are serving Queen and country?" Devon asks, "Just kidding, it's in the paperwork, a consultant's weekly retainer plus reasonable expenses, with a GST receipt of course."

"Ha, gotta keep the bean counters happy," Tom laughs, then he narrows his eyes, "Did you set this up to call Koro off?"

"No, it's all George's idea, but that's a good point," Devon realises, "You better have a word with him because you don't want Koro to blow your cover."

"Roger that. So, what is my cover?"

"Just some random guy on crutches who frequents cafés, I haven't thought that far," Devon adlibs.

"I guess we can come up with something," Tom shakes his head. "I certainly didn't see this coming."

"And with you on the case, Kendrick won't see it either."

\*\*\*

*Monday Lunch*

The cold concrete bench seat sends a chill through his body as Tom waits, observing the pedestrians walking either side of the cenotaph. Many are scurrying to their next meeting or racing to cafés for a hurried lunch.

He checks his watch, and reports in to Devon via text on his new phone: 1200 no sign of him yet.

On the back of his neck is a rising irritation. He scratches it. 'Damn this vest is itchy! I must check out why, and I might see if Dev has a foam pad for these damn cold benches.'

Across the road sits the old government buildings, now inhabited by a sprawling network of Victoria University departments. He scans the parade of people walking his way, finally spotting his blue-suited prey. He taps a quick message: *K heading from Lambton into Whitmore – following.*

Checking that the earbuds are Bluetooth-connected to his phone, Tom gathers his crutches and ambles to the busy pedestrian crossing to wait for the green light. His heart rate increases as he is hit by a wave of anxiety. His fretful inner monologue natters, 'Don't stuff this up man. Dev is counting on you. Come on lights I can't lose him yet.'

The crossing buzzer sounds and Tom joins his fellow amblers, his crutches swinging in perfect rhythm with his legs easily setting a determined pace. Ahead, Tom catches a glimpse of the blue pin-stripe suit before it is obscured by a building.

Catching the next crossing as it turns green, Tom quickly makes his way across, his phone buzzing. Pausing, he taps the earbud and continues his pursuit, answering, "Yeah?"

"Do you still have him in sight?" Devon asks.

"No, he's crossed Whitmore heading down Stout Street, I'll be there soon," Tom answers.

"I'll stay on the line, I'm heading to the car now and I'm about five minutes away, bro," Devon responds.

"Roger that," Tom concentrates on his rhythm, rounding the corner into Stout Street, "There he is, he's across Ballance and heading towards the entrance of… the Big Super Ministry."

"Interesting," Devon replies.

At the street corner, Tom stops near the rain shelter, noting the colour of a lanyard flapping in the Wellington breeze and reports, "K is now shaking hands with a BS official and they are heading inside. Should I follow him in?"

"Yep, there's a café on the ground floor, I'll meet you there."

A courier van passes. Tom waits, then crosses first Ballance Street, then Stout, steadily closing the distance to the entrance steps. "How far away are you Dev?"

"Two minutes, bro."

The automatic doors to the Ministry open. Tom watches Kendrick and the ministry official leave the reception desk and walk towards a nearby meeting room. Scanning the entrance lobby, Tom nods at the approaching security guard.

"Do you need some help there, sir?" the security guard asks.

"All good mate, meeting my brother for a coffee," Tom answers, quickly reading his name badge.

Frowning, the security guard says sceptically, "Well that's okay, I guess."

"Thanks Dave, he said he'd be here shortly and to wait in the café, can you tell me where it is please?" Tom asks innocently.

"Oh, it's just around the corner to the left past the reception," Dave replies, walking with Tom towards the desk, and giving the receptionist an appreciative eye, "He's okay Sally, say when are you due for your next break?"

"Thanks," Tom nods, as he makes his way towards the table nearest the meeting room. He notes that the door is still ajar and pulls his phone out, laying it on the table with the microphone aimed at the door. He switches on the voice recorder.

Casting a glance around the open space, Tom sees a constant stream of public servants pouring out of one of the lifts, others leaving the building or heading for a coffee, while some of the slimmer ones tackle the stairs.

He notices two self-important black-suited men with long BS coloured lanyards swinging from their necks, walking towards the meeting room. He picks up his phone and snaps a photo of them, while he appears to be scrolling on his phone's screen.

The two men walk into the room closing the door behind them. At the same time, Devon strides through reception, flashing a BS coloured ID card at a surprised Dave and Sally. He casts an experienced eye over the room and heads directly for Tom.

Devon sits down opposite Tom, who holds out the phone and brings up the photos he took. "Recognise any of these guys?" Tom asks as he slides his phone across the table to Devon.

Deftly picking up Tom's phone, Devon swipes through the photos, "No one I know."

Nodding towards the reception, Tom says, "I bet Sally does."

"Quick work bro, I didn't know you liked red heads," Devon teases.

"Ha, good one Dev, but I don't think I've got a snowball's chance in hell," Tom fires back, "Did you not see Dave chatting her up?"

"Brother, you are good at this game!" Devon's phone starts to chirrup, "Damn, that's the boss... Hello... yes sir... not yet sir... roger that. I'm on my way."

"Is that George?"

"No, it's my immediate boss, Robin. He's got a bee

in his bonnet and I've got to get back." Devon stands. "Great work, Tom. See if you can get a name or two out of Sally, but don't get sprung by Kendrick. Call me if you see anything else, but let's debrief at the gym."

"Roger, see you about 1730," Tom, slips back into military parlance easily. "Make sure you look angry when you go past reception."

Devon looks confused, "Okay bro." He strides out of the building, flashing a grumpy look at Sally.

Tom takes his time. He picks up his phone and crutches and winds his way around the tables back to reception.

"Hi Sally, I must apologise for my brother. He thought he had booked that meeting room over there." Tom points towards Kendrick's meeting room, "But he must've been bumped out, which is why he's so mad."

"Oh dear, let me have a look at the meeting room schedule," Sally replies naïvely, tapping on her keyboard, "No... no... sorry, I can't see any other booking for that room, just the Space Agency boys. Mind you, they would have first choice because they are a special category team."

"Oh well, thanks for your help, Sally," Tom beams at her as he swings off towards the exit.

'Kendrick meeting with the New Zealand Space Agency? What's that all about?' Tom wonders as he turns left and makes his way to the street corner. Looking about, he leans against one of the fallen pillars outside another Government building and casually observes the BS ministry's front entrance.

Taking his phone out of his pocket, he opens the voice recorder and listens via his earbuds. Adjusting the volume, he can just make out Kendrick's American accent, "...goddamn lax security... I don't care! ... huge investment..." another kiwi voice closer, "Hello Mr

Waldergrave, it is good to ..." and then the sound of the door closing.

Thinking to himself, he attaches the recording to a message and sends it to Devon, tapping: can you clean up the recording a bit more, something about security and a big investment, and Sally sends her regards, those suits were NZ Space Agency that had double booked the meeting room.

A black Chevrolet Suburban SUV pulls up outside the BS Ministry's front entrance, Tom pulls himself up onto his crutches and half-hiding behind the pillar focuses on the vehicle and takes a quick photo, then another few as a large man in a black suit exits the car and holds the rear door open. Kendrick leaves the entrance and climbs into the rear seat. Then sliding out of view behind the pillar, Tom waits for the black Chevy to drive past his position. He snaps another photo as the Chevy comes alongside him and another as it pulls out into traffic on Lambton Quay and speeds away.

'Well if that doesn't scream CIA, then I don't know what does,' Tom thinks.

His tummy rumbles in complaint, 'I wonder how much the expenses will cover?' Back into his easy swinging motion, Tom turns and heads further up Lambton Quay looking for an eatery.

\*\*\*

*Monday Afternoon*

"Tāmati Yelich?" A weary looking middle-aged man asks.

"That's me," Tom answers as he hikes himself up

onto his crutches and follows the man down the equally tired-looking hallway to his consulting room.

"Take a seat please, Tāmati, I'm Dr Peter Cleeland, please call me Peter," he invites.

"Thanks Peter, I go by Tom."

"Ah, that's right, you're a referral from Megan, a conscientious lady there." Peter checks his computer, then gets up and pulls the curtain to screen the bed from his work station, "Okay, lets run through this physical, if you can strip down to your underwear and hop on the bed, I'll get this paperwork started."

Tom sits on the examination bed and starts the laborious process of getting undressed, "Geez Peter, I thought I'd already filled out enough paperwork in the waiting room."

"There is always an excessive number of forms for anything to do with the government, Tom. Now what exactly are you applying for?"

"According to the Middlemore doctors, and the Americans in Afghanistan, they reckon I won't be walking, let alone running ever again. Well, not without crutches. I get these jolts of severe pain in my leg, but what really worried me was I had a bit of a turn, an episode, I don't know what to call it, last week."

"What happened?"

"I was at the gym and I had a moment where I thought I was actually back in Afghanistan. It felt so real, like I could hear the gun shots and smell the cordite and everything." Tom explains the whole situation.

Peter listens carefully, gently probing while he checks Tom's reflexes, blood pressure, and other vitals, noting the results. After he is satisfied with his examination, he instructs Tom to get dressed and sits back at his workstation to complete the paperwork.

"All done Doc. What's the verdict?"

"You have the most extensive scaring down your left leg that I've seen since I worked in the Emergency Department of Auckland Hospital fifteen years ago. And from what I've seen, you may not be able to run again, but you could walk unaided if you continue the strengthening work at the gym, so keep that up."

"Cool, I'll do that," Tom confirms.

"As for your sudden onset leg pain, I believe that is probably nerve damage from the shrapnel. Your severed nerves are healing, but will be sending incorrect messages to your brain causing the electrical jolts of pain. Sorry, but that one's going to take some time to heal properly."

"How long Doc?"

"It varies from patient to patient, it could be years Tom. Now I've written you a referral to a Clinical Psychologist, Sandra Williams, because you may very well have a form of PTSD from the trauma you experienced in Afghanistan. But she will make that diagnosis. Now if you can sign this form, I'll scan it back to Megan for you and here's a copy of a medical certificate which you will need for Veterans Affairs."

"Wow, do you really think I might be able to walk without these sticks?" Tom asks hopefully.

"It will take a lot of effort, Tom, but I have seen an industrial accident where a young man who got his leg crushed by a forklift managed to get back to walking again."

Tom's eyes grew moist. "Thanks Peter, I think that's the best news I've heard in a very long time."

***

*Monday Evening*

With his thigh muscles quivering under the stress, Tom grits his teeth and pushes the resistance plate away from him once again, hissing the count… "Five."

"Do you have three more Tom?" Taylor dubiously asks.

Slowly easing his legs back to a ninety-degree angle, he braces for the next push… "Six".

"Come on brother," Devon urges, "nearly there!"

Their voices are barely heard as Tom focuses solely on his objective, edging his legs back into position for their next push… "Seven."

"This is crazy progress," Taylor shakes her head in amazement.

Lessening the pressure for his last repetition, noticing both thighs are now visibly pulsating, Tom gathers his strength and drives his feet forward, crying out triumphantly…"Eight!"

"Go you good thing!" Devon joins in.

"Wow, that's just… well I haven't seen that before," Taylor shakes her head, then noticing Tom's thigh is still pulsating, directs, "Devon grab the plate please and hold it firm. Here Tom let me help." She supports his legs as he carefully twists himself free from the seated leg press machine.

"Thanks Taylor," Tom grunts, exhausted but feeling a sudden excitement at her electric touch.

"Are you okay Tom?" Taylor asks, passing him his drink bottle.

He nods and tips the bottle up taking a long drink of

water, before wiping his mouth with the back of his left hand. "Thanks again," he puffs. "I needed that... yeah, sure, I'm okay."

"How's the leg bro? Any pain? Your left one is still jumping," Devon's concern evident.

Tom massages his trembling thigh with his left hand. "It's okay. Not so sore at the moment. Man that was hard work."

"I don't want you to overdo it Tom," Taylor warns. "You're making steady progress and the last thing you want is to have a setback at this stage."

"Save your breath Taylor, Tom can be as stubborn as a mule when he's set himself a goal," Devon advises, "I could tell you some stories."

Frowning, Taylor admonishes, "Devon, there is a fine line between encouragement and macho bullshit, and I mean it, I'm not having any of that crap in MY gym."

Tom laughs, "It's all good Taylor, but he is right, I can be stubborn. Go on Dev, I'd like to hear what story you have up your sleeve."

Intrigued despite herself, Taylor says, "Okay, I only listen to true stories."

"Oh, which one do I choose?" Devon exaggeratedly scratches his chin looking wistful. "Okay, when we signed up for cadets, Tom was a skinny little runt. He could hardly carry his full kit when we went on exercise. After about five kilometres, he would be wobbling around and lagging behind the rest of us. We thought we had real pricks for instructors and they said to the rest of us, Don't help Yelich or you'll be on a charge, if he can't make it to our objective tonight, he's out."

"That's so unfair! Aren't you meant to be there for your army buddies?" Taylor asks.

"What we didn't know at the time, was that it was a test not just for me, but for the rest of the intake," Tom chips in.

"Yeah, one of the instructors said we couldn't carry any of his load, so I thought about it and decided that I'd walk beside Tom and just encourage him," Devon recalls. "The rest of the crew carried on and we had one instructor walking behind us keeping an eye on what we were up to."

"How long was the march?" Taylor asks.

"Twenty-five kilometres, with pack, webbing and rifle. Forty kilos," Tom replies, "I wouldn't have made it without Devon there."

"Bullshit brother, when you get that look in your eye and I've seen it plenty of times since, you just go for it. Just like you did tonight."

"Wow and you guys were just kids. You made it obviously, or you wouldn't have had an army career."

"Yeah, I did and that started Devon on his way up the ranks. He got a promotion by showing real leadership."

Devon hands Tom his crutches. "Anyone would've done it."

"But they didn't, did they Devon?" Tom quickly responds, "And that's what generates great leaders. Compassion and the willingness to walk in someone else's shoes."

"Come on, let's hit the showers and get cleaned up," Devon deflects.

Pushing himself up on his crutches, Tom makes his way to the door, "Thanks for tonight Taylor. With both your help, I'm sure I'll be walking without these sticks sooner rather than later."

"I still think that doctor of yours was out of line for telling you that," Taylor shakes her head, "But who knows, with the right attitude and lots of hard work, and from what I just witnessed, you might just make it."

'Oh I'll make it alright,' Tom thinks to himself, 'and then I might just be able to ask you out.'

\*\*\*

"You boys are looking a bit tired. Have you got enough energy for some kaimoana?" Koro asks.

"Always plenty of room for some kaimoana, Koro, eh Tom?"

"Āe, I'll be up for that." Tom drops his gym bag by his armchair and makes his way to the dining table.

"Devon can you please get the plates?" Koro asks.

"Sure Koro," Devon gets the crockery and cutlery and takes it to the table, setting them in front of three of the chairs.

Tom puts his phone on the table and slides it towards his friend. "Check out those new photos Dev." He passed over the loaf of white bread, still in its plastic wrapper, and the chipped china butter dish.

Scrolling through the gallery, Devon's eyes widen slightly. "Could it be any more obvious? A black Chevy Suburban."

"Check out the passenger opening the car door for him," Tom points out.

"That headset is so noticeable with that marine buzz cut. Hey, did you see what he's carrying, bro?" Devon asks.

"Yeah, the bulge in the back of his suit jacket and the way he carries his left arm makes it obvious."

"Put that phone away boys and tuck into this," Koro interrupts, placing a large steaming bowl of mussels in the centre of the table.

Tom opens the bread bag and tosses a couple of slices towards each of their plates, hitting them dead centre.

Koro shakes his head and complains, "Bloody dead-eye dick here eh? Where's your manners?"

Laughing Devon agrees, "Give him a rifle or a packet of bread and he'll hit the bulls eye every time!"

"Aroha mai Koro, but it's a bit hard to get up and down at the moment," Tom apologises.

"Less talking and more eating," Koro grumbles good-naturedly, "What's so important on that phone?"

"Just someone we are taking an interest in," Devon tries to cover.

"That bloody Kendrick I bet. Where is he?" Koro demands.

"Yeah, about that," Tom starts, looking at Devon for assistance, "Koro, no one is meant to know that he's in New Zealand."

"So what? I bloody well know and that's enough," Koro replies belligerently.

"How about I make you a deal, Koro?" Devon asks.

"Pass the butter while I'm listening," Koro picks up his knife.

"How about you let Tom and I find out what he's up to first. Then once we have everything we need, I'll personally tell you where you can find him?"

"Huh, let me think about it." Koro answers, spreading a thick wedge of butter onto his bread.

"These mussels are awesome, Koro," Tom tries to divert the conversation. "What did you put in them?"

"Plenty of garlic and chilli in a butter sauce. Pretty good for an old fella, eh?" Koro smiles, "But I'm not that senile boy, when I get a hold of that Kendrick…"

"Okay Koro, just what will you do?" Tom calls his

bluff.

"You don't learn to fight just in the army, boy. We got plenty of practice in the union," Koro counters.

"Hey, settle down, you two," Devon mediates. "But, I am wondering about union fights. What's the story?"

Koro calms down and explains, "I've worked mainly for the Railways all my life and joining the union was compulsory until the eighties. The bosses have always held the power and back when I started there were only a few managers who knew what they were doing, so us workers got a raw deal." Koro pauses to pull another mussel from its shell and wrap it in buttered bread, "When that happened, the union called us out on strike and we would picket outside the front gates to stop any scabs from working."

"What's a scab, Koro?" Tom asks.

"That's what we called a person who worked while we were on strike," Koro explained, "And of course the bosses would encourage scabs to work and get the cops to break up our pickets."

"More fighting with the police Koro? You're a real rebel, eh?" Devon teases.

Koro pulls his hair back and points to a hidden scar running back into his hairline. "Got this from the Nazi pricks in seventy- eight. The bastards wouldn't let the paramedics see us for hours. Not until they had processed us at the station and charged us."

"Holy shit!" Devon exclaims. Tom shakes his head.

"We learnt to take the law into our own hands and never trust a cop or a boss," Koro recalls. "We had many bar fights with the cops when they were supposedly off duty. A bunch of the bastards would show up at our pub and start pushing us around, winding us up until someone reacted. Then it was all on. You had to stand up for yourself and back your mates or they would smash you into the ground."

"I never knew," Tom says, both boys taken aback.

"It was hard on your Gran. She couldn't take it in the end," Koro softly admits, a tear coming unbidden to his eye. "That's why she left me and went back up north to her whānau."

"I don't remember Gran much, Koro, just her warm hugs and her tangi that you took me to when I was about six…" Tom falters.

Reaching across the table, Koro places his hand on top of Tom's, tears candidly falling, "I know Tāmati, it was only six months after your parents' tangi. That was a terrible year."

"That must have been real tough," Devon sympathises trying to hold the tears back himself.

"I don't remember much, Dev," Tom wipes the tears from his face. "There was the car accident with Mum and Dad, moving in with Koro, then Gran leaving and then her tangi, I really don't remember much at all from back then."

"Sometimes that's a good thing," Koro replies, then more firmly, "Come on you two, your kai is getting cold, eat up!"

\*\*\*

# Chapter Nine – Given Notice

*Tuesday Morning*

WITH THE MORNING sun warming Tom swings his way down the Wellington Waterfront Walk, admiring the old wharf buildings' architecture, 'man we are lucky to still have these.'

His thoughts range randomly. He nods to some of the other walkers exercising, who greet him occasionally with friendly hellos and bright fluro active wear.

Faltering on his crutches slightly as a memory surfaces, Tom stops, a distant look in his eyes as he recalls a series of disjointed memories. His parents in the front seat of the Holden Kingswood laughing, a loud bang, the car rolling and being tossed around like a rag doll, his father's head twisted at an unnatural angle, his mother half hanging out the front window and blood everywhere, men's voices, then the fire engine and hiding under the seat blocking out the awful reality.

He shakes his head to clear the horrific memories and drags himself back to the present, wondering, 'If only I had of stayed with Koro and Gran maybe they wouldn't have had the accident. Oh geez, come on Tom, snap out of it, it was in the past and you can't change it. Come on man, you promised yourself you would make it to Te Papa and then have a coffee as a reward.'

With a deep intake of breath, Tom sets off again, and

starts taking an interest in the people around him.

At Queen's wharf, Tom slows to avoid the influx of passengers disembarking from the Eastbourne Ferry, heading in all directions, some well-dressed women stop at a turquoise coffee caravan parked next to a small pohutukawa tree. Following his nose he smells the distinctive aroma of espresso. The sign atop of the caravan reads, Micco's Turkish Treats.

As the new crowd disperses and thins, he recognises a distinctive number-one haircut. Raking his brain he recalls with surprise, 'it's that young Israeli from the café. I wonder what he's up to?'

Initially, Tom manages to keep up with the Israeli spy, but gradually the distance between them increases, as they saunter down the Quay. 'That is one old suit. Good, he's going my way towards Te Papa.'

Concentrating on his rhythm, Tom determinedly increases his pace for a few minutes, then goes back into his easy stride, noticing his busy internal mental chatter, 'Oh, his gaze is focused ahead. He must be following someone. Damn that's an old suit, looks like it's from a charity shop, it certainly doesn't disguise the pistol he's packing. I must ask Devon if that's normal. Shit, I better report in.'

In front of Shed 5, Tom leans against the bench seat and fishes his secure phone out of his shoulder bag, tapping a quick text: following one of the Israeli guys from the café last week, passing Shed 5 heading towards Te Papa.

He pops his earbuds in, turns the Bluetooth on and slips back into his crutches. He is about to resume his pursuit, when he sees another familiar face. This time it is one of the Frenchmen. He taps out another message: Now there's a French spy following the Israeli.

His phone chirps, and a reply comes through: Be

careful bro!

He takes a good look around him and wonders, 'How many other spies are out here?' Not seeing anyone else he recognises, he continues his pursuit.

As he nears Shed 6, Tom sees both the Israeli and Frenchman veer to the left taking the harbour side path heading towards Frank Kitts Park. Picking up the pace, Tom narrows the gap to the Frenchman who seems to be slowing as he reaches the corner.

Getting closer to the Frenchman, Tom sees the Israeli standing by the stairs leading up to the rear of the TSB Stadium. Tom's sniper training kicks in. He notes the angle of both spies, and realises that they are both looking at someone else.

He slows down, he looks ahead. A swarthy complexioned man is standing near the water's edge talking into a phone. 'Who the hell is he?' He takes a quick photo of each of the spies and pockets his phone. He notices the Frenchman dial a number on his phone. Tom chances it and makes his way closer, slowing as he passes, to overhear, "…je ne sais pas… Algérien… Oui, oui… "

Not breaking stride, Tom carries on towards the Israeli, noting that the Algerian is on the move again, continuing towards the Museum of New Zealand. Everyone follows him.

As he passes the lighthouse slide at the park, the Frenchman overtakes him and the distance begins to grow again. His earbud chirps in his ear, tapping it, he hears Devon's voice "Talk when you can, but what's happening?"

"It's almost comical bro, I'm following a Frenchman, who's following an Israeli who's following an Algerian!" Tom chuckles, "but they're getting way ahead of me now."

"Damn, you're good at this brother. How'd you know

it's an Algerian?"

"I overheard the Frenchman talking on his phone, oh and he's a Parisian, the way he chopped his Oui was the givaway. Looks like my schoolboy French came in handy after all."

"George is going to love this Intel."

"Dev, I'm losing them. I'm too slow man, I can't keep up on my damn crutches." Tom anxiously replies.

"See if you can find out anything else. Where are you now?

A quick look around shows Tom where he is. "The Wahine memorial." Then he continues onward to chase his prey. "Damn, they've split up Dev. The Frenchman has gone right towards the city-to-sea bridge. The other two have gone ahead across the walkway. Where do I go?"

"Follow the Frenchman. He could be getting to high ground to observe the others," Devon rapidly answers.

"Great. More stairs," Tom sarcastically replies as he pushes himself forward.

"Go on, its good exercise for you, and Taylor would approve," Devon taunts.

As he negotiates the steps next to the Albatross fountain, Tom looks up to see the Frenchman rapidly climbing to the top of the stairs.

Back into his stride, Tom rounds the corner of the Whairepo Lagoon and heads to the next set of stairs. "I've lost him, now for the stairs."

"Taylor would be impressed, I can hear her now, Come on Tom, one more set," Devon teases as he does a poor impression of Taylor's Canadian accent.

Tom puffs derisively, "Funny guy, you should do stand-up comedy for a living."

"That reminds me, there is an open mic night at one

of the clubs in Allen Street tonight. Do you want to go?"

At the top of the stairs, Tom scans the area, "No sign of him, Dev. Hang on I'll head over a bit further. Are you seriously talking about going to a comedy club?"

"It took your mind off the stairs, didn't it? But why not? You keen?"

As he heads towards the southern end of the bridge, Tom stops and takes another look around. "There he is, Dev. I doubt if I'm going to catch him but I'll try."

"Where is he now?" Devon asks.

"He's raced down the ramp and is heading towards Te Papa between a couple of buildings. You know the one with the bar and restaurant."

"By the Mac's Brew bar?"

"Yeah, that's the one." Catching his breath, Tom says frustrated, "Okay bro, I've seriously got to find a faster way of getting around, but I'll keep following them and if I catch up I'll call you."

"Roger that. Catch you after work and remember bro, call me if you need back up," Devon hangs up.

As he carefully navigates the ramp towards the stairs, Tom notices a kayaker paddling around the lagoon. His crutch slips. He puts his left foot down too hard to balance and a terrible pain shoots through his body, stopping him in his tracks.

Taking in deep breaths to fill his lungs and breathing out slowly, Tom gradually regains his composure, thinking 'Damn it, I have to be more careful.' He takes stock and decides to take his time and finish his original goal of making it to Te Papa and having a coffee, unless by chance he sees one of the characters he was chasing.

\*\*\*

Relaxed at an outdoor table enjoying the sun, Tom surveys the lagoon casually, watching a couple of kayakers paddle around half-heartedly. A few seagulls land nearby, their raucous screeches imploring him to feed them. He makes a call on his phone, he hears his friend's voice, "Are you still on the chase?"

"Nah bro, I couldn't find anyone around Te Papa, so unless you call bird-watching the chase, I'm having a well-earned break at the café by the lagoon."

"Look at Casanova, eh? Is she a blonde or a brunette?" Devon baits him.

"The feathered variety bro," Tom sighs.

"Kinky all right, I didn't know you had it in ya," Devon laughs.

"Ha! As if you would know," Tom fires back. "So are we doing this comedy club tonight?"

"Ah… about that," Devon takes a breath, "Aroha mai brother, we are both working tonight."

"What? Since when?"

"Since George said so about ten minutes ago," Devon explains, "He wants a word somewhere private at 1900. Do you think Koro would mind if we met at your place?"

"I think it will be okay, I'll check and get back to you," Tom replies a little embarrassed, "you know it's not flash."

"Oh, and send me any photos you have from today and I'll run them through our computer and see what pops up," Devon brushes Tom's concerns aside.

"Sure, sure, okay Dev. I'll call you back once I've spoken with Koro."

\*\*\*

*Tuesday Afternoon*

The Station is chaotic with public servants who have clocked out early, rushing to make their trains, mixed with high school students lazily meandering around looking for any excuse to avoid their journey home. Tom and Koro push their shopping trolley and weave slowly across the concourse from the Metro supermarket.

"The price of those tomatoes is criminal!" Koro complains.

"I guess they can set whatever price they want in there," Tom assumes. "I mean, we all pay the cost for the convenience."

"I know you're right," Koro grumbles, "but it's just not on."

"Uh oh, here's Mr Happiness himself," Tom observes, seeing their Kiwirail nemesis waiting by their door.

"Tēnā koe i tēnei ahiahi Dunkell," Koro greets.

"Stuff off with your woke murray rubbish. You won't get me speaking anything other than the Queen's English," Dunkell opens.

Bristling, Tom angrily replies, "Just where do you get off talking to us like that, you Pommy prick?"

"Oh look who's racial now. The yellow war hero himself," Dunkell beams, turning Tom's words back at him, he chalks up an imaginary point in the air, "One nil to me."

"I think you will find it's 'racist' not 'racial' in your Queen's English," Koro counters, "But I'm sure you aren't here for an English lesson Dunkell, so…"

Taken aback with the rebuke, Dunkell agrees, "You're right, I'm here to give you the good news myself. Start packing your bags Yelich. You'll both be out by this time next week."

"Oh what for this time?" Tom asks. "Have you made up some fancy story to try and evict us again?"

Sporting an evil grin, Dunkell triumphantly delivers the news, "After my submission, the Council has re-zoned the whole Railway Station for commercial use only. So, your cosy little residential flat can no longer legally exist here and I'm going to turn it into office space."

Speechless, Tom and Koro look at each other. Koro slowly answers, "So, you finally managed it Dunkell. Well, I'm not packing a thing until I see something in writing."

Pulling an envelope out of his jacket pocket, Dunkell hands it to Koro, "Here you are Yelich. The Council decision and a letter asking you to vacate within a week, signed by Mr Harrop himself."

Taking the envelope from his foe, Koro replies, "If you're right, I'll miss our little fracas. Oh, by the way, that's an Italian word you English co-opted."

Dunkell looks puzzled at that last comment and walks off saying half-heartedly, "One more week Yelich."

Tom is worried as he unlocks the door. "Has he won Koro?"

Koro is unloading the shopping bags from the trolley. "Let's not give up too easily, Tāmati," he says with determination.

***

*Tuesday Evening*

"Stop fussing boy!" Koro yells angrily, "And turn that bloody hoover off! You look ridiculous!"

Tom pushes the off button with the end of his crutch. The loudly complaining machine's whine slowly trails off, "I'm just having a little tidy up Koro."

"You would think you had a girl coming around with all this nonsense," Koro complains, waving his arm around. "Look, if the man can't handle things a little jumbled around here, then he's not welcome in my whare!"

Tom sighs and sits down. "You're right Koro, it's just... well... he was my CO and I guess in my mind he still is, and I kinda wanted to make a good impression."

Koro sits beside him and gently reminds him, "Remember what I told you before you went away to the army?"

"Which piece of advice are you talking about? Ah, don't get yourself shot?" Tom kids.

"Well, you ignored that and got yourself blown up," Koro smiles, "no, the other one."

"You're right Koro, as usual," Tom concedes, "The mana of a man is measured by his actions, not the whare he comes from."

"Now, I'll put that hoover away. You get the kettle on, get the biscuit tin out, and turn the warmer drawer on," Koro commands, pushing himself up and dragging the vacuum cleaner away.

After preparing the supper and setting the table, Tom checks his watch and heads downstairs, yelling out, "Koro, they'll be here in a few minutes, I'll just open up."

At the bottom of the stairs, Tom hears a rapid knock at the door. Unlatching the lock, he opens it to reveal his friends.

"Tom, good to see you," George extends his hand.

Tom resists the urge to salute and firmly shakes his former Commanding Officer's hand, "Likewise George.

Please come in," he indicated the stairs, "Go on up. Hey Dev."

Devon leans in close, whispering, "Brother, has Koro calmed down or is he still anti the army?"

Tom shrugs, "I think he'll behave."

They troop upstairs, George leading the way, "Interesting place you have here, Tom, I didn't know there was any residential apartments at the Station."

Koro is in the living area where he greets his guests, "Kia ora George, Devon, please come take a seat."

George approaches Koro, puts his attaché case down and extends his hand and as he shakes Koro's hand, he leans in and greets Koro correctly with a hongi, lightly touching their foreheads and noses, pausing and mingling their breath, saying softly, "Kia ora Rangiwahia, it is an honour to finally meet you. He toa taumata rau."

"Āe e hoa, bravery does indeed have many resting places, nau mai, please sit down, George."

With his attaché case in hand, George crosses to the dining table, pulls out a chair and sits relaxing, "Ah, this has a homely feel, Rangiwahia."

Taken aback, both Devon and Tom, still standing stare at each other, "What just happened? Did you school George up?" Tom asks.

"Not me brother," Devon shakes his head equally puzzled.

As Koro takes a seat opposite George, he turns to them, "Well, where is your manaakitanga boys? You don't keep the manuhiri and the kaumātua waiting!Kia tere!"

Spurred into action Devon reaches the kitchenette first, Tom follows, instructing, "Open the warmer drawer bro, the plate is on the side."

The aroma from the oven's contents, fills the room.

"Mmm," George sniffs the air, "is that fry bread I smell?"

"If we are breaking bread for the first time, might as well enjoy it," Koro smiles.

As the jug clicks off, George pipes up and opens his briefcase, "If I may be so bold Rangiwahia, perhaps we could hold off the tea and refresh our palates with a little of this." He passes a gift-wrapped bottle to Koro, "I hope it meets with your approval."

Clearly surprised at receiving a gift, Koro carefully removes the wrapper, "Very thoughtful. Hmm what have we here..?" He reveals his old favourite, scotch with the Black and White Scottish Terriers on the label. He calls to Tom, "Hold the tea Tāmati and get us all a glass... the good ones." Turning to George he asks, "How did you know?"

Looking very pleased with himself, George answers, "A lucky guess. My uncle used to work in the Railway Workshops in Ōtāhuhu until they closed it in ninety-two. It was his favourite tipple."

"You're not related to old Eddie Gillies, are you?" Koro asks incredulously.

George looks a bit baffled, "Yes, did you know him?"

"Huh, Eddie was a bit of a rough diamond, and boy could he put a pint away, but a true stand-up man," Koro recollects, "He used to bring the overhauled D-class electric units back down to Wellington, and stay the night. Of course, we would show him a good time at the Waterloo across the road and then back here for a night cap or three."

"Sounds like Uncle Eddie," George replies with fondness.

Koro pours the golden liquid into the four glasses. "A wee dram, then we have a serious kōrero. This is not one of your Flash Harry single malts Devon, but I'm sure you'll like it." He lifts his glass up, and intones, "Slàinte Mhath."

Everyone joins him.

The smooth blended whisky leaves a slight burn all the way down his throat, which Koro enjoys. He smiles, then turning serious, asks gruffly, "All right George, enough with the pleasantries. What's this meeting all about?"

"As you wish. I'm going to take a chance here and put all my cards on the table. I trust that it will never leave this room," George states, "We have a major work problem, someone is leaking information from the SIS to both the Americans and the Russians and probably the Chinese as well."

Koro looks shocked. "Really? Who is it?"

"If I knew that, they wouldn't be still leaking information," George replies irritably, "That's why I asked Tom via Devon, if he could do a little work for us. We are running him 'dark' which means no one at the Service knows he is working for us."

"How dangerous is this job? Hasn't he already given enough for his country?" Koro demands.

"He certainly has given more than was asked for, and has saved countless lives as a result. To be honest, I don't know how dangerous this assignment will be. But I'm sure that his SAS training will keep him safe," George confesses.

"If you haven't noticed, he's on crutches. He's hardly able to hold a gun," Koro points out.

"It's Tom's observational skills that are key here. They have already yielded some fascinating Intelligence." George pulls out a manila folder and puts it on the table, patting it without opening it.

"So where do I come into this?" Koro shrewdly asks.

"Very perceptive, Rangiwahia." George pauses to take a sip of his whisky before continuing, "And I am getting there. Tom has uncovered two foreign operations in Wellington in less than a week. I've kept the information under wraps for the moment because of our leaks. And I want to run a larger covert counter operation to discover what's actually going on in OUR country. I really don't like the fact that the American's, Israeli's and French think they can do whatever they please in Wellington, without us knowing about it."

"Aren't they meant to be on our side?" Koro asks.

Devon and Tom exchange a look at each other, fascinated at the turn of the conversation.

Chuckling, George continues, "There are no sides in the Intelligence world. Oh we have alliances, but information is king and whoever has it first, holds the advantage. This is where you and Tom come in. I want to have a secure facility or base where we can run this counter operation, and I believe the best place for that base is right here in your apartment."

Koro raises his eyebrows in surprise, "Eh? Here?"

"Yes, right here. It's central and no one would suspect it," George enthuses, "I noticed a large space downstairs that appears unused that would be perfect. Of course, we would pay a generous rent for the use of the space and a stipend for your time."

Tom interrupts, "Unfortunately, we have a slight problem with that idea."

Koro adds, "I've just been given notice. We have to be out in a week." Then thinking on his feet, asks hopefully, "Unless of course, you could pull some strings?"

Deflated, George replies, "Oh, well, I'm not sure…"

Interrupting, Devon asks, "Can I have a look at your eviction notice Koro. There's got to be a loop hole somewhere."

Reaching behind him, Koro grabs the envelope from the sideboard and hands it to Devon. "Fill your boots Devon, I couldn't see a way out of it myself. Might be time for a second dram."

"Don't mind if I do, thanks Rangiwahia."

Koro picks up the whisky bottle and pours everyone a measure.

"Tom, can you google the Wellington Council's definition of 'commercial premises' please?" Devon asks, reading the eviction notice and other papers.

Tom rapidly taps scrolls through his screen, "Yeah, here it is…" Devon leans over and scans the information.

"It baffles me George, what these young fellas can do on those things," Koro comments, "But tell me, what's my part in this spy game of yours?"

"Well, I wouldn't put you in harm's way, but I know you have a lot of contacts in this city, and that could come in handy. What I also haven't mentioned is that we would need a few extra people involved."

"Like who?"

George adds, "Okay, now as for staff, clearly they can't have any obvious link to the Service. Devon, remember that gamer computer guy you questioned last month?"

"The hacker? Connor wasn't it? Are you sure?"

"Yes, I believe he would be willing to 'serve' his country and stay out of jail," George grins, "and Rangiwahia, do you know a Francesco Vettori?"

Koro narrows his eyes, "Not the cop?"

"Retired police officer now, I believe you may have crossed paths before." George smiles.

Koro laughs, "You could say that. More likely crossed fists a couple of times. But Frankie's honest enough for a cop. I dunno if he would want to work with me though."

"I'll get Devon to arrange for them to meet you all tomorrow," George confirms, "You may need a front person, receptionist or such to keep up the appearance of a legitimate detective agency."

"Who did you have in mind?" Tom asks.

"My niece, Danielle. She's just back from her OE and is looking for work," George explains.

"A bit dodgy having a Gillies on staff, isn't it?" Tom queries.

"She's my sister's daughter, surname Franklin. She's from up Shannon way and doesn't want to settle down with a farmer yet." George is thinking to himself, 'plus it would be good to get her off my couch.'

"Sorry to interrupt, but I think I've found it," Devon inserts himself into the conversation, "According to the Council reg's, if you can start a business and run it from downstairs, you can legally live upstairs if there is existing accommodation."

"But we can't start a business and run a covert operation in the same space. This isn't Hollywood bro," Tom laughs.

"We could, if it's the right business," Devon thinks, "Okay, we need a business that runs at odd hours and doesn't need someone to 'mind the store' during business hours."

"Don't laugh," Koro muses, "but what about a detective agency?"

"That... could... work," George replies a bit surprised, then more determined, "No, seriously, that would actually work."

"Really?" Tom asks in disbelief.

"Yes, it would. Now Tom you would have to apply for a private investigator's license, but I can speed that up.

There is probably a form to fill out at the Council... and of course, you would need a tax number and maybe even set up an actual company," George brainstorms, "Yes, it's very do-able."

"Ha, that would stuff up Dunkell's plans," Koro chuckles, "How fast can we set this up?"

"Officially, maybe three days, so by Friday maybe Saturday, all set to open business on Monday."

"I like it... a lot," Koro beams. He stands and puts his hand out, "George you've got yourself a deal. Put it there."

George reaches out to shake Koro's hand, when Koro asserts, "On one condition, Tom's name goes on the business and he gets my share, I'm on the pension and I don't want to pay any more tax."

"Why not, if Tom's agreeable," George confirms.

"So, what are you going to call this detective agency of yours brother?" Devon asks Tom, gently elbowing him in the ribs.

"I dunno bro," Looking around the room for inspiration, Tom sees one of his favourite books on the shelf, "How about 'White Rabbit Investigations' to honour one of my childhood heroes, Wing Commander Yeo-Thomas."

"I like the irony, the Special Operations Executive undercover spy in World War Two," George nods, "Hiding in plain sight. Very good."

Raising his glass, Koro toasts, "Here's to White Rabbit Investigations and all who sail in her! Slàinte!"

"This is really going to happen," Tom states, shaking his head, "Oh, I've got an appointment tomorrow morning at nine-thirty, so any time after that for the staff meeting."

"Devon, get a hire van tomorrow morning and meet me at the BS Ministries All of Government office supplies facility on Sar Street at 0900. Rangiwahia we should be here about nine-thirty with some office furniture for downstairs. Tom what time are you due back?" George asks.

"Just after ten hundred sir," Tom slips back into military speak.

"So, staff meeting at ten thirty," George states, then putting the manila folder back in his briefcase, "I'll brief you all on the contents of this folder then."

\*\*\*

# Chapter Ten – New Friends

*Wednesday Morning*

"TAKE A SEAT Tom, I'll be with you in a moment," the Doctor announces, leaving Tom alone in her office.

Swinging himself over to the wall, Tom inspects the framed degrees and certificates, thinking, 'Well she's one well qualified shrink.' Then he squares himself over the chair and lowers himself onto the spongey cushion.

The door swings open and the Doctor brings in two hot cups of tea, "Sorry, we only have peppermint tea. Is that all right?"

"Sure Doctor Williams," Tom takes the offered cup from her.

"It's Sandra, please. It's not often I get a combat referral."

"Nice tea, it's very, well… pepper-minty," Tom falters, then gathering himself, "So how does this work?"

"Today, we talk," Sandra explains. "I'll ask a series of questions, so I can complete the assessment and hopefully provide you with a diagnosis. Then we can plan how you want to tackle any issues we discover."

"Great, so you decide if I'm a nutter… geez I feel like a loser already," Tom sounds depressed.

"Tom, you aren't a nutter. You've suffered an extremely traumatic experience and have a serious injury as a result.

How could you not come through that unscathed?" Sandra asks rhetorically.

"I guess you're right," Tom admits grudgingly, "Have you ever treated combat veterans before?"

"Not soldiers, but I have treated people who have suffered physical violence, like police officers, gang members and many battered partners, as well as rape and assault victims." Sandra takes a sip of her tea. "PTSD is a disorder that arises from trauma and the individual's response or lack of response to cope."

"Of course, when you put it like that, I suppose there are a lot of people out there," Tom gestures to the window. "This PTSD, what are some of the symptoms?" Tom asks, trying to get to the point.

"It sounds like you're ready to start," Sandra, rests a clipboard on her knee and takes a pen from her desk. "Just answer yes, no, or very briefly to these questions. We can go into detail later."

"Sounds like a tick box exercise, but fire away." Tom settles into his chair.

Smiling, Sandra begins, "Do you have insomnia and or nightmares?"

"Yes to both."

"Uh ha, what about flashbacks?"

"Yeah, I had one last week at the gym."

"Right, do you startle easily?"

"Ah, I dunno. I'm very observant. I do look around me a lot."

"That's sounds more like Hypervigilance," Sandra makes another mark on the paperwork. "What about memory loss?"

"No, I remember exactly what happened," Tom looks a little pale.

"Do you get angry or irritable?"

"Well, yeah, but then there is a lot going on.' Thinking a moment, Tom continues, "I mean I've lost my Army career. I'm back living with my grandfather and I've lost my mobility, so yeah actually I'm quite pissed off."

"I can imagine." Sandra's pen scratches some notes. "Would you say you are more of a positive or negative person?"

"I'm finding it really hard to stay positive, I mean, I hear some good news and it's like fleeting you know, it just doesn't seem to stick," Tom shakes his head.

"Okay what about risky behaviours?" Sandra asks.

"Such as?"

"Like drinking, drugs, gambling, unprotected sex, high adrenaline activities?"

"I do like a drink. You can't escape that in army life, but I've got that under control with my best mate Devon. Never touched drugs, my Koro used to follow the horses, but I never have. Sex, ha, no time for a relationship in SAS, and now, I don't think any girl would look twice at a cripple." Tom decides not to mention his recent undercover work. "And I'm not jumping out of a plane any time soon."

"Okay, I think we have enough to work with. Just give me a minute." Sandra's pen keeps moving over the clipboard. "Now, you say you live with your grandfather?"

"Yeah, he's my only surviving whānau, Mum and Dad died in a car crash when I was six. That's when I moved in with Koro and Gran, then Gran left and went up north but she died soon after that," Tom takes a deep breath.

"I'm so sorry to hear that. It must have been very tough," Sandra sympathises.

"Yeah, it sure was. Oh I had a flashback of the car accident a couple of days back, so sorry that's two flashbacks this last week."

"What? You were in the car when your parents died?" Sandra queries.

"Ah, yeah," Tom replies slowly.

"Oh my god, that must have been horrific," Sandra cries, then collecting herself, "I'm sorry, that wasn't very professional."

"Well, that's good. It shows me that you're human," Tom smiles. The questions continued for another half an hour before Tom finally asks, "So what's the verdict?"

"Well Tom, you've got a full house. I've ticked off so many PTSD symptoms, and there are a lot of questions I'd like to explore further."

"So where do we go from here?"

"I would suggest a weekly therapy session, and to help with your sleep, I'm going to refer you to a psychiatrist for medication," Sandra advises.

"Not another doctor. Can I hold off on the medication for the moment and just go with the therapy?"

"Well, I suppose we could try that, but if you aren't making progress, then I would recommend you see the psychiatrist," Sandra decides. 'They have a lot of good prescription drugs nowadays and they're not addictive, if that's your concern.

"Just so long as we can stop the flashbacks. They really freak me out."

"Let's see what we can do," turning to look at her computer, "how does ten thirty Wednesday next week sound?"

"Oh, none today?" Tom asks a bit deflated.

"Sorry Tom, this is an assessment appointment, next week we will have a full hour dedicated purely to therapy," Sandra replies, then offers clicking the print button on her computer, "But I've got a handout on sleep hygiene which may help at night. And please try and get some exercise each day as that does make a vast improvement to your mood."

Gathering his crutches and the handout, Tom pushes himself up, "Well thanks Sandra, see you next week."

***

Tom stops at the open doorway, amazed taking in the transformation.

Directly in front of him two desks face the entry with partitions behind them to screen off the stairs. A small gap partially reveals more office space. In the reception area, are a small two seater couch and low coffee table to one side and a spreading, tree-like pot plant to the other.

He swings through the gap in the partitions, and finds two more desks, both supporting a computer, and an oval meeting table. Here Koro sits looking inside a set of file drawers. The walls are decorated with a book shelf, a large whiteboard and two large cork boards.

"Wow, you guys have been busy!"

"Like you wouldn't believe brother," Devon pops up from under one of the desks. "You know how George is. I'm just running an extension cord for this computer to get it working."

"How did it go with the shrink?" Koro asks, turning from the filing cabinet.

"I think she's going to be okay. I see her again next week. It's looking alright."

"Is that some optimism I'm hearing in your voice?" Devon asks.

Thinking a moment, Tom decides, "Yeah... I think it

is."

"About bloody time," Koro declares. "You've been a right sad-sack since you got home."

"Really?"

"Really! You've had us both worried brother." Devon confirms, "I know this is not something you can just snap out of, so it's a good sign."

"And I'm an impatient, grumpy old man, but I know you have a long winding road ahead of you Tāmati. That's why I think all this will be good for you." Koro gestures at the room, "It'll give you something to focus on."

"Thanks for hanging in there and putting up with my moods guys. I guess I've been so wrapped up in my own misery, I didn't notice how gloomy I've been."

"Why do you think I pushed you to go to the gym?" Devon asks.

"And I've got you on tea-making duties, so you don't feel like a spare prick at a party," Koro adds.

Tom sits down at one of the desks. "So, you two have been putting up with my crap and gently encouraging me all this time… did you plan this?"

Looking a bit red-faced, Devon explains, "Ah yeah, I came and saw Koro when I first got down here to start work. You had me really worried when I visited you last time in Middlemore. Koro… well, we had a bit of a chat."

"Devon explained things to me, how you were in hospital, how tough the flight back home was on you with the cockup in Townsville, how you got shafted by that bloody army. It's no wonder you're feeling down boy." Koro walks over and pats Tom on his shoulder. "You're carrying a hell of a lot up top. It will be good for you to have a proper kōrero with someone independent, even if it is a shrink."

Overcome with emotion, Tom reaches across and pats Koro's hand on his shoulder, "Thanks Koro. I don't know what I would do without you both. Devon my bro, you're one stand-up guy."

"Brother I can never repay you for rescuing me after school that day. I was about to give up," Devon confesses, "I want to thank you too Koro, for letting me stay when Tom brought me here all those years ago, and for making me feel part of your whānau."

Koro wipes the tears from his own face. "Come on my boys, I can see that I taught you well. We are whānau and we bloody well stick together and help each other. Look at us three sook's, eh? Come on clean yourselves up before the new fellas arrive."

Looking at his family, Tom feels the bonds of love that tie them to each other. He pulls his handkerchief from his jeans pocket, and wipes his face. He hears Koro blowing his nose. The joy rises up within him; fills him with a new-found confidence that he hasn't felt for a very long time. Determined to help he asks, "Devon, do we have any notebooks and pens yet?"

"Yeah, I've put them in the top filing drawer, I'll just plug this cord in."

"I'll get them," Koro offers.

"Good, let's spread them around the table and get a couple more chairs in here," Tom directs.

There is a knock at the door. Tom looks over his shoulder.

"Hey dude, is ah… Devon here?" A pale, gangly youth with dark unkempt hair saunters in carrying a skateboard under one arm. He has a good look around.

"Yeah, in here, are you…" Tom begins

Devon pops up from under the desk, "Connor, come

on in." He points to the others, "This is Tom and Mr. Yelich. Guys this is Connor. He's going to help us with these computers."

"Come on in, boy," Koro invites gruffly, extending his hand which Connor grabs and shakes firmly, "Nothing like a good handshake Connor. Call me Koro."

"Ah, nice to meet you Mr... ah... Koro," Connor stumbles, walking over uneasily to Tom, "Don't get up dude."

Shaking hands, Tom confirms, "Nice handshake bro, grab a pew. We're waiting on a couple of others."

Connor takes a seat by the large computer. "Hey, do you mind if I have a look?"

Devon on his way out to collect some more chairs, turns at Connor's voice, "Yeah, please, I think I've hooked it up okay."

"We'll see if you have, dude," Connor smiles, his hands flying over the keyboard in a flurry of activity. "Dude, this PC is dank!" he says with pleasure. "But the connectivity is a bit slow, where's the router?"

"I take it that 'dank' means good?" Devon asks, then points to the corner, "The routers over there by the bookshelf."

Another knock at the door sounds. In Tom's mind he sees George with an attractive blonde entering the room, turning he sees a large older man cautiously entering the office.

Koro turns and momentarily freezes seeing the familiar face. After a slight pause, he says, "Come on in Frankie and meet the whānau."

Chuckling the bear of a man saunters into the room, "Well I never thought I'd see the day when I'd be invited into your place without a warrant, Rangi." He extends his hand to greet Koro, and they both perform the ritual hongi, then stand back, laughing together, clapping each other's upper arms.

"Boys this is one of the toughest bastards to ever wear a copper's uniform," Koro declares, "Frankie, this is my moko Tom and his friend Devon, and that's Connor by the computer."

Shaking Tom's hand, Frankie remarks, "Looks like you've been in the wars, Tom."

Tom fires straight back, "Afghanistan actually, Frankie."

Frankie raises his eyebrows with respect, "Really? I didn't see anything on the news."

"Huh, you only see what they want you to on TV Frankie," Koro replies.

"We're just waiting on the boss and the…" Devon starts as he brings in a nest of four chairs.

"And here we are," George calls out.

Tom looks over towards the newcomers, his breath catching and an eerie sense of déjà vu comes over him when he sees the blonde haired woman with George.

"Come on Danielle, through here," shepherding his niece in, before he closes and locks the front door. Once behind the partition he does the introduction. "Good, we're all here. Everyone, this is Danielle, Danielle this is Francesco, Rangiwahia, Tom, Devon and Connor."

"Hi everyone," Danielle waves, enthusiastically. "This is so exciting!"

"Okay Mr. Gillies," Frankie asks, "Just why are we all here?"

"Before we start, Devon can you please pass around these forms for everyone to sign. Then you'll get the full story," George suggests.

Dani surreptitiously glances around the room noting the two young men her age. The taller one passing the forms around and the cute one on crutches whose eyes look strangely familiar.

Glancing at the long form with tiny print, Koro comments. "George I'm not going to read all this, give me a quick run down,"

"Essentially, you are signing a Non-Disclosure Agreement to say that everything you learn about or do in this agency, you will keep quiet about or you may face some legal penalties," George summarises.

"And just what legal penalties are these?" Frankie asks, his legal background piqued.

"Well, we don't shoot people for treason anymore," George pauses to see the effect of his words. He makes sure has everyone's attention and continues, "But we do lock people up for a very long time."

Connor is the first to speak up, "Hey Dude, you said if I work here, I won't have to go inside."

George fixes Connor with a steely gaze, "I'm a man of my word, Connor. Just keep up your end of the bargain and you will get paid legitimately for your unique set of skills." Then looking at each of the room's occupants, "Each of you have valuable expertise and talents that combined will answer the questions I have regarding some of the dubious activity happening in our city."

Frankie asks, "George, can you get to the point. Koro and I aren't getting any younger."

"You are now part of a Top Secret operation to find out what other country's spies are up to in Wellington," George explains. "No one in the New Zealand Intelligence community knows about this, apart from Devon, myself and the Director General. As such, this is all about watching people and gathering information. What we call Intelligence, and then working out what is going on - analysis. Then we, in the SIS, can take action if necessary to keep our country safe."

"Uncle George, you didn't tell me this job was going to be so thrilling!" Danielle comments.

"Dani, I said to drop the uncle." George is a little embarrassed. He puts his attaché case on the table next to the corkboard. "Devon, can you pass me some drawing pins please."

"Sure thing Boss," Devon replies, locating the pins in the filing drawer.

George pulls some large photos out of his briefcase and pins them to the corkboard, "This is Eitan Freidman, Mossad, that's Israeli Intelligence, and this is Henri Chevalier, DGSE, that's French Intelligence. They were following this man." He pauses and taps the photo. "We don't know who this man is, or why the other two spies were following him. He may be Algerian. The Algerians have no diplomatic presence in New Zealand, but it doesn't mean they aren't here spying. I want to locate this man, find out who he is and what he is up to."

"Judas Priest, straight to business," Frankie declares, "How dangerous is this job, George?"

"Hopefully it's not too dangerous, Frankie. Your role, as I said is information gathering. But the last DGSE operation we missed in this country, resulted in the bombing of the Rainbow Warrior in Auckland and the death of one of her crew." George looks at everyone again. "I don't want to miss anything like that and have to live with the consequences on my conscience."

Breaking the deathly silence that follows, George continues, "Officially, you all work for Tom who runs this detective agency, 'White Rabbit Investigations'. I'll get you all to fill out some paperwork shortly to apply for a Private Investigator's licence, which I'll get fast-tracked. I've tasked Devon to this assignment and he will be the official link back to me, but I'll pop in occasionally for a briefing on your investigation. And for safety, Devon will get your sizes for a vest and some other PPE, Tom would you like to say something?"

"This is all a bit surreal, but hell, this is our first assignment and I can't wait to crack on."

Koro interrupts, "What about Kendrick?"

"Yes, Rangiwahia," George picks up another photo and pins it on the second corkboard, "This is Theodore Kendrick, CIA, last known assignment was Operation Crimson Sky, Afghanistan which Devon, Tom and their team were intimately involved in, and where Tom received his injuries."

"That bastard will pay for what he did to Tom," Koro promises.

"That he will, Rangiwahia, that he will. But only at a time of our choosing." He stops and points to the photo, making sure he has everyone's attention. "Currently he is somewhere in Wellington. Probably at the embassy. I will confirm this through SIS back channels. However, we know, thanks to Tom, that he has been in contact with high level BS Ministry staff involved with the New Zealand Space Agency. What exactly about? We don't know yet. This is our second assignment. Any questions?"

"How big is the IT budget?" Connor asks, "I mean, this is a good computer, but it's limited, especially if you want smart phone connectivity."

"Give Devon a list of what you need and I'll see what I can scrounge," George replies.

"Any idea of where we can find this Algerian?" Frankie asks.

Tom interjects, "I've had a thought on that. Let's check if there is an Algerian community group or restaurants and cafés. Then we can watch them and see if he shows up."

"Good thinking Tom." George looks at his watch. "Perhaps extend that out to Middle Eastern cafés and the like. Tom, can I leave you to organise this and task everyone. I have an invitation to deliver."

"Thanks George, we won't let you down," Tom announces, then empowers the team, "Right, everyone, grab a notebook and pen. Now, no idea is a dumb idea and don't be shy, I want everyone speaking up."

The office becomes a hive of activity, everyone quickly melding into a chaotic crew as they brainstorm ideas and grow their roles. Devon and Tom relate their experiences and share some of their skills, during which they have fun practicing role-playing, and later Frankie tells some tall tales of his stakeouts while they relax with a cuppa in the late afternoon.

*** 

George walks confidently into the US Embassy reception, past the Marine standing at ease. He smiles at the receptionist.

"How may I help you today, sir?" The blonde woman asks, her beaming smile showcasing the many thousands of dollars spent on her teeth.

"Could you get me your manager, please? I have an invitation to pass on," George asks politely.

"Do you have an appointment sir?"

George puts his attaché case on the counter and opens it. He pulls out an envelope, "I don't need one, your manager will want to see this."

The Marine guard smartly approaches George barking, "Hold it sir! Let me see what is in the bag!"

George flashes his warrant card, firmly replying, "Stand down son." He places the envelope on the counter, "I suggest you get your manager."

The wide-eyed receptionist jumps up from her seat and opens the door behind her, stammering, "Ah s-sir, there's a gentleman here from the…"

"I'm coming," a dishevelled man comes out of the room, tucking the tail of his shirt into his trousers and approaches the counter. "What seems to be the problem?"

George sizes up the man. "I have an invitation for you to pass onto Mr Kendrick, I believe he is currently working here."

"For who, sir?" the manager asks.

"Mr Theodore Kendrick. He is cordially invited to present himself and his credentials to the Director General this afternoon at three," George grins.

Looking at George quizzically, "We don't have anyone working here by that name."

"Tell your Ambassador that we know Kendrick is in the country masquerading as a Mr Waldergrave and that he's been meeting with some of our officials." George fixes the manager with his steely gaze, slapping a photo down in front of him of Kendrick outside the BS Ministry shaking hands with an official, "And if he wants to avoid an embarrassing leak of photographs to the Capital News Network about unauthorised CIA operatives running around our country, he'd better present Kendrick at the invitation's time this afternoon." He waits momentarily for a response. "Do I make myself clear?"

***

*Wednesday Evening*

"Come on Devon, put some more power in that movement," Taylor admonishes, "That's it Tom, one more set of hip rotations."

Both the boys redouble their efforts, concentrating on their technique to get the best out of each exercise.

"Good work. Now stay on your backs, extend your legs straight and keep them that way through the exercise," Taylor instructs.

"That's easy. Now what?" Tom asks.

"Push the backs of your knees to the floor while flexing your feet and pulling your toes back towards you."

"These are good wind down exercises after the workout on the machines," Devon comments.

"True that bro," Tom confirms.

"Just mixing it up for you boys, or you might get bored," Taylor smiles, "Good, now a couple of deep breaths... and one more set to finish."

"Too easy," Tom says brightly starting his last series of leg stretches.

"Can I ask what's up with you two?" Taylor asks.

"What do you mean Taylor," Devon queries.

"Well, it's like... Devon, you seem more relaxed and Tom, well, it's like something has clicked up here," she taps her head. "You are so much more committed to the exercise routine. But there's something else I can't put my finger on."

Finishing the set, Tom sits up, looking at Devon wondering how much he can say, fumbling, "Err, I've found a good shrink?"

Covering for them both, Devon speaks up, "You're

right Taylor, something has clicked for my bro and it's good to have the old Tom back." Then trying to divert the conversation, "Hey, what are you doing Friday night? We were thinking of catching a couple of acts at one of the stand-up comedy clubs. Would you be keen?"

Taken aback at the offer, Taylor asks, "Are you asking me out for a date?"

Blushing slightly, Devon recovers, "No, no, that wouldn't be professional. It's just, well, we haven't had much of a social life in the army and I thought we might try something a little different, like a comedy club, but you're probably already booked up."

Thinking for a moment, Taylor replies, "Actually guys, I might take you up on that offer. I've spent the last two years focused so much on building this place up from scratch, I haven't had a good night out in ages. Let's talk more tomorrow eh?"

"Sure thing," Devon stands, offering his hand to Tom, "Come on bro, let's get you showered and home."

\*\*\*

*Wednesday Evening*

The nearly empty Station echoes with the sound of their footsteps as they cross the concourse. A few late stragglers saunter towards their trains, looking a little worse for wear from either the long hours on the job or one too many after work drinks.

"I knew you were after her, bro," Tom states.

"What?"

"Asking Taylor out, it's so obvious man," Tom insists.

"Nah brother, I did that for you," Devon deflects,

lightly punching him in the arm.

"Mate, no woman will look twice at me, but you on the other hand. You could have them eating out of your hand," Tom counters. "But, seriously, I don't know if I'm up for going down Courtenay Place on a Friday night just yet."

"You'll be fine Tom, I'll keep an eye out for ya," Devon smooths.

Deep in their conversation, neither of them notice the figure approaching them until his voice intrudes, "Trying to slip an illegal tenant in afterhours, are we war hero?"

"Geez-us, don't sneak up on me like that, Dunkell," Tom exclaims, "Are you trying to give me a heart attack?"

"I saw all that extra furniture going into your flat this morning," Dunkell begins, then looks at Devon, "So you've moved in have you?"

"Ah no, I'm just giving Tom a helping hand…"

"Spare me your pathetic excuses," Dunkell dismisses Devon, turning back to Tom, "Tell your pops that I can't wait until next Tuesday, when I can get the cleaners in and finally disinfect the Yelich stench from my Station."

"Dunkell, you do know that you have a real problem, don't you?" Tom holds his antagonist's gaze, "you should see someone about it. Come on, Dev, we've got more important things to do."

Tom swings his way around Dunkell, and both he and Devon cross the final few metres to their front door.

"I hope I'm here when Koro finally drops the news on him. Can you imagine what his face will look like?" Devon quietly remarks.

"Ha, his head will probably explode." Tom laughs as he lets them into the reception. An immense surge of pride rises up from within him, and he swings ahead into the office pausing to look at the corkboard's development. "You know bro, we made some real progress today."

"Yeah, we all really bonded. Even young Connor seemed to come out of his shell." Devon agrees, "I think we might have to keep an eye on him though."

"What's his story? Anything I should know?" Tom eases himself into one of the chairs next to the busiest looking corkboard.

"Well, he hacked into the Deputy Prime Minister's computer and was about to hand over the contents to a journalist when we caught him," Devon begins.

"Geez-us, what did he have on that prick?"

"Just some copies of his dubious internet search history and some images he had loaded onto his computer."

"Let me guess," Tom suggests. "Porn? How embarrassing."

"Some very borderline porn, verging on school-girl fantasy stuff. Definitely a career limiting scandal if it had got out." Devon shakes his head, "But it wasn't that which George was concerned about. It was what we found on Connor's computer when we investigated that."

Wide-eyed, Tom says, "Okay spill."

"The clever little bugger had worked out the access code to the Waihopai Communications facility. He'd only just got into the intranet index to look, but hell, if we hadn't caught him with the Deputy PM's porn, who knows what he could have accessed?" Devon shakes his head.

"I'm glad he's on our side then."

"Yeah, but he's young. We'll need to keep an eye on him."

"Oh, you mean like when Trev joined our unit?" Tom recalls, "They think they are ten feet tall and bulletproof."

"Āe, a real know-it-all," Devon agrees.

"You're right, but emotionally immature," Thinking a bit, Tom chuckles, "Good call. He did bitch a bit about getting here by seven-thirty tomorrow."

Koro calls out as he makes his way down the stairs, "I thought I heard someone down here. Why are you making an old man take these stairs more than I have to eh?"

"Aroha mai Koro, we were just thinking we may have to keep an eye on young Connor," Tom explains.

"Huh, he'll be alright, I'll keep an eye on him," Koro takes a seat at the table, "It's that young Dani that you'll have to watch."

"Really Koro?" Devon asks, "What did you notice, apart from her over-eagerness?"

"That she was eyeing both you boys up," Koro winks, "So what would 'Uncle' George say if either of you started courting her?"

"You're dreaming, Koro. If you think she has any interest in me."

Devon looks slightly pale. "Oh no! George would have my balls, if I tried anything on with her."

Ribbing his friend, "Is that why you asked Taylor out, Dev? A bit of diversion."

"Hey, I didn't choose the skux life bro. It chose me," Devon wisecracks, holding his hands up in mock surrender.

"I'm just saying keep an eye on her," Koro says sagely.

"So, what about you and Frankie, Koro?" Tom asks.

"We respect each other, even if we were on different sides of the fence in the past. We'll be okay," Koro informs them confidently.

"He certainly knows his way around town," Devon comments.

"Just look at his waistline. He must know every restaurant in the city!" Koro jests.

Laughing Tom adds, "He'll also provide some good legal input if we need it."

"I still think it's a bit dodgy with Dani's link to George. I mean she is dossing on his couch," Devon comments.

"I've been thinking about that," Koro contemplates a moment, "Tom, ring Sheila on your phone and pass it to me."

Tom dials the number, puts it on speaker and passes his phone towards Koro, "Just speak out loud, so we can all hear."

"Don't get too bloody fancy boy," Koro begins, then hearing Sheila answering, "Sheila, Rangi here. Hey is that old room out the back of your place habitable?"

Sheila asks sternly, "Rangiwahia, have you and Tom fallen out?"

Laughing Tom interrupts, "No Aunty, Tom here, we have you on speaker. Koro and I are all good."

"Oh Tāmati, so what's this about my spare room?"

Koro puts on his sweet-talking voice, "Sheila, I'm just thinking about you. Maybe you might like a bit of company in the evening. Also you'd be helping out a friend of Tāmati's, a young girl, Danielle. She's looking for a place in the city to stay."

"Well does this girlfriend of Tāmati's have a job? I'm not a charity and I only just get by on the pension."

"She's not my girlfriend!" Tom protests. Devon laughing, makes a heart sign in the air pointing at Tom.

"Yes, she does and your place is close to her new job," Koro replies.

"And close to young Tāmati, too. Hmm, well I shouldn't get in the way of two young lovers. Tāmati, best you bring her to visit tomorrow and we'll see if I approve of this match."

"Thanks, old girl, see you then," Koro replies, looking at the screen in bewilderment, "How do you turn this thing off?"

Sheila snaps, "Enough of the OLD girl, Rangiwahia and remember you owe me a game of Cribbage," And the line then goes dead.

"She's not my girlfriend, Koro," Tom mutters.

"Sheila doesn't need to know that, if it gets Dani some digs now does she?"

"What if they don't get along?" Devon asks.

"Then you might have to give up that flash apartment of yours and you move in with Sheila," Koro replies.

Laughing Tom kids Devon, "I don't think Sheila would approve of you bringing Taylor back to her place skux."

"Come on you two, your kai is getting cold. You can sort your girlfriend troubles out later, kia tere. Come on, up the stairs with you," Koro hustles them.

"Oh yeah, Koro," Tom remembers and he picks up his crutches, "We ran into Dunkell on the way home."

"Don't spoil my appetite," Koro mutters, "Let's eat first."

\*\*\*

# Chapter Eleven – The French Connection

*Thursday Morning*

"MAN YOU HAVE one real Nazi arsehole out there," Connor complains as he walks into the reception area, with his skateboard tucked under his arm and a large black backpack hanging from his right shoulder.

"Are you okay?" Tom asks, making his way to the door and looking out, "Oh, that's Dunkell. He's a pratt."

"Nosey parker wanted to know what I was doing here. Thought I was a tenant." Connor is indignant.

"What did you say?" Tom asks, closing the door.

"Nothing, I just skated around him and gave him the finger," Connor replies, then excitedly, "Hey I've got some cool stuff for the computer. Can I go and set it up?"

"Sure, sure. You want a coffee or tea?" Tom asks.

"Nah dude, I've got my supply of energy drinks." Connor pats his backpack.

There is a loud knock on the door. Tom turns angrily and swings back, opening the door, expecting Dunkell. "Yes?"

"Talofa, delivery for ah White Rabbit Investigations?" A large Samoan man, points at a trolley jack stacked with boxes, "I'll need a hand with a couple of big boxes still in the van."

"Ah, yes, just inside here to the left please," Tom

replies apologetically, reads his name badge then calling out, "Connor can you come and help Joseph please."

Connor comes back in and assists Joseph to stack the boxes.

"Hi Connor, Hi Tom," Dani greets them as she arrives, "Need some help?"

"We'll be okay, miss," Joseph replies as he and Connor head out to the van.

A little embarrassed, Tom asks, "Dani, could you please help move some of these boxes through to the office?"

"Sure." Dani places her handbag on one of the front desks, thinking aloud, "It must be hard being on crutches and not being able to help lift things."

"It's damn frustrating at times," Tom replies a touch bitterly, as they move through to the office space, "If you can put them on this desk, please, I'll find a packing knife to open them."

Tom rifles through the filing cabinet, then he has a thought. "Dani, we need to cover the corkboards, before the delivery guy gets back."

"What if I turn these brainstorming sheets of art paper around, and cover the photos?" Dani asks.

"Great idea!" Tom agrees, announcing his discovery, "Found one."

"Coming through," Connor announces as he backs into the office carrying a large flat rectangular box with Joseph on the other end.

"Boss, we have two more just like this and then can you sign for them?" Joseph asks Tom.

"No worries, Joseph."

Unpacking the boxes and setting up the new equipment keeps both Dani and Connor occupied for the next half hour. Connor patiently explaining where and how the different parts of the computer function, keeping both Tom and Dani struggling, at times, to keep up.

"Essentially, with these components, I've upgraded the old computer to the highest spec gaming PC," Connor explains.

"It's not something I've gotten into Connor," Tom starts, "and I'm not sure you will have much time for gaming."

Looking at Tom with an incredulous expression, "Where have you been dude? Under a rock? Did you not get any time off in the army?"

"Mate, we used rocks for cover from real bullets and our downtime was usually spent in a bar where we could have a quiet cold beer." Tom pauses with a faraway look in his eyes and quietly adds, "You don't really want to play at war on a console after you've experienced it."

"Sorry dude, I didn't mean to…" Connor begins.

"Just forget about it mate. Tell me more about this souped up computer."

Regaining his enthusiasm, Connor continues, "It's way faster than my old PC and that was a one of a kind, so I'll be able to run multiple dense programmes at the same time. But I need to ask if it's okay to access the dark web and to add some of my software."

Dani frowns. "Isn't the dark web full of porn and where all those pedo's hang out?"

Laughing, Connor explains, "Well, yeah there are those weirdo's there, along with alt-right Nazi's, porn stars and black market versions of eBay where you can get anything. It's also where my hacking mates hang out."

"I'm not sure Devon and George would want you reconnecting with them Connor. We aren't meant to be breaking the law to do what we've been asked to do," Tom advises, "so what's this about?"

"I thought I could find some decent facial recognition software through my mates or maybe hack into something like Interpol to see if we could find a match for that mystery Arab guy, George was talking about."

This could get out of hand real fast, Tom thinks. "Nice idea, but let's hold off on any hacking just yet," he cautions. "I think we had best get approval from Devon or George first before you go and break any more laws."

Despondent, Connor slumps into the chair behind the main computer and listlessly clicks around with the mouse.

"But I do like the idea of facial recognition software, Connor," Tom concedes, "So how will we use it?"

Connor's face lights up, "Well, we don't have any cameras of our own yet, but I thought if we 'shared' the City Council CCTV network, we might find anyone we are looking for a lot quicker than sitting around in cafés by ourselves."

"He has a good point Tom," Dani concedes, "although I was looking forward to a Frappuccino or two."

"I'm sure we'll all get a few coffees on the firm Dani," Tom reassures her, then turning to Connor, smiles, "Lets hold off until I talk to Devon about this, but I do like it."

"Okay, I'll mount the big screen on the wall over there," Connor points to the gap between the two corkboards, "Then we can put anything you like up there when you're having one of those serious planning talks, like last night."

"In the army we called them SITREP's short for situational reports, but I guess we could call them briefings or meetings?" Tom asks uncertainly.

There is a knocking at the door. "I'll get it," Dani offers. She strides through to reception, and opens the door a little surprised, "Hi Frankie, why didn't you just come in?"

Looking a little embarrassed, he replies, "I guess I'm still getting used to the idea."

"We're just in the office. What's in the box?" Dani asks.

"All in good time, Bella," Frankie lowers his voice, "Between you and me, it's a peace offering for Rangi."

As they walk into the office, Tom turns to Dani, "Dani, are you still looking for accommodation?"

"I sure am. Do you know somewhere affordable?"

"I know someone that is looking for a boarder."

Overcome, Dani starts frantically waving her hands to fan her face, blinking back some tears, "Wow, this is just too much. A job and a flat in two days! Oh, you're the best Tom."

"We'll go and meet your potential landlady after the morning meeting."

"Is everyone here yet?" Koro calls from the top of the stairs.

"Just waiting on Devon," Tom calls back.

"Good, I'll bring the coffee down in a minute."

"I could rig up an intercom for Koro if you like," Connor offers.

"That might be a good idea, but you'll have to be patient while you teach him how to use it," Tom chuckles.

"One for the front door might be a good idea too," Frankie suggests.

Pulling a CCTV camera up out of one of the boxes, Connor grins, "I've got that covered, and it'll be up and working later today."

The front door opens and Devon calls out, "Just me."

Dani darts up the stairs, "I'll help Koro. Back in a

tick."

Devon surveys the office taking in the new boxes, "Good, looks like the tech turned up."

"Dude, you really delivered!" Connor raves obviously impressed, "This QLC SSD drive is crazy fast! Hey can you give me a hand to mount this monitor?"

Devon and Connor get to work fixing the large screen to the wall and hooking it up to the PC system. Koro and Dani return, carrying a large plunger of coffee each, Dani with hers on a tray with a collection of mismatching coffee cups and sets them up on the oval table. Frankie adds his cardboard box to the morning tea, "Rangi, have you ever tried sfogliatella?" He lifts the lid on the box and turns it towards Koro.

"Can't say I have Frankie, but they look whakawaiwai!" Koro exclaims, then seeing the blank look on Frankie's face, adds "that means delicious, you old bugger. Thank you."

Relieved, Frankie comments, "I got one for each of you and two for Rangi here, he's looking a bit thin to me."

"Cheeky bugger!" Koro growls.

Dani pours the dark brown liquid lightning into the cups and announces, "Coffee's ready, help yourselves."

"And get a taste of real Italian pastry!" Frankie reminds everyone.

"Damn this is good Frankie!" Koro compliments.

"I know right," Connor agrees.

"Okay you lot, listen up," Tom rallies everyone.

Quietening down they all turn to face Tom, except Koro, who reaches into the box and starts on his second pastry.

"Devon has a new phone for each of you. Connor, can you please set them all up with each of our phone numbers, work email accounts and maybe a secure messaging service. I want you to use them for business only. When can you have them ready?"

"Maybe in an hour?" Connor answers hesitantly.

"Good man. When Connor has them ready, get a photo of these people," Tom points to the photos on the corkboards, "All of them are your targets.

"I'll load the images up," Connor offers.

"Excellent. We also have some new kit for you, which Devon will train us up on later. Today, we'll all be hitting a series of cafés and restaurants trying to locate any of these people, but especially these two," Tom indicates the Arab and Kendrick. "Listen closely, you're not to take any chances. If you see any of them message Devon and myself and wait for further instructions."

Devon stands up. "Remember this fact, these people are very dangerous and highly trained spies. They could very well be guarded by colleagues, or they could be being watched by another agency. Your job is just to keep your eyes open and report via the phone what you see."

"Now, the plan is to send me a text at least three times for each place you visit, the first text to me is the name of the café and the word 'arrived'. The second text, is when you are halfway through your coffee and either 'nothing' or the code name of the spy you see. To make it easy, they will be Arab, Frog, Yank and Zion. The third text is when you are leaving the café, text me 'left', any questions?" Tom asks.

Dani wide-eyed, speaks up excitedly, "Are we all going out today?"

"Yes, today I'm pairing Koro and Frankie together, Devon and Dani and Connor you're with me," Tom replies.

"This is real on-the-job training," Devon adds,

smiling, "If you pick it up well, you may be going solo soon."

"We have a lot of places to cover over the next few days, so hopefully you are all quick learners," Tom grins.

"So do we get a gun like 007?" Connor asks.

Devon laughs and holds up his phone, indicating the sides of the device, "This is your weapon. If you get into trouble, first squeeze both these buttons together for at least three seconds. It will send an emergency alert to all of our phones with your GPS coordinates so we can get to you ASAP. And then I'll show you how to use these babies." He holds up a pepper-spray device in each hand.

Frankie adds, "Sorry son, not even these foreign spies are legally allowed to carry a firearm in New Zealand, only the Police, Army or DPS…that's the Diplomatic Protection Squad."

"One of the American's I saw last week was definitely carrying a pistol in his shoulder holster." Tom looks slowly around the room, eyeballing everyone, "That's why everyone will wear their vest at all times. I don't want anyone taking unnecessary chances. Got it?"

Punching Frankie in the arm lightly, Koro proudly states, "See I told you he was good."

Nodding, Frankie agrees, "So what happens if we find one of these characters?"

"Text me and I'll organise the rest of us to set up a tail. Don't worry, I'll keep you in the loop with what's going on," Tom reassures the team, "Anything else? No? Cool, Dani, finish up your coffee, we have a meeting."

\*\*\*

*Thursday Morning*

"Just to warn you Dani, Koro told Sheila that you were my… err… well… girlfriend," Tom is a little embarrassed.

"Is that what Koro thinks?" Dani asks astonished, as they walk up Pipitea Street, Dani carrying a bunch of flowers.

"No, no, it's a… well… he has Sheila on all the time and she's just got the wrong end of the stick."

"I suppose a girl should be flattered," Dani says hesitantly.

"And don't get me wrong here, Dani. You're an attractive woman, but… I'm just not in the right space at the moment," Tom fumbles over his words.

"Just so you know Tom, I'm not in the market for a boyfriend at the moment either," Dani replies, thinking to herself, 'not after that bastard Brummie bricklayer.'

The silence between them stretches, as they confront their own inner demons of self-worth, slowly making their way into Murphy Street.

Back in the present, Dani looks around. "This is a nice area, close to work. I hope she likes me."

The spell broken, Tom realises where they are, "I think the flowers were a nice touch Dani, I'm sure Sheila will appreciate the gesture, and it might just swing the deal." Tom points, "Her place is just up here. The red door on the left."

Dani reaches the door first, looks herself up and down, smoothing a crease from her skirt a little with her free hand, before knocking firmly on the wooden door.

Sheila opens the door only a few moments later,

pushing her grey curls from her forehead. Welcoming them, "Kia ora rā kōrua, you must be Danielle. Please come in."

"Ah, thank you Miss…" Dani begins.

"Call me Sheila. Now, straight through to the kitchen," Sheila instructs. Turning to Tom she growls, "Kia tere Tāmati, get a move on boy."

"Alright already Aunty, I'm coming," Tom replies as he swings up the steps and follows Dani down the hallway, passing the multitude of framed photos, commenting, "Mmm, something smells good Aunty."

"You just taihoa there boy," Sheila mockingly grumbles following them up the hall.

In the large sunny kitchen, Dani walks over to the red-flecked formica dining table, pulls out a battered chrome framed mid-century chair and holds the bouquet of carnations out to Sheila when she bustles into the room.

"Aren't they pretty? How nice of Tāmati to buy them for you," Sheila smiles.

Looking confused, Dani starts, "Oh, no, I bought them for…"

Sheila cuts her off, rounding on Tom, "Tāmati! You made her pay for her own flowers? How could you?"

Patiently Tom explains, "Aunty, Dani brought the flowers for you. And Koro is winding you up, Dani isn't my girlfriend."

"Thank you Danielle. That is very kind of you." She takes the offered flowers from Dani, and walks over to a cupboard to get a vase, "I thought it was odd you having another girlfriend so quick. After what's her name, that Canadian girl?"

Dani shoots Tom a surprised look, "Tom, didn't you just say…"

"Taylor, sorry Aunty. She's not my girlfriend either,"

Tom apologises.

"Well I can't keep up with you young ones these days, swapping partners and running around all over town." Sheila turns the electric jug on and takes the lid off a large tea pot on the breakfast bar. "So Danielle, please tell me a little about yourself."

"Ah… well… I grew up in Shannon. My parents are sheep farmers and have a small place out the back by the power station. I worked in the petrol station after school and when I left high school I saved every penny I could so I could travel to the UK and Europe.

There I worked in pubs and bars pulling pints or waitressing in cafés, even office temping sometimes, almost anything really just so I could save enough to go on lots of guided bus tours throughout Europe.

Unfortunately, I got caught at the border trying to get back into the UK after my working visa had expired. So I had to come home."

Sheila spoons a green and brown coloured mix of tea into the teapot. "If you don't mind me asking, why aren't you back home with your whānau in Shannon?"

Dani smiles, "After living in London and Edinburgh, Shannon is a bit small, so I'm planning on living in Wellington. Now I have a job, I just need a place to stay."

Placing the pot on the stand in the centre of the table, Sheila then walks back to the oven and takes out a tray of steaming hot scones.

"Hmm, let's take a look at the room Danielle while Tāmati sorts these scones out for us. Follow me." Sheila leads the way back into the hallway.

Dani scrambles up from her chair to follow Sheila. As they pass more framed photos, she asks, "Who are all these people in the photos?"

Sheila stops to look at a large old sepia photo of a handsome young man in uniform, "These are my whānau and tīpuna. This one is my Uncle Teoti... he didn't make it back home... he's somewhere in Italy. He signed up the same day with Tāmati's great granddad..." She pauses for a moment, rebuking herself, "Listen to me, an old wahine carrying on. This is your room through here."

Sheila opens the door and stands to one side to usher Dani into the room.

"Oh, it's just lovely," Dani cries, looking at the wallpaper patterned with light pink and blue coloured birds, then the single bed with a slightly faded yellow candlewick bedspread. A dark stained rimu tallboy cabinet at one end of the bed and a small wooden single drawer bedside table.

"There's no cupboard for hanging your clothes, but there is space in the tallboy," Sheila offers.

"That's perfect. I don't have many clothes as I've been travelling light for years."

"That's good. Now be straight with me, Danielle," Sheila begins.

"Please Sheila, Dani is fine."

"Dani, if Tāmati isn't your boyfriend, who is? I can't believe a pretty young girl like you is single."

"Can we keep this between us?" Dani asks hesitantly.

"Of course my girl, us wāhine have got to stick together."

"I had a bad break up with my Birmingham boyfriend. That's the real reason I left Britain, he was..." Dani admits looking a little tearful.

"Oh my girl!" Sheila exclaims, opening her arms offering a hug, "Come here."

Dani falls into the welcoming warmth, tears now streaming down her cheeks as she sobs softly into Sheila's shoulder, "it was so awful."

She pats her gently on the back. "There, there my girl," she soothes, "Don't tell me now, we will have plenty of time later when you're ready to talk. I think you should move in here and let's get you back on your feet, eh?"

Feeling the genuine concern in Sheila's voice, Dani makes her decision. She pulls back and wipes her eyes, "Really, you'll let me stay?"

Sheila smiles, "On one condition, no sneaking anyone in here at night... without telling me first."

"There's no chance of that. I'm off men for a long time."

Ever hopeful, Sheila asks, "So you might help me find someone for Tāmati?"

"I don't think he's looking for anyone right now, but when he is, maybe we can help. He is kinda cute."

"Good, now let's see if he's found the jam and cream for the scones."

"So, can I move in soon?" Dani asks as they head back into the hallway.

"Anytime, before seven tonight as Rangiwahia owes me a game of crib," Sheila offers entering the kitchen. She surveys the table, "Good boy Tāmati."

Noticing Dani's puffy eyes, Tom is concerned. "How did it go?"

With a deep intake of breath, Dani replies, "All good."

Taking the teapot's handle Sheila turns it properly. "Dani will have to move in before Koro arrives, so you make sure to let her off from that job early. Are you coming along tonight?"

"What and get thrashed by you two pro's! No chance Aunty. Besides, Dev and I are at the gym tonight." Tom turns to Dani, "Don't let them talk you into playing, Dani.

They are both sharks."

Pouring the tea, Sheila looks hurt, "Tāmati, you are so mean to your Aunty."

Looking at the steaming green liquid in his cup, Tom sniffs the brew cautiously, "What concoction have we here?"

Sheila shakes her head, and turns to Dani, "You see what I have to put up with. Such disrespect! You like kawakawa tea, don't you Dani?"

Dani picks up her tea cup and warily tastes the contents, surprised she replies, "Mmm, that's really nice. It's a bit, well peppery."

"Kawakawa, or as the pākehā call it Macropiper excelsum, or the pepper tree, it is good rongoā," Sheila informs them.

"I can see I'm going to get a crash course in te reo living here, Sheila you might have to put up with me asking you questions all the time," Dani states, "What is rongoā?"

Sheila laughs, "That's all right girl, you will keep me on my toes. Rongoā is traditional māori medicine, Tāmati is using some for his wounds."

"Really?" Dani asks incredulously.

"Yeah, I've been following her instructions for a week and I know it's really helping. Devon and Taylor are amazed at the progress I'm making. Hopefully I'll be down to one stick soon."

"I'm a qualified nurse, Dani, I learnt the pākehā ways and then when I saw it failing a lot of māori, I went back to my kuia and learnt the old ways."

"Wow, that's amazing," Dani exclaims.

"Sheila has always been our first port of call when Koro or I haven't been well, and she runs a clinic at the local marae on Tuesday mornings," Tom explains proudly.

"Enough of that now," Sheila cuts them off. "Come on, these scones are getting cold. Eat up the both of you!" She hands around the plate of steaming goodness.

\*\*\*

*Thursday Midday*

"Good to see this weather is holding," Frankie comments as the group walks along the Wellington waterfront. The sun warms them, and a very light northerly breeze occasionally ruffling their hair.

"Okay, as we practised, we will pair off into the next three cafés, Tom states. "Come on Connor, we're first." Tom swings towards the vibrant coloured eatery.

Connor follows Tom, pulls his new phone out and asks, "Do I still text you, even though you're with me?"

"Yes. In fact, you lead and I'll follow."

Quickly tapping a message onto the screen, Connor flicks his long fringe to one side and walks over to a free table. He takes a seat and signals to a waitress.

Tom follows, scanning the crowd as he takes his seat at the table. He places his own phone in front of him, checks the screen and asks, "Okay Connor, tell me why you chose this table."

"Because, I've got my back to the wall and can see the front door easily." Connor notices the waitress approaching and turns his phone over so the screen is down. "Two double shot espresso please."

When the waitress leaves, Tom says, "Nice move with the phone, and good reasoning. You're a quick study."

"To be honest Tom, this is the first real chance anyone has ever given me and you actually treat me as a person, not a kid," Connor grins. "I don't want to stuff this up."

"That's good to hear bro, because I know George has kinda forced you to work with us, but I'd rather that you want to work with us. Being a tight team is the thing that makes the difference when we are under pressure."

"Yeah, that George laid it on real heavy. I got the message loud and clear," Connor concedes, "But dude, you guys are so much older than me, I'm not sure I'll fit in, but I'm trying."

"Connor, I'm only eight years older than you. It seems a lot when you're eighteen, but before you know it you'll be my age." Tom laughs, "But it looks to me like you get on with everyone, so who's the one you're worried about?"

"It's Devon," Connor admits, "I can see you and Devon are tight, but he scares me, man. He watches me like a hawk. I know if I slip up then he will tell George and then I'll be sent inside. I don't think I could handle that."

"Yeah. We are tight, known each other since school, and he was my Sergeant in the Army. If I know Devon, he's keeping a close eye on you because he doesn't want you to make a mistake again." Seeing the look of disbelief in Connor's eyes, Tom explains, "Think about it. You got caught because you made a mistake. If you make a mistake working for us, then one of us might be at best compromised. Or at worse, put in danger. So really he doesn't want you to make a mistake. That's why he's spending so much time with you."

"Oh, I didn't see it that way." Connor looks relieved.

"I wanted to give everyone a taste of what it's like out in the field, because then you and Dani will have a real idea of what it's like for us when you are coordinating things from the office," Tom expands, "We'll be relying on you both to keep us up to date. It's a big responsibility."

"So, we will be stuck in the office then." Connor looks a little disappointed, "I mean I know my IT skills are being put to best use, but it's kinda exciting doing this operational stuff."

Chuckling, Tom teases, "Oh so you want to be the Kiwi version of the Kingsman's Eggsy, or Alex Rider eh?"

Connor's face turns a bright red. He replies softly, "Well, I guess a kid can dream."

"Sorry man, that was a bit mean," Tom apologises. "But you will get a chance every now and then. That's why you have to wear that vest. So on that, two tables over there is a couple having a deep and meaningful talk. Show me how you would get a photo of them without them noticing. Remember to get their faces for easier identification."

"Too easy Dude," Connor picks up his phone, he glances around the café to locate the couple, then stands up saying loud enough for everyone close by to hear, "No, no man, you stay there, I'll get it."

As everyone turns to see what Connor is up to, he quickly leans over to take a selfie with Tom but angles the phone to capture the couple at their table, "Say cheese!"

Sitting back down Connor opens the gallery and smiles. He turns the phone around for Tom to see a perfect photo of the couple looking towards them.

"Well done Connor, but you may have just blown our cover."

"No way Dude. All they will see is a skateboard punk and a dude with crutches," Connor explains, "No one will recognise our faces."

"Yeah, you are probably right and I like the selfie idea, I tried that myself, so good to see we're on the same page."

Connor spins his phone around and taps a quick message, then picks up his espresso and gulps it all down.

Tom's phone vibrates, checking it he sees the message from Connor, "Good you didn't forget, alright let's get back to the office."

\*\*\*

*Thursday Midday*

With the rest of the team straggling behind them, Tom and Connor reach the top of the station's steps. As they approach the open front doors a man in black with a Hi-Viz vest steps out in front of them.

"Okay, just what are you Yelichs up to?" Dunkell demands. "Are you taking in vagrants now?"

"Excuse us Dunkell, we have other things to get on with," Tom politely replies, manoeuvring around the verbal obstacle.

"This punk was skateboarding in the concourse this morning, and that's prohibited... Hey I'm talking to you, war hero!" Dunkell yells starting to follow them.

Frankie steps up beside Dunkell, taps him on the shoulder and flicks open his pocket notebook, "Excuse me sir. Do you wish to lay a complaint with the police?"

Surprised, Dunkell stops. "Yes... why yes, I do. That young punk was..."

"Yes, yes, I have that, now your full name and address please," Frankie slyly winks at Koro as he walks past, "and contact phone number... do you have your driver's licence on you?"

"Shouldn't you be talking to that skate boarder?" Dunkell asks as he reaches for his wallet to show Frankie his driver's license.

"Don't you worry sir. You leave it leave me. I just need

your complaint and I'll be in touch," Frankie closes his note book and slides it back inside his suit jacket pocket, before following Devon and Dani inside the station. Dunkell, left bewildered, stands there scratching his head.

Inside the station, as they cross the concourse, Devon comments, "Slick move there, Frankie. You sounded like you were still on the force."

"Old habits die hard," Frankie replies, as they enter the office.

Devon asks, "You know you can't imitate a police officer. What are you up to?"

"Technically, I didn't impersonate an officer of the law," Frankie begins.

"Dude, thanks for helping," Connor interrupts. "That guy is a real prick. But like Devon said, won't you get in trouble?"

"No, no, all I did was ask him if he wanted to lay a complaint. I didn't say I was an actual police officer," Frankie smiles.

"But won't he smell a rat, when he sees you coming and going from here?" Tom asks.

"Who cares? If asked, I'll just say I'm making enquiries." Frankie takes a seat at the meeting table surrounded by an assortment of chairs.

"You always were a tricky bugger," Koro laughs, "Hopefully that should keep Dunkell off our backs until next week. Tom have you done all that paperwork yet?"

"I've sent most of it off, Koro. Just a bit more to look over tonight after the gym," Tom advises, then calls the team together, "Okay, well done out there team. This afternoon, Frankie, Devon and I will be out canvassing more cafés. Koro can you team up with Frankie, Dani and Connor, you guys will be minding the store. We'll need you to help coordinate our moves so if you can, please find a café nearest to the ones we are in and let us know any information that comes up."

Connor's hands fly across the keyboard and he asks, "Devon can you turn the main screen on please?"

"Sure, what are you up to?" Devon asks.

As the screen comes to life, Connor opens a window with a satellite map of the Wellington CBD, he zooms in on the station where a collection of coloured luminous dots pulse. Next he opens another window with a search engine of Wellington cafés. His wizard-like fingers tap their magic commands on the keyboard and result in a sprinkling of orange flags. "Okay how's this? The flags are the cafés and the different coloured dots are all of us, so we will know exactly where everyone is!"

"Oh you are GOOD!" Devon praises him.

Dani pipes up, "Connor, can we import those cafés into a spreadsheet that I can work on at the other computer?"

"Sure can, I'll send it through now," Connor replies with a big grin on his face.

Koro turns to Frankie, "It's just bloody magic all this computer stuff to me."

Frankie nods, "The young ones make it look easy. Mind you, they grow up with it. A computer was the size of a house when I was at school. But we had to use them in the force. I used to spend hours typing up my reports with two fingers."

"I dunno if I'll ever get the hang of this flash phone," Koro admits.

"That's why you're with Frankie, Koro," Tom explains, "Alright we'll see you all back here at four o'clock for a quick debrief to see what we've learnt."

Frankie leans over to Koro, "Don't worry Rangi, I'll

show you that you can teach an old dog new tricks."

"Connor, can you please send us a text with our first target café." Tom asks. "Okay team, let's get going."

\*\*\*

The car door creaks as Koro pushes it open, and complains even more when he closes it.

"You ever consider using a bit of oil on these hinges, Frankie?" Koro inquires as he makes his way towards their target.

"I'll get around to it one day," Frankie absently replies as he puts a couple of coins into the parking meter.

Moving to the side of the glass door to let a young hipster couple exit, Koro asks, "I just realised that I don't know much about you. Tell me about your whānau, any kids?"

Frankie passes the trendy couple as he walks towards the café entrance, looking a bit surprised and sad, he deflects, "Let's get a cuppa and I'll tell you a story."

They enter the café, walk up to the counter and order a cup of tea each. Then take a sea by the window.

"Not many punters in here," Koro comments.

"Look over here. I'll show you how we send the first text," Frankie offers and with simple directions he instructs Koro on the task.

Once the tea has arrived, Frankie takes a deep breath and begins, "Not a word of this to anyone Rangi."

"Alright Frankie, what's the secret?"

"My wife got cancer twelve years ago," Frankie begins getting a touch tearful, "It was a long slow miserable ten-year death sentence, which took its toll on both my daughter and I." Taking another deep breath to steady himself, he continues, "My daughter Isabella was only five when this started and was fifteen when Maureen joined her god. I lost my faith after what happened."

"Frankie! I'm so sorry to hear of your loss!" Koro gives real meaning to that simple phrase.

"Thanks Rangi." Frankie gratefully replies, "On top of the worst thing to happen in my life, losing my Maureen, I then had to bring poor Isi up by myself."

"I can sympathise, as you know about Tom living with me after his parents car crash," Koro consoles, "That must have been tough."

"It was. For a start I couldn't cope with a teenage girl becoming a young woman. We argued all the time and then I buried myself at work to try and escape the pain."

"That doesn't sound very healthy. Was there no support?"

"Nothing from the church, I mean we supported everyone else through their troubles but when it was our turn, there was nothing. Not even a casserole. The Priest just wanted to know when we were coming back and if we wanted to sponsor a pew in Maureen's name, greedy bastard. That's when I really left the church." Frankie continues.

"So how is Isabella now?" Koro asks.

Swallowing a sob, Frankie takes a moment, then adds, "Isi couldn't stand living with me. I understand why, I was a miserable grumpy old man, who was always on her case, so she left home last year and I haven't seen her since."

"Where is she? I mean she can't just disappear," Koro pipes up.

"She's living somewhere in Newtown. A couple of my old police friends tracked her down. She asked if she could take out a restraining order on me, as she didn't want to ever see me again." Frankie has tears in his eyes. "Legally she couldn't of course, as I hadn't done anything to her, but that was her wish. So, I was advised to let her be, and wait until she wanted to reconnect."

"Maybe Tom and I could help?" Koro offers.

"Thanks Rangi, but I think it's a waiting game." Frankie digs in his pocket for a handkerchief. "It's just so hard. I love her so much and miss her dearly."

"I bet you do, Frankie. Oh talk about bad timing," Koro comments quietly, "Look at the guy walking in."

Wiping his eyes, Frankie turns and clocks the new patron walking up to the counter, "Judas Priest, you're on the money Rangi. Now watch this."

Looking like two old men trying to work out how to use a new smart phone, they don't attract the newcomer's attention. Frankie gets a series of photos which he sends to Dani and Connor and then he sends Tom a text 'Frog'.

\*\*\*

The phone's ringtone startles both Dani and Connor as they are looking at the photos coming in from Frankie. Dani reaches across and stabs at the answer icon, "Hello?"

"Hi Dani, where are they? I know they're at the Emporium café, but I don't know where the hell it is," Tom urgently relays.

Glancing at the large screen, Dani replies, "It's up on Abel Smith Street. They got some good photos too. It's definitely the Frenchman."

"There's no way I can get up there soon on my crutches, I'll try and get a taxi. Is Devon closer?"

"Yes, if he ran, he could make it in ten minutes." Dani makes a snap decision, "Get a taxi, I'll phone Devon."

\*\*\*

"So, what do we do now?" Koro whispers.

"Just talk normally, but maybe a little quieter, Rangi. We have to act normal. Just like we were before, or we might attract his attention."

"Oh, so you can still show me how to work this phone?" Koro asks.

Frankie chuckles, "Let's get a couple more photos, and use your phone this time."

The barista delivers a coffee to the French agent, and Koro lines up his phone pressing the camera button and holding it down a fraction longer, causing it to take a series of photos. "Oh balls, what did I do there?"

Frankie shakes his head. "I don't know, but let's have a look."

Taking Koro's phone, Frankie points out, "Look this icon opens the gallery, and oh, you've taken a burst sequence. See how they all look the same just a fraction of a second apart."

Frankie's phone chirps. He opens the message and reads out quietly to Koro, "Devon and Tom are on their way, just stay in the café and don't follow FROG."

"But what if he leaves before they get here?" Koro asks.

Thinking for a minute, Frankie lays his ideas out, "If this is where he has regular meetings, we can always watch the place and catch him next time."

Koro sits back in his chair, and sips his cool tea. He looks around carefully, "Hmm, I guess you're right."

\*\*\*

Devon weaves around another pedestrian and pushes the vibrant purple e-scooter to its maximum speed. He launches past another person and the scooter gets airborne. Devon flies from the footpath onto the road parallel to the pedestrian crossing. An angry middle-aged man racing across Vivian Street shakes his fist, "Watch where you're going you lunatic!"

Ignoring his heckler, Devon merges back onto the footpath heading up Cuba Street thinking, 'Thank goodness the foot traffic is lighter here.' He speeds up the footpath to the next intersection, where he dismounts and pushes the e-scooter around the corner. He places it in a stand and leaves it behind. It's a short walk towards the café. He scans the area as he goes.

His phone vibrates and Devon taps his earbud to answer the call. "What's happening Dani?"

"Tom's stuck at the lights. He's not going to make it anytime soon."

"Damn, we need at least two people for a quick tail…" Devon starts.

"Heads up. He's leaving the café," Dani interrupts.

Devon moves closer to the building. He turns and looks into the window, noticing it is a dry cleaners. Angling himself to take advantage of the windows reflection. He sees the French Agent emerge from the café, softly informing, "Got him, it's definitely Henri."

Devon grabs his phone. He holds it up and appears to be looking deeply into the screen, while he follows the French Agents progress away from him. He snaps a couple of photos, and starts off in pursuit. Nearing the café entrance, he sees Frankie's car, "Dani, ask Frankie and Koro to get in their car and get ready for instructions."

"Connor's just phoning them now. I've got you on speaker here."

"Damn, he's crossing the road. Looks like he's heading

for the side street ahead. I can't remember the name."

Following Devon's progress on the big screen, Dani asks, "Footscray or Kensington? Footscray loops back on itself."

"The one closest to Victoria Street," Devon replies as he crosses the road quickly.

"That's Kensington Street. It looks like it's got a walkway through to the highway."

Devon curses, "I've just made it to Kensington and he's disappeared."

"Frankie and Koro are in the car waiting for instructions. What do you want to do?" Dani asks.

Thinking as he walks through to the footpath by the highway, Devon scans the area. There is no sign of his quarry. "Tell them to wait for Tom and me. We could do with a lift back to the office."

\*\*\*

"Just give me a couple of minutes," Connor suggests, as he works feverishly at his terminal.

Tom taps Devon on the shoulder and nods towards reception. They both make their way there, leaving Koro and Frankie telling their café story one more time.

"Dev, I felt useless man, I just couldn't get there and these damn sticks just slow me down." Tom shakes his head. "I just don't know if I'm up for all this," he quietly admits. "I mean its fine in theory, but the reality is, I'm hopeless."

Devon looks Tom straight in the eye. "Brother, you are just too damn hard on yourself. I only just got there in time and I was heaps closer."

"I dunno man," Tom replies a bit sceptically.

"True story. Save the pity party for later. We can work that out at the gym. Now get back in there and work your magic with your team," Devon commands.

They make their way back into the office where Connor announces, "Check this out. I've put everyone's photos all together in time sequence."

Everyone turns to look at the big screen and watch the slide show.

"This is where I was practising using that flash phone," Koro skites.

"Yeah, that's definitely Henri Chevalier," Tom comments.

"That's when he got his coffee, man he must like it sweet. He's just picked up all the sugar sachets," Frankie commentates.

"Wait a minute. Connor back up the slide show," Tom instructs, "That's it. Now play one at a time, coffee next… sugar next… there, stop. Does anybody see what I see?"

"Just like I said, Henri has a sweet tooth. He's used all the sugar," Frankie observes.

"Where are all the empty sugar sachets?" Dani asks.

"Exactly!" Tom confirms in triumph.

Devon chuckles, "I told George you were good at this."

"What am I missing here?" Koro asks.

"The lack of empty sachets means that they aren't empty, he took the lot," Tom explains.

"So he's a cheapskate, he pinched all the sugar. What of it?" Koro rasps.

"Devon, can you explain the proper term please," Tom asks.

"Okay, this is a classic 'Dead Drop', which is like a spies letter box," Devon begins, seeing the lack of comprehension in some of the team's faces, he expands, "The sugar bowl at that table is the letter box, what we didn't see was the previous patron at that table. They would've put a message in a sugar sachet and placed it in the sugar bowl, then Henri Chevalier comes in afterwards and collects the mail. Koro and Frankie saw the last half of the transaction."

"But why wouldn't they just send an encrypted message via their phone?" Dani asks.

"Because it's often safer to pass a message physically rather than risk an electronic message being intercepted," Devon explains.

"But now we know their mail system, we can watch it and track the first person," Tom notes. He turns to Connor, "Could you rig up a surveillance camera in the café?

"Sure can," Connor replies eagerly, pulling a small box from the desk drawer. "I can try out one of these babies."

"Okay, let's get two of those in there first thing tomorrow morning. A great day's work team. Let's knock off a bit early and start early tomorrow."

***

# Chapter Twelve – Mediterranean Tagine

*Friday Morning*

FRANKIE AND CONNOR enter the office in high spirits, laughing. Connor addresses Tom, "Dude, you wanna see how this old man drives. He's a regular Sébastien Ogier."

"The rally driver? In Wellington traffic? You gotta be kidding," Tom replies disbelievingly.

"Well, I didn't want to be late for the meeting," Frankie explains deadpan.

"I can't get you off any speeding tickets, Frankie," Devon frowns.

"Oh, you should've seen that skateboard Nazi's face... Priceless!" Connor continues.

"What have you done to Dunkell?" Koro asks Frankie sternly.

"I might have ah... borrowed his car park," Frankie looks a touch bashful.

"More like cut him off by drifting into his space. Man, was it a buzz!" Connor explains.

"Did he see you two together?" Tom asks, shaking his head.

"No, he swerved to miss Frankie and hit the carpark fence," Connor laughs, "He was too busy looking at the ding to his car."

"Your car is pretty distinctive Frankie," Koro warns,

"Expect him to track you down."

Looking at the camaraderie developing in his team, Tom feels a surge of pride in his chest. He pushes himself up from his chair, and addresses his smiling, playful crew, "Hey, good work yesterday team. Connor, how did you get on with installing the camera?"

Turning serious, Connor slides into his chair at the computer. "All good dude. Frankie distracted the barista while I put the cameras into position." He taps at the keyboard for a moment, then points at the big screen, "Here, check this out. They're on opposite walls."

Opening a new window, Connor clicks his mouse a few times and the fuzzy grey turns to vivid colour, displaying the café's interior from two directions, both focusing on the table where the Frenchman had been seated.

"Excellent! That's a job well done you two! Now that frees us up to cover more cafés," Tom smiles, and turning to Dani he suggests, "How about you tell us our next destinations?"

"Connor can you bring up the map please?" Dani authoritatively begins, "Koro and Frankie, you are up in Jessie Street first, the Agraba. Devon you have the Miznon in Bond Street and Tom you are out at Greta Point at the Marrakech. Anything else Tom?"

"Dani and Connor, you watch the Emporium. Message me if you see the French agent and try to work out who his contact is. Okay team, let's be careful out there."

***

Scanning the menu, Tom decides on a late breakfast, addressing the waiter, "Thanks for your patience, can I please have the pan fried fish?"

"Certainly sir, would you like anything to drink with that?" The waiter is all efficiency.

"A large flat white while I'm waiting, and maybe a bottle of soda water," Tom orders. Leaning back in his chair, he gazes around the restaurant observing the busy staff readying the orders, the bustling crowd of pensioners all talking over each other and a couple of walking mums who are deep in conversation.

His phone vibrates with incoming messages and he confirms everyone is in position. The lull in activity gives him much needed time to contemplate some nagging concerns that are stacking up in his mind, neatly parked but threatening to overwhelm him if they get loose. 'Am I really fit for this new role? I mean I've been swept up in all the action... I really let the team down yesterday by not getting to the café in time... Am I putting everyone in danger? Maybe Devon and Taylor could run some self-defence classes for us... Is Koro really up for this? He talks up his union tough guy image, but will it be enough? And as for Frankie, he looks like he's carrying a bit too much weight to be running after younger agents... Dani is sweet, very pretty and has something about her... I can't put my finger on what it is... Young Connor is a worry, I hope he doesn't try to be a hero. He's far too scrawny... but he knows his computer stuff! I must ask Devon about that facial recognition software and see if he has access to any... Oh, far out, we are meant to be taking Taylor and Dani to the comedy clubs tonight! I wonder if Devon is after Taylor... or Dani for that matter... not that I'd have a chance with either of them...'

The waiter interrupts Tom's thoughts, sliding a cup and saucer across the table towards him, "One large flat white, sir."

"Oh, cheers," Tom abruptly comes back to reality. He looks around the room. The walking mums are getting up to leave, still actively engaged in their conversation. One in particular is gesticulating wildly to make her point.

A suited businessman enters the restaurant, a newspaper tucked under one arm and large smart phone carried in the other. Tom notices that he takes a seat at a table for four close by. He is shortly followed by a swarthy older man wearing an open neck white shirt. He bursts through the front door, brandishing his very hairy grey chest like a badge of honour, calling out, "There you are Stefanos!"

As he strides over to join him at the table, Stefanos stands and greets the visitor, "Yassas Erasmos, kaliméra." They shake hands firmly and slap each other on the shoulder.

Tom quickly takes a photo before the two friends sit down, wondering to himself, 'What are those two friends are up to?' Then opening his smart phone's search engine, looks up the origin of the name 'Stefanos', seeing the result is a Greek male name, Tom nods to himself. He looks up from his phone, and is startled when he recognises the next person entering the restaurant. The man is wearing a familiar grey jacket. He checks his phone to avoid eye contact, and his thoughts rapidly coalesce, 'Geez-us! The Algerian!'

He taps in the code *'Arab'* and sends it to Dani. A surreptitious scan of the room surprises him. The swarthy Algerian joins the two Greeks at their table. Tom hastily takes a photo as they all stand and formally shake hands.

Tom thinks as he sips his hot brew, 'Talk about luck, I'm so close I can just about make out some of their conversation.'

His smart phone vibrates again, seeing an incoming call from Dani, Tom taps his earbud, answering softly, "Hi, can't talk."

Hearing two enthusiastic voices, Dani excitedly comes through, "Shh Connor. How are you Tom? Oh, you can't talk, silly me. I've phoned Devon, and Connor is talking to Frankie now. Devon is getting a taxi and will get there as soon as he can. Frankie and Koro should be there in about ten minutes if their car is parked close... What's that Connor?"

"Tom, Connor here, well I suppose that's obvious, hey, Frankie asked if he should park where he can observe the entrance so he can follow the Arab when he leaves?" Connor breathlessly spurts out.

"Good idea. I'm sending you some photos, can you get copies of these to them and print some out for the board please," Tom instructs as he sends the photos to Connor.

"Right, I'll let them know," Connor's voice trails off and can be heard in the background talking to Frankie.

Dani comes back on the line, "Ah, what do we do now, Tom?"

"We wait," Tom replies, then adds before ending the call, "I'll send you a message."

Popping his earbud out, Tom sips his coffee again and attempts to listen, above the noise of the pensioners, to the conversation two tables over. He sends a message to Dani, *Sorry Dani, too hard to talk, I'm trying to listen to their conversation, the other two men are Greeks.'*

Wondering what two Greeks and an Algerian are meeting about, Tom listens in, catching snippets of their conversation.

Stefanos is the loudest, "... As Aristotle once said, a common danger unites even the bitterest enemies... ahh coffee!"

As the waiter takes their order, Tom attempts to listen in to some more. But the pensioners are loudly laughing at an old dad joke. The Algerian moves in closer to hear and Tom faintly makes out Stefanos saying, "…due in port next week… don't worry, Erasmos is the new Captain…"

The waiter interrupts his eavesdropping as he delivers Tom's fish, "Here you are sir, I hope you enjoy your meal. A small favour if you wouldn't mind, can you please leave a review on our website."

Tom nods to the waiter, "Sure, sure." He picks up his utensils, and the waiter retreats back to the counter.

With a mouthful of fish, Tom refocuses on the conversation at the adjoining table, "…yes, yes… Chabarha…"

Tom downs his coffee, taps some notes into his smart phone He sends them to Dani, thinking, 'I wonder where Chabarha is? Maybe India?'

The men all burst out laughing, as the waiter arrives at their table with their espressos.

Tom's phone vibrates and he pops his earbud back in and answers the call with half a mouthful of fish, "Yesh?"

Dani asks, "Is it Chabarha or Chabahar?"

"I'm not sure, why?"

Connor replies, "Chabarha looks like it's an Indian surname but Chabahar is a major port in Iran."

"What's the context, Tom?" Dani asks.

"Shit, it's the second one. I'd better sign off," Tom whispers quietly as he ends the call. His mind races, 'What the hell are the Greeks and Iranians up to?'

His phone vibrates again. He takes a quick look at the text message from Koro, *'In position,'*

Tom breathes a sign of relief, 'Good, at least we can

follow one of them.' He shovels in another mouthful of food, and sends a reply, *'You two follow the Arab wearing a grey jacket.'*

Quickly eating the remainder of his fish, Tom watches the men drink their coffee while making small talk. Putting his cutlery on his plate as he finishes his last mouthful, he grabs his crutches and makes his way to the counter to pay, before the men finish.

"Great meal thanks and can I get a GST receipt, please," Tom compliments the hard working waiter.

Chairs scrape across the wooden floor. Tom guesses the men are coming towards him. Without looking behind him, he heads out the door as a taxi pulls up with a familiar face in the back seat. Rapidly closing the distance, Tom says to Devon as he opens the door, "Scoot across bro," and he climbs into the taxi.

Addressing the astonished taxi driver, "This might sound weird, but can you keep the meter running and just wait here a moment please?"

The driver looks at Devon, questioning, "Is this okay, sir?"

Devon laughs, winking at the driver, "It's okay Trang, I know this character. Next thing, he'll ask you to do is to follow a car. Just like a real old-school detective. Let's just humour him, eh?"

Trang shakes his head. "As long as you are paying sir."

Turning to Tom, Devon raises his left eyebrow questioningly.

Tom opens the notes app on his phone and shows Devon, Two Greeks, one a ship Captain, common enemy, Chabahar, Iran port, not Algerian, Iranian.

Devon nods. "Good work brother, now the real work

begins. Here they come."

The three men exit the restaurant, shake hands and head in different directions.

Tom calls Koro, "Okay, the two heading away from you are yours. We've got the single."

Devon asks, "Trang, you see that man in the grey jacket? When I tell you, can you please slowly follow him?"

Wondering what is going on, Trang asks, "Are you allowed to do this? Is this legal?"

Pulling his wallet from his jacket pocket, Devon sorts through his cards and shows one to Trang, "It's okay, we are licensed investigators."

Looking at the official card with Devon's photo ID, Trang replies, "All right. This is a first for me."

Frankie and Koro pass them going in the opposite direction, "Thanks, now he's getting into that blue car, when he pulls out, count to three and then follow him."

Tom zooms his phone's camera in on the car and snaps a couple of photos. "I'll send these to the office and see if we can trace the number plate when we get back."

Trang eagerly turns his engine over, "Well this is exciting. A real detective car chase!"

"Hopefully, we won't be doing a high-speed chase, just following slowly so we don't get noticed," Tom replies.

"Oh, of course," Trang sounds a little disappointed, "There he goes."

"Count to three!" Devon reminds him as Trang starts to pull out.

Trang looks behind him, to make sure the road is clear. A red car passes them as Trang manoeuvres the taxi out behind it onto Evans Bay Parade slowly shadowing the blue car.

Tom sends the photos to Connor, then looks up from his phone. They are passing a dog exercise park. Just ahead, the blue car indicates a right turn into Rata Road.

"Where's he going?" Trang asks, "Shall I still follow him?"

"Yes, but slow down. We are getting a bit close," Devon instructs. The red car passes their target and goes straight ahead.

Slowing and indicating the same turn, the blue car speeds in front of an oncoming car leading a trail of traffic from the lights, the offended lead car sounds his horn in surprise at being cut off.

Trang waits for the line of cars to pass, then makes a turn into Rata Road eventually. "I think we might have lost him." He sounds disappointed.

"Let's see once we get around the corner." Tom opens his phone and selects an app.

Driving up the hill they turn the corner to discover that the blue car has disappeared.

Pointing to a street coming up on their left, Trang asks confused, "Which way Sir?"

"Straight ahead please, Trang," Devon says. "And could you go a little faster?"

Trang powers his Toyota Prius up Rata Road to the next turn, rounding the corner, he cries out, "There, there, do you see it?"

Devon grins, "Good work Trang. Let's see where he goes."

Following at a safe distance, they see the blue car turn left into Kainui Road. Tom has the map app open on his phone and does a search of the nearby area.

They turn into Kainui Road. Trang cries, "It's gone again!"

"Just head up to the intersection," Tom instructs, looking at his phone.

At the 'Give Way' sign on the next intersection, Trang deflated asks, "Which way now?"

"Turn right into Waipapa," Tom instructs. "I think I know where he's going."

"If it's safe, you can speed up a little Trang," Devon advises.

"That's it, veer left into Arawa Road and straight on past the school."

"Just as well it's not three, or we wouldn't be moving at all with the yummy mummies picking up their precious little kids," Trang observes, "Which way now?"

"Turn right into Hataitai Road, then right again into Te Anau," Tom directs.

"Where are you taking us?" Devon asks.

"You'll see bro."

The Toyota's wheels squeal slightly as Trang tightly corners into Te Anau, excitedly yelling, "There he is!"

"Okay Trang, slow down a little and keep driving past him when he turns off to the right down here," Tom commands.

The blue car pulls into a short driveway on the right, stopping before a gate, which is slowly opening automatically. Tom snaps a quick photo as they drive past heading downhill.

"What now?" Trang asks.

"Keep going around a few more corners until we are out of sight," Tom tells him, then turning to Devon, "What do you want me to do now, bro?"

Thinking for a minute, Devon decides, "Okay, let me off down here, I'll walk back up and see what I can, and I'll meet you both back at the Haitaitai Road intersection and we'll take it from there."

\*\*\*

*Friday Midday*

"We almost lost them twice," Koro leans back in his chair at the office table.

"Where was that?" Connor eagerly asks wide-eyed.

"Once at the lights coming off Evans Bay Parade and then again we almost got in the wrong lane coming around the Basin Reserve," Koro recounts.

"If you hadn't seen him change lanes, Rangi, I would have missed the turn off to Cambridge Terrace," Frankie concedes.

"So where did they end up?" Dani asks.

"They darted across to Hania Street and parked in between the Greek Community Centre and the Orthodox Church," Frankie answers.

"So over here," Dani pushes a pin into the map of Wellington on the cork board, then pins a photo of the two Greek men next to the map and ties a red ribbon from the men to the pin on the map.

The front door bangs open as Devon and Tom return from their tailing of the Iranian. They make their way into the office, and Tom slumps down into a free chair.

"How did you get on?" Tom begins, then seeing the photos and red ribbon, compliments, "Oh, good work, so what's there?" He points to the map.

Connor looks up from his computer, "Apart from the Greek Church and Community Centre, there is also the Greek Embassy… not many secrets from Uncle Google. How'd you guys get on?"

"We tracked the 'Algerian' to the Iranian Embassy in Te Anau Road," explains Devon.

Tom rubs his face with his hands. "Now the hard work begins, trying to work out what are the Greeks doing talking with an Iranian agent?"

"Brain storming time, team. No idea is a bad idea," Devon adds.

"So, what do we know about the Greeks and the Iranians in general?" Tom asks.

Dani pins up another photo and extends more red ribbon to the Iranian Embassy's map position.

Silence envelopes the office as everyone thinks of something positive to contribute.

Connor's finger tips are at work on his keyboard.

Frankie clears his throat, "The only thing I know is that Alexander the Great, invaded Persia back in the day and Greece controlled a huge area there for many years. But that was a few hundred years BC."

"Thanks Frankie, what about more recently?" Tom asks.

"Here's a regional map," Connor points to the screen, "and Turkey is the only country between them."

Devon remembers, "Of course, you're right! When we were in Syria Tom, the Iranians were supporting Assad's regime and Turkey was supporting the Sunni rebels."

Dani excitedly adds, "Ow, ow, I visited Cyprus eighteen months ago. It's still split in two. The Turks are in the north and the Greek Cypriots in the south. Beautiful beaches and the clearest blue water I've ever swum in," Dani recalls, "When I was talking with some of the locals over a glass of ouzo in the taverna, they were still pretty dark on the Turks."

"So is it possible that Turkey could be their common

enemy and they could be working together?" Connor asks.

"Yes, but on what?" Tom muses thinking aloud, "Something to do with that Greek ship Captain."

"I might be able to help there," Koro offers. "I'll check with my wharfie mates tonight at the pub. Do you want to come, Frankie?"

"Depends on the pub Rangi... and who's buying."

"We'll also have to put a watch on both the Embassies," Tom suggests, 'and somehow follow the Iranian agent."

"Yeah brother, he's the key," Devon agrees. "We have to find out what he's up to. But we don't really have enough resources to watch the embassy twenty-four-seven."

"Er... Connor showed me something while you guys were out, that might help us," Dani hesitantly discloses.

Everyone turns to look at Connor, who turns a bright shade of red, "Well... I was going to ask, but... well, I just couldn't help myself," Connor hesitates, then takes a deep breath, "Let me show you, and if you don't like it, I can delete it." Connor opens up new windows and activates his new software programmes. He begins cautiously, "Devon, don't shoot me man... okay, if we take these photos and drop them into this facial recognition programme, they become targets that can be picked up by this CCTV network."

"Ah, what network are you in Connor?" Devon asks.

"Oh... a few. There's the City Council's and Regional Council's networks, the NZTA traffic network, which will also pick up the number plate recognition programme here. Oh and the Metlink cameras," Connor confesses nervously, "I haven't started on the private security camera systems yet."

"I don't want to rain on your parade, Connor, what you've done is impressive... but it's illegal and we can't really cross that line," Devon gently remarks.

Seeing the rejection on Connor's face, Tom quickly thinks, then pipes up, "Hang in there Connor, I've got an idea.

"I know that look Tom! What are you up to?" Devon asks.

"Look Dev, it would save us a lot of time and give us a shit ton more flexibility." Tom picks up his phone and sends a text. He looks up at Connor. "Okay Connor, let's put those two number plates into your computer, and put Kendrick's photo in as well."

Dani walks over to Connor, saying softly, "See I told you they would listen."

"Must be time for a brew," Koro announces, "I'll get the jug on."

***

*Friday Early Afternoon*

"That's a remarkable achievement," George nods after hearing the briefing, his gravelly voice breaking the silence that followed. "And as for the acquisition of the CCTV networks and other surveillance software Connor…"

"I know it's not strictly legal sir," Tom starts, "But Connor showed some good initiative."

"It absolutely isn't," George interrupts. "Legally you can't use it."

"But then what these other agents are up to isn't legal either," Frankie adds.

Drumming his fingers on the edge of the office table, deep in thought, George muses, "As this is a 'Dark' operation and deniable from the government's point of view, I think you might have a little leeway here… Hmm…"

"We haven't picked up anything yet, but we only started using it an hour ago," Connor concedes.

George stops drumming his fingers. "Devon, get a copy of the ethical surveillance policy from work and get everyone here to sign it. Dani, set up a register and I want every photo and number plate recorded that you feed into that software along with any results it turns up, be exact with dates and times. This will give you all some guidelines and accountability."

"Thanks sir, it might just help even the odds for us," Tom adds, "I want to run this software as ethically as I can, because you are our only real oversight."

"Connor, I'm glad you are working for us, keep up the good work," George looking at his watch sighs, "Sorry I can't stay. Another policy meeting to round out the week."

"The joys of being a public servant, eh?" Koro says cheekily.

Laughing, George replies as he turns to leave, "Touché Rangiwahia. Touché."

A beaming Connor calls Dani over, "Let's get started on this register."

"I guess I'd better get that policy wording sorted this arvo," Devon sighs, "Nothing like more paperwork."

"I can type it up if you like Devon," Dani offers.

"I'm starting to feel a bit redundant here Frankie, what about you?" Koro asks.

"What time will your wharfie mates be at the pub, Koro?" Tom asks suggestively.

"Huh, any time these days. There isn't a defined shift timetable since they broke the unions up in the eighties. Stevedoring is all private contracting companies these days and mostly temp work," Koro relays, not reading between the lines.

"So, we could go now, then? A late liquid lunch perhaps?" Frankie asks.

"Now you're talking! I'll just get my jacket," Koro replies enthusiastically.

Laughing, Tom makes his way over to Connor, "Alright, let's see what CCTV coverage we have around those two embassies."

***

*Friday Early Evening*

Looking up from the computer that Connor is working on, Tom sees Devon pulling his suit jacket on, "What time are we taking the girls out Dev?"

"I'm picking Taylor up from the gym at eight, and we'll meet you and Dani back here just after that."

"Fast work skux! Dani is hot!" Connor compliments Tom.

Devon bursts out laughing as Tom protests, "Not you, too! This is a bloody conspiracy. Dev did you prime him?"

Devon holds his hands up defensively, "Not me brother, he's worked this one out himself."

"Come on, spill the tea dude," Connor prompts.

Taking a breath, Tom collects himself, "Sorry Connor, no gossip to tell. Dev and I thought we'd catch some stand-up acts a bit later tonight, then we invited Taylor our gym instructor and Dani to join us. It's definitely not a date."

Suddenly a red banner flashes across the top of the main computer screen.

"Hey, what's that Connor?" Devon asks.

Connor swivels back to read his screen, "Looks like

you guys might be late for your date tonight. That's the number plate recognition alert. The Iranian car has just passed Hataitai Beach on Evans Bay Parade. What do we do?"

Rapidly thinking on his feet, Tom says, "Shit, Frankie and Koro are still at the pub. Dev, can you get a car from George?"

"Not after five-thirty bro. All the pool cars will either be allocated for operations tonight, or the day shift have taken them home for the weekend."

"He's just passing the Yacht club, heading towards the lights," Connor advises.

Tom grabs his phone and his crutches. He stands and runs a hand through his hair. "Connor, you stay here and message us updates. I'll phone Dani to come back in. Dev race out and grab a taxi."

"Dude this is just the best job ever! Good luck," Connor pulls up his phone and plugs the USB cord into a port on his computer.

***

The white hybrid taxi quietly glides through the Mount Victoria tunnel, buffeted by the occasional car horn as its echo rebounds around the artificially lit vehicle warren.

"Have you decided where you're going yet?" The taxi driver asks.

Reading the latest message from Connor, Tom replies, "Sorry mate, Miramar shops please."

"So, it's not the airport," Devon comments. "That's good," Devon comments.

"Yeah, but we're still at least ten minutes away. Oh hang on," Tom taps his earbud.

"Tom, it looks like he's gone past the petrol station," Dani enthusiastically informs him. "Still on Miramar Ave, there's two more cameras we're watching and Connor is searching for more in the area."

"Thanks for the update Dani. Any word from Frankie and Koro?"

"Frankie said, they might be onto something there and he said he's not in any shape to drive, so it's just you two on this one."

"Roger that Dani, I'll call you when we get there," Tom taps his phone screen to end the call.

"It's your lucky day, that's two green lights in a row," the driver comments.

Tom looks out the window marvelling at the different wind sculptures, the Zephyrometer indicating a light southerly breeze.

"I hope he's not out just getting a feed," Devon comments.

Feeling a little foolish, Tom replies, "Hell, I never thought of a takeaway run! Let's hope not."

His phone vibrates and Tom glances at the screen, then addressing the driver, "The Roxy please."

"I wonder what's on? Hopefully it's not a re-run of Lord of the Rings," Devon remarks.

"Don't you want to see those elves prancing around the screen? I thought you had the hots for one of them?" Tom teases. "What's her name? She played the girlfriend of the big green man in that other movie."

"Settle brother, we're nearly there," Devon turns towards the driver, "Can you just pull in there, by that café please. How much?"

Tom pushes the door open and after fitting his crutches, hops out of the taxi, taps his phone and starts making his way towards the corner of the block.

Taking long strides, Devon catches up with Tom and asks, "Okay brother, what's your plan?"

Scanning the parked cars, Tom points. "Look, there's the blue car. He's got to be here somewhere. How about you cross the road and check over there and I'll go this side?"

They part ways, and Tom slows to look through the windows of the Thai restaurant on the corner. His eyes dart over each of the patrons, in search of his prey. Failing to locate him, he moves onwards, his hypervigilance driving him forward.

Finding the bakery closed, Tom swings around the short queue outside the ATM. Heading for the Roxy Cinema, a sinking feeling in his stomach, 'Maybe he's seeing a movie?' His phone vibrates. Tom stops and looks at his screen then taps his earbud, "What's up Dani?"

"We've just found his car in the carpark next to the Roxy," Dani replies, "Connor thinks he saw him go inside the cinema. Oh, and we can see you too now."

"Thanks, we found the car and are searching for him, I'm about to check out the Roxy. Can you message Devon please?"

Taking stock as he pockets his phone, Tom admires the Art Deco theatre and slowly makes his way through the open wood and glass doors towards the ticket counter. He casts a quick eye over the café crowd and identifies two people. Looking back to the ticket counter, Tom moves over to check the 'What's On' movie itinerary, his mind racing, 'What the hell is going on? Rookie mistake charging in here like I just did… Have they seen me yet?'

Devon strides in towards Tom, scanning the café as he approaches, then quickly turns his face away from the café patrons. He reaches Tom and picks up a copy of the movie itinerary and comments quietly, "Come on brother, let's get a table way over there and join the surveillance." Tom swings in beside Devon and they make their way over to a table against the wall and take a seat.

Tom snaps a few photos and sends them to the office then taps a message, We have company, two Mossad watching the Iranian talking to two men.

"Well bro, at least he's not here seeing a movie," the relief is clear in Tom's tone.

"True that. I wonder if it's a coincidence Eitan and his Mossad mate are here," Devon speculates.

"After seeing them in action in Syria, I wouldn't think so."

"Damn it, you're right. Just wishful thinking I suppose," Devon sighs.

"So who are the two newbies? Recognise either of them?" Tom asks.

"Ha, I don't know every agent in town," Devon chuckles.

Tom takes a longer look at the newbies. "They look pretty nervous. Hawaiian shirt guy is carrying a stack of weight and the short one looks like he's sweating buckets."

"Trust the sniper to notice the little things," Devon compliments. "Yeah, you're right again. So, they probably aren't professionals, which means the Iranian is likely a Case Officer running his own spies that he's recruited here."

"Look, the Israelis are leaving," Tom urgently whispers.

"So, maybe it was a coincidence?"

"Right, so as we have a huge team available," Tom begins with a touch of sarcasm, "Let's prioritise and just concentrate on the two newbies."

"Agreed. How about I go and wait across the road and see which way they go and if Mossad are waiting, we can take it from there."

Tom looks at his crutches and agrees with a touch of bitterness, "Sure, sure… Man, I have to get off these damn sticks."

"Chill brother. Your brain is working overtime and making up for any loss of mobility. Text me when they leave." Devon stands and makes his way outside.

\*\*\*

Tom's phone vibrates, swiping open his screen he reads, We've updated the board, any news?

Mossad have left, Tom taps in. Devon's outside waiting to follow Iranian contacts. Hang in there, it's a waiting game.

With a long slow breath, Tom falls back on his SAS training, restoring his patience and observation skills, thinking, 'Just like a recon op but the camouflage is very urban.'

Refocusing on the Iranian's contacts, Tom notices a black and green striped lanyard partially tucked into the larger man's open necked Hawaiian shirt, taking another photo to capture it, he forwards it to the office team with a message, Have you seen these colours on a lanyard before?

The shorter man stands first as their meeting looks at an end. He sends an alert text to Devon, and picks up the movie list, appearing to take a deep interest in it.

\*\*\*

Devon is observing from a recessed doorway across the road from the Roxy while waiting to make his move. He sees the Iranian contacts leave the cinema and turn left to walk up Park Road. The Iranian returns to his car.

Texting Tom, Wait 5 then head left.

The Iranian starts his car, pulls out onto Park Road and heads right, indicating a turn into Miramar Ave.

Keeping to the shadows of the Pohutukawa trees, Devon slips away from his observation spot and follows his targets, seeing the shorter man talking animatedly to the larger man in his brightly coloured Hawaiian shirt as they cross Tahi Street.

As he nears the next tree, Devon pauses and looks back to see if anyone else is on the move. He thinks, 'Good, no sign of the Mossad team.' He lengthens his stride and makes it to the next tree, keeping pace with the two men, who turn left into Byron Street. He sends a message to Tom, 2nd left Byron.

Devon waits for a couple of cars to pass, crosses Park Road and checks at the corner. The two men are still talking as they jay walk across Byron Street. Then they stop at a white picket fence, and open the gate that leads to a battered weatherboard house. Devon snaps a quick photo.

He moves back down the road and around the corner to wait for Tom. Soon a taxi pulls in beside him with the rear window automatically lowering. "That was quick brother, move over."

"Did you lose them?" Tom asks.

"No, they got home safely," Devon shows Tom the photo. "Looks like we need to do a little research. Ah driver, can you please go down Byron and then head to the Railway Station?"

"Sure thing Boss," the Polynesian driver replies.

"Excuse me bro," Devon mutters as he leans across his friend to get more photos of the old house.

"So that's it?"

"For tonight," Devon answers, then seeing the look on Tom's face, he expands, "We have some time. Look, if they were up to something tonight, they wouldn't have met at the Roxy."

Tom sighs and nods his head, resignation evident on his face, "Yeah, you're probably right. I guess we must be getting closer."

Devon smiles, "Besides, you've got a hot date tonight and we can't miss that!"

"It's not a… Oh, you're on the wind-up," Tom realises belatedly, then attempts to turn the tables, "Now you and Taylor on the other hand…"

\*\*\*

*Friday Evening*

"Can you spare a dollar, sir?" The unkempt homeless man grins, revealing three missing teeth. A filthy sleeping bag is wrapped around his shoulders.

Devon stops and pulls a five dollar bill from his wallet, handing it over. He looks pointedly into the man's eyes, "Please… spend it on food."

Wide-eyed, the man bobs his head, "Sure thing boss, thank you, thank you muchly."

The foursome walk on, as the homeless man, picks up his meagre belongings and shuffles off.

Taylor breaks the silence, challenging, "That was very nice of you Devon, but how do you know he won't spend it on booze or drugs? Aren't you just wasting your money?"

Devon pauses to think carefully before replying, "I don't know what he'll spend it on, Taylor, but do I know what it's like to live on the street and have everyone think those very same thoughts. You get to learn to read people quickly when you are hungry and don't have much energy left to beg from every passer-by."

Taken aback, Taylor asks innocently, "Really... wow... when was this? Sorry, I don't mean to be rude."

Dani listens to this exchange. She looks at Tom wide eyed. He nods as they continue down Courtenay Place towards the cinema complex.

"Yeah, it's all good Taylor. Life was pretty shit at home in my teens, my dad was in a gang, so there were lots of drugs, booze and beatings. After one real bad night, I decided the street would be better than home, so I packed a few extra things in my school bag and never went back."

"So how long were you on the street, if you don't mind me asking?" Taylor asks.

Devon shudders slightly as he remembers that time, "Ah, a while, I kinda lost track of time after a bit, until Tom found me."

Turning to Tom, Taylor asks, "Were you looking for Devon?"

"That's a very sanitised version," Tom starts, "We were in the same Science class and I noticed his uniform wasn't well washed for a couple of weeks. Then he stopped coming to class."

"Ha, it wasn't often our clothes got washed at home," Devon comments.

"Well, I knew where he lived, so I went over to see if he was alright. Dev's mum came to the door, wearing sunglasses, but I could see the black eye she was trying to hide. She said that Dev had run away and good riddance,"

Tom relayed, "So I started looking for him. It took me three months."

"Far out!" Taylor exclaims, "I know you guys are tight. You must have been good friends."

Thinking for a moment, Devon replies, "Nah, not really… I mean we used to play 'force back' at lunchtime with some other mates. I was hiding up in an abandoned derelict house at night and was half-heartedly looking for some food out the back of a café, pretty crook and starving, couldn't see a future or really any point in carrying on. Then this skinny little runt turns up and invites me back to his place for supper. That meal saved my life. Tom's just one in a million."

"Once I got Dev home, Koro got Devon talking over dinner, then offered him a bed for the night. Tom adds, smiling, "We couldn't get rid of him after that."

"Ha, I nearly left the next day when Koro got Aunty Sheila to come over with her concoctions. But she's one tough wahine! Wouldn't take no for an answer with her rongoā," Devon adds, "Oh, up here on the left is Allen Street. I think we could all do with a laugh after that tale."

"So that's why you call each other brother so much," Taylor concludes, then she touches Devon on his arm, "Thanks for being real and sharing that with us."

Feeling a little embarrassed at revealing so much so quickly, Devon points, "Ah yeah… sure… hey, the club is just a few more doors down."

\*\*\*

# Chapter Thirteen – Observations and Preparations

*Saturday Morning*

THE THUMPING IN his head and the dryness in his mouth finally gets bad enough that Tom reluctantly opens his eyes to discover where he has landed, groaning in his mind, 'Thank god I'm in my own bed.'

He turns to see if he is alone or not and the pain from the sudden motion jars his brain and obscures his vision. He gently massages his temples and squints to see that he is, in fact, the only occupant of his bed, 'Thank god I'm by myself... unless...' The thought of Koro entertaining one of his lady friends briefly crosses his mind, 'Nah... surely I'd hear something.'

He gradually eases himself to the side of his bed, grabs his bedside glass of water and shakily downs the remnants. He gathers his crutches, and carefully pushes himself up onto his feet. He takes the stairs, deliberately, one pace at a time. Each step sends a shaft of pain through his brain, slowly. Eventually he makes his way into the living area and heads for the kitchenette.

"Ata mārie Koro," Tom croaks as he fills a glass full of water, then drains it completely before refilling it.

"You and Devon made a hell of a racket when you waltzed in at three," Koro grumbles.

"Aroha mai Koro. Did we wake you?"

"I think you guys would have woken the dead at Bolton Street, bloody giggling and carrying on like two school girls," Koro complains.

Draining another glass of water, Tom refills and then turns the jug on, "Sounds like you need a cuppa Koro. Have you eaten yet?"

Wobbling a little as he stands, Koro joins Tom in the kitchenette. "Pass me a tall glass boy," he grumpily commands as he takes an egg in each hand from the carton sitting by the stove. In one fluid motion Koro cracks two eggs into the glass, then sprinkles salt and pepper over the top. He reaches for the Worcester sauce. Koro asks, "Do you want one too?"

"No thanks Koro. I prefer my eggs cooked." Tom shudders slightly watching Koro down the concoction in one long draft.

"Well if you're offering, I'll have a couple of fried eggs and some baked beans on toast with that tea thanks." Koro shuffles back to the dining table and starts to read his newspaper.

"Roger that," Tom acknowledges, grateful for the silence while he prepares their breakfast. The dull thump in his head recedes as the rehydration gradually takes effect.

Tom carries a steaming plate of hot food over to the table. Koro looks up from his paper, raises his left eyebrow and marvels, "Don't tell Tom, but he's only using one stick."

Placing the plate on the table, Tom realises what he has just done. "Wow." Using one crutch, Tom makes his way back to the kitchen bench and returns with the other plate, getting more confidence he turns and collects the teapot.

"Well, there's some good news. Much better than this dismal lot, another bashing of some poor immigrant," Koro observes as he tosses his paper onto the old battered sideboard.

Tom sits at the table and picks up his cutlery to start on his breakfast. He recites a kai karakia, before tucking into the fried food.

"Good boy," Koro acknowledges as he begins his breakfast.

Between mouthfuls, Tom asks, "So how did you and Frankie get on?"

"We ran into Hamish at the pub," Koro begins.

"That grizzly old soak. Geez, no wonder you're sculling raw eggs this morning."

"He sure can drink, that old Scotsman," Koro agrees, "But he did introduce us to a couple of new guys."

"Anyone interesting?" Tom enquires.

"Yeah, one guy was shouting everyone, reckon he'd had a win on the ponies."

"Ah, so he's the hangover culprit," Tom observes, sopping up some tomato sauce with a piece of toast.

"Yeah, we egged him on a bit. But the funny thing was when I started talking horses with him, he didn't know shit," Koro explains, "So he's getting his money from somewhere else."

"Nice work. Does this guy have a name? And what does he do?"

"Darryl Bigham and he's a container crane driver, you know one of those Straddle Carriers like Hamish drives," Koro answers, "I'll keep an eye on him at the pub and see what else I can pick up."

"More tea?" Tom asks as he pours himself another cup beaming, "I'm pretty stoked I can get around with one crutch."

"Now don't you go overdoing it boy, I don't want this gain to end in tears," Koro warns, "Anyway, tell me about that Arab?"

"It appears I got that wrong, Taylor was telling us at the club that Iranians are Persians not Arabs… don't look at me like that!" Tom demands and then fills Koro in on the previous day's activities.

\*\*\*

*Saturday Midday*

"Thanks for coming in everyone," Tom begins, "There's plenty of coffee for those that need it."

Frankie gets up from his chair gingerly and helps himself to another steaming mug.

"Did everyone pull an all-nighter? You all look wrecked!" Connor asks, sipping on his energy drink, then screwing the top back on.

"Whose idea was that last round of Jäger shots?" Devon asks as he pops a couple of paracetamol tablets from a blister pack and swallows them with a coffee chaser.

"Taylor's," Dani replies massaging her temples. "Remind me to eat properly before we go out again."

"Quit your moaning. It was all self-induced," Koro brusquely states, "Now, what's today's plan?"

Tom stands and using one crutch, ambles to the corkboard with the map.

"Hey, look at you," Dani announces, "Mister one crutch!"

"Congrat's brother!" Devon applauds him.

"Thanks guys, lots of hard work and support from

Taylor and Aunty Sheila is paying off. Just like yesterday with us…" Tom updates everyone on the events in Miramar and at the Thistle Inn. He turns to Connor and asks, "How many cameras do you have left that can work outdoors?"

"Five, but to be safe, their batteries need swapping out every six days. I'll set the laptop up so we can go mobile."

"Cool, bring up Byron Street on the map and let's see where we can place the cameras for maximum effect. I want to know where these two guys work and what they're doing for the Iranian."

Tom's enthusiasm is becoming contagious as everyone joins in debating camera placement, and their respective hangovers recede.

"What about this Darryl Bigham character?" Frankie asks.

"I think we need to keep a close eye on him," Koro adds.

"Yeah, you're right Koro, can you and Frankie handle another session?" Tom asks.

"Does the Pope wear a funny hat?" Koro fires back, then turns to Frankie, "Ah, no offence, Frankie."

"None taken, Rangi."

"Tom, you and Devon need your own car, if Frankie and Koro are at the pub," Dani states the obvious.

"Sorry, no pool cars left at work," Devon apologises.

"What about that rent-a-dent place down Thorndon Quay?" Connor asks.

"Yeah… that would work. Good idea," Devon agrees.

"Nice! You can get a different car each time. Good stuff Connor," Tom agrees. "Dev, can you please get us a car for the four of us, Connor obviously you'll be installing the cameras and Dani we'll need you to help us keep watch, so we don't get spotted."

"Yay, on a mission! Devon, can you get a van please? We'll also need a ladder. Is there a hire place close?" Connor asks.

"Oh, oh and a Hi-Viz and hard hat for each of us as cover," Dani adds excitedly.

"Looks like this team is coming together nicely," Tom proudly observes, as he writes up all the items on the whiteboard.

\*\*\*

Sitting in the passenger's seat, Tom swipes the keypad on the open laptop and checks the screen, waiting for the camera to connect.

Devon stands at the bottom of the ladder bracing it against the concrete post while Connor is up top mounting the camera.

An elderly neighbour walks to the end of his driveway next to the lamp post. Tom calls to Dani, "Heads up."

Dani sees the approaching man and walks over to him brandishing her clipboard, "Excuse me sir, do you have a minute to answer some important customer service questions?"

Startled and caught off guard, the grey-haired man replies, "Ah, no thanks, but can you tell me what you're up to?"

"We are just installing a monitoring device to check the quality and volume of telephone and internet traffic on the lines. Are you sure you wouldn't want to answer some questions? They would really help us improve the quality of our dependable service to our valuable customers," Dani breezily answers.

"No, no, I've got to get back to my... um... garden."

The man makes a hasty retreat back towards his home.

As she walks back past the van, Dani comments to Tom, "I wonder why people don't want to answer any of my questions."

"It's a sad indictment of our society today that no one wants to help improve a corporate's performance," Tom responds, deadpan.

"It's a shame, I've written out a whole series of questions… just in case," Dani winks.

"Okay, all done. Tom how does it look?" Connor calls out as he climbs down the ladder.

Looking at the screen, Tom checks the angle and replies, "Perfect, let's go!"

"All right, that's four down and one more to go." Devon folds the ladder and carries it to the rear of the van.

Connor swings open the rear doors and climbs in swiftly to help Devon as they stow the ladder. Dani climbs in beside Tom and fastens her seat belt, "What's next after the last camera?"

"I guess we check everything is working back at the office and then chill," Tom answers.

"We make a pretty slick team, eh boss?" Connor calls from the back as Devon climbs into the driver's seat.

"Not bad at all Connor, not bad at all."

The van pulls away from the kerb, back onto Park Road and Devon asks, "Are you sure about the placement for this last camera?"

Thinking a moment, Tom replies, "I know it's a long shot, but it's a tourist attraction and you never know just who might drop in."

"Ha, I doubt that Kendrick will go there. Go on admit it, that's who this camera is for," Devon grins, joshing his friend.

"Okay, yes you're right, but you never know."

The kerb-side carparks are full, so Devon drives up onto the footpath. "Connor and Dani, can you set out a couple of traffic cones, please? There are a few tourists about."

A distinctive clicking sound fills the air as Devon pulls the hand brake on quickly, springing out the driver's door and pulling open the rear van doors.

Connor passes the four bright orange cones out the door as Dani arrives, together they efficiently place the cones, and ladder into position. Connor checks his tool belt and scrambles up the ladder with his last device in hand.

Dani walks smartly back to the passenger's door and collects her clipboard. A crowd has gathered outside the side doors to the attraction. "Have you done a tour there, Tom?"

Tom glances across Camperdown Road to Weta Workshops. "No, I haven't really had the time."

"Neither have I. We should go sometime," Dani breezily invites, then realising how it might sound, covers herself, "Ah, that's if you want to of course."

"Yeah, that might be fun... I'd like that," Tom thoughtfully nods and smiles to himself, thinking, 'yeah, I'd really like that.'

Connor breaks the spell, yelling, "Hey Boss, how's it look?"

Coming back to reality, Tom checks the laptop, all business-like, "Just a touch to your right please."

Connor adjusts the camera slightly and calls, "What about now?"

"Perfect! Okay team, let's get outta here," Tom instructs while he closes the laptop and with half his mind on the job, the other half goes back to thinking about spending more time with Dani.

\*\*\*

*Sunday Midday*

"Thanks for coming in guys," Tom greets, "I just want an extra pair of eyes to make sure that Koro and I are all set for tomorrow."

"If you don't nail that meeting and wind up losing this place then George will be pissed," Devon admonishes.

"And I'll be out of a job," Dani replies sternly. Then she gets all business-like, "So, let's see what you've done. Come on Tom, spread all the documents out on the table."

There are screeds of paperwork in the manila folder Tom is holding. "Here's the IRD stuff, so that's GST and tax number, ah… Companies Office and City Council… oh there's three here for them, and the Kiwirail application form, with business description and plan, bank accounts and… that's the lot. What have I missed?"

"Well I'm seriously impressed." Devon claps Tom on the back. "How have you managed all that along with gym training and this rollercoaster investigative work?"

Looking a bit worried, Tom confesses, "To be honest, I'm not sleeping that well, so I've been catching up then."

Concern creasing his face Devon asks, "Are you having those village nightmares again?"

"What village nightmares?" Dani's curiosity is piqued.

Tom takes a breath, "That would be me reliving events in the Afghan village where I was injured."

Dani is shocked. "Oh, sorry Tom that must be awful."

"So, when are you seeing a doctor about this?" Devon asks.

"I've got an appointment on Wednesday to see the shrink," Tom answers.

"What about a regular doctor? Can't you get some sleeping pills to help?" Dani asks naïvely.

"I tried them in Middlemore, Dani and they kinda made things worse, because I couldn't wake up properly, so I stayed in the nightmare longer and then I wasn't getting any real sleep anyway so I was shattered."

"Oh, that's terrible!" Dani sympathises.

"Have you told Aunty Sheila about this?" Devon asks.

"No, geez, you're right Dev," Tom realises and slaps his forehead lightly.

"How about you phone Aunty, and Dani and I'll take a look through this lot, eh?" Devon advises.

"Roger that bro," Tom pulls his phone from his jeans pocket.

\*\*\*

# Chapter Fourteen – Miramar Meetings

*Monday Morning*

TOM SIGNS FOR a delivery and takes possession of an envelope from a courier driver, "Thanks mate."

Dani and Devon emerge from the crowds of commuters, crossing the concourse from the direction of the car park, "Ata mārie e hoa," Dani greets them. She turns to Devon and asks, "Did I get that right?"

"Ask this Māori." Devon nods at Tom. He's the one that grew up with te reo."

Chuckling, Tom answers, "Ata mārie Dani. Yes, you did get it right, and Dev is just teasing. He knows plenty of te reo."

"Yay, for me!" Dani looks pleased with herself.

"Come on, let's get inside. Koro is bringing the coffee down," Tom smiles.

Closing the door behind them, Tom opens the envelope he has just received to confirm the contents, then once everyone has left reception, he tears the brown paper wrapping open from the first large package. Satisfied he calls out, "Come and check this out guys." He stands back to take in the artwork featuring a running white rabbit stretching over the top of the wording, 'White Rabbit Investigations' and in smaller print underneath, 'Private Detective Agency' and a telephone number.

"That's dank dude," Connor says appreciatively.

"Wow, so cool! When do we put that up?" Dani enthuses.

"After our meeting at midday. I'm sure we'll find time then."

"Looks very professional, boy," Koro arrives with the coffee. "Shame we can't put it up right now."

"While you're all here, you might as well take one of these... Connor, Dani..." Tom calls them one by one and hands them an A4 page from the envelope.

"Whoa, Licensed Investigator certificate. Mum will be so proud," Connor beams.

"Wait until we get our ID cards." Devon grins. "They look real flash."

"We get ID cards too?" Dani asks with a sense of wonder.

"Of course. Otherwise, we could get had up by my old colleagues," Frankie answers, "But these certificates are good for starters."

"George really came through. Now you have everything you need for that meeting," Devon confirms.

"We're really going to swing this boy." Koro sounds determined. "Nobody is taking our home from us."

"Connor, can you please scan a copy of everyone's certificate and then you can all take the originals home. Dani, if you can print off copies and frame them for the reception wall," Tom asks.

Connor returns to the office. Shortly, he calls out, "Ah Dudes, we've got a hit!" And he sits behind his screen, "The Miramar boys are on the move. Damn where have they gone?"

The team race back into the office and grab some personal items. Frankie snatches his jacket from the table, "Come on Rangi, you're with me."

"You ready, brother?" Devon asks as he grabs his keys and Tom's shoulder bag, "We're parked over by platform nine, I'll carry this to the car."

"Great thanks," Tom replies collecting his second crutch leaning against his chair, seeing Dani's quizzical look, "I can go faster with two at the moment. Call us in five."

***

*Monday Morning*

The traffic is crawling slowly towards them as they follow a taxi on State Highway One heading towards the airport. The colourful metallic windsocks catch Tom's eye. They appear to march up out of the sea, almost like a troop of predatory robots about to swarm the road to catch their victims.

The smart phone buzzes, startling him back to reality, swiping to accept the call, Tom hits the speaker icon, answering, "Team, what's happening?"

Dani's voice sounds anxious as she asks, "How far away are you? Frankie and Koro can't find them."

"Geez, that guys a hoon," Devon comments.

"So where are they?" Tom asks, swiping his laptop's keypad to look at the Miramar map.

"They're on Park Road, nearly at the Miramar North Road roundabout," Dani replies.

"Okay ask them to swing back around the roundabout and backtrack to the Roxy, just in case they missed them. We're just turning into Miramar Ave. Dev turn up Tauhinu Road and we'll check Byron Street again."

Tom can hear Connor talking to Koro in the

background passing on the instructions. "Okay Dani, run through what Connor's cameras picked up again."

"Just the one activation so far from the camera above the bus shelter on the corner of Park and Byron. It looked like they were heading north on Park Road. Then nothing. I thought they would be catching a bus to work or something."

"We're just turning into Byron Street now, nothing yet," Tom advises.

"The others are just about at the Roxy. Frankie's insistent that he wants to check Miramar Ave," Dani informs them.

"Maybe they were fast walkers and are still walking up Park Road," Devon theorises.

"Yeah, well there's no action at their flat." Tom makes a decision, "Okay, we'll continue up Park Road... ask Connor to check the other cameras are all working, just in case."

"Okay, Connor..." Dani's voice fades into the background as Tom and Devon scan both sides of the road searching for their quarry.

"They can't just disappear, unless of course, they got picked up by a car," Devon speculates, driving north through the roundabout.

"You could be right Dev. That is a gaping hole in our surveillance plan," Tom agrees, mad with himself that he hadn't thought of it earlier.

"Got them!" Connor yells.

"Where, where?" Dani asks frantically.

"There look, they're outside Weta Workshop."

"Did you hear that, Tom?" Dani asks.

Devon puts his foot down and accelerates up towards the corner.

"Sure did. Nearly there," Tom replies.

"Frankie and Koro will be there soon. The targets have gone north up Weka Street," Dani informs them.

"Great, we're turning into Weka now… there they are," Tom points, "Okay, there's a carpark near Manuka Street. We'll pull in and see if they go past us."

"Where do you want Frankie and Koro?" Dani asks.

"Maybe have them park on Camperdown Road and let's see what happens."

Both Devon and Tom adjust their rear view and side mirrors to watch the approaching duo on the footpath. The shorter man looks to be talking as he gesticulates with his hands to make his point. The larger man is sporting an orange and black Hawaiian shirt this morning and nods as the shorter man continues his one-sided conversation, oblivious to being observed.

"Bro, use your recorder on the phone, you might pick up something, if short-arse doesn't shut his trap," Devon advises.

Tom taps off the speaker function and sets up the voice recorder. Crooking his arm out the open window, he palms his phone resting it on the sill, angling it towards the talkative on comers.

Listening carefully, Tom hears the shorter man say, "It's all very well for them, they're on a permanent contract. Ours finishes this week."

"Ray, it's still risky man," the larger man doubts.

"Yeah, but as I keep saying, with the cash from this, we can survive in the States and score a sweet job over there," Ray cajoles.

"Okay, okay, look we're nearly at work, so let's just keep our heads down and I'll get that swipe card off Marty today," The larger man warns.

"Good on you, Theo. Without that swipe card, we won't get near that computer," Ray replies.

"I know, I know already," Theo grumbles frustrated, "Now give me a break from all this talking so I can think."

The pair turn into Manuka Street and disappear from view.

"Go Dev, go," Tom whispers.

Quickly and quietly opening the driver's door, Devon slips out of the car and walks smartly to the corner to follow the pair from a distance.

Popping his earbud in and syncing it to his phone, Tom asks, "Did you hear any of that Dani?"

"Not really.

"The short one is Ray and the large one is Theo, Theo is getting a swipe card off someone called Marty to get at a computer, Devon is following them… oh he's coming back… hang on." Tom looks at his friend waiting for his information.

"Weta Digital," Devon advises.

\*\*\*

Koro's tokotoko stick clacks on the tiled floor of the Railway Station concourse, as the four men make their way back to the office.

Their nemesis approaches them demanding, "What's this meeting at midday with Mr Harrop all about? Just what are you good-for-nothing Yelich's up to? Trying to plead for more time, I bet. Well you're out of luck on that front!"

Tom bristles, "Now that's just about…"

Koro talks over the top of Tom, "Dunkell, you will find out soon enough. Now, if you don't mind, I have a meeting in Mr Harrop's office to get prepared for."

Turning to Frankie, Dunkell confronts him next, "And when are you cops going to arrest that skate board punk? I saw him again this morning."

"Did you now? Well, I guess I'd better go and have a word with him then," Frankie replies walking passed the loud mouth.

Dunkell scratches his head. "Ah… yeah… you do that."

Devon holds the front door open for everyone before closing and locking the door behind him. "Just say the word Koro and I'll shut his toxic mouth once and for all."

Koro eyeballs both Tom and Devon, growling, "It's not worth the both of you getting locked up. I don't want either of you to touch him, no matter what he says." He pauses for effect. "Got it? Good, now let's have a quick feed and get ready."

"You go on up Koro, I'll just have a quick debrief with the team," Tom tells him.

With Koro disappearing up the stairs, Devon leans over to Tom, "I guess Koro is right, but man I could smash that prick."

"I'm hearing you, bro," Tom thinks aloud, "It's almost like Koro knows something he's not telling us."

"What's this?" Dani asks as they congregate in the office.

"Dunkell? Oh it's nothing," Tom dismisses the subject. "Okay team, we now know the first names of the targets and where they work. Connor and Dani, can you guys source any available information on them while Koro and I are at our meeting."

Connor tapping away at his keyboard calls out, "Already on it."

"Frankie and Devon, can you two see what you can

find out about the Greek contacts and we'll all meet back here at one- thirty." Tom looks around at his motley crew and hobbles for the stairs, "Great teamwork this morning."

"Dani, check this out," Connor reports, with Dani moving in to look over his shoulder at the screen.

\*\*\*

*Monday Midday*

Tom taps his fingers erratically on his crutch, absently looking at an imaginary spot on the wall his mind emptying, almost in a meditative state, an old Army trick he learnt while waiting for a dressing-down from one of the training non-commissioned officers.

"Stop fidgeting, boy," Koro growls quietly, attempting to divert some of the building tension.

Snapping back to reality, Tom blinks rapidly, "Oh, aroha mai Koro."

Koro pulls his sleeve up slightly to look at his watch, grumbling, "They didn't use to be this late for a meeting when I worked here."

As if Koro had spoken the magic words, the office door bursts open, a tall man in a navy suit with one hand on the door handle, laughing towards the room's occupant, "That's a great idea for the spinnaker Paul. I'll see you down the club on Friday."

"Will do Greg, see you there..." a salt and pepper haired Paul replies as his large frame fills the doorway, "Ah Mr Yelich, sorry to keep you waiting. Please come in."

Koro stands and walks towards the door, "Mr Harrop this is my grandson Tom, Tom... Mr Harrop."

"Please, it's Paul. My word, looks like you've been in

the wars young man."

Using one crutch, Tom approaches Paul and extends his hand, "Afghanistan, we were the last Kiwi unit out."

Shaking Tom's hand firmly, Paul looks him directly in the eye and offers, "Good to meet you Tom, damnably difficult war from what I could tell. Thank you for your service. It's good to see you are on the mend. Please come in and take a seat."

Inside the office, Tom notices the three large windows that look over the pohutukawa trees lining the entrance to the Railway Station. He takes a seat next to Koro at the large oval table and whispers, "Are you ready?"

"I've got this," Koro nods back, as he opens his battered leather briefcase and places a thick manila folder in front of him.

Paul lowers himself into the chair at the head of the table, gathering some of his paperwork together and tapping it on the table to straighten the pile up. "Mr Yelich, I know you have been a long-term tenant and previously a valued member of staff. However, with the conservative government's drive for more profits from all State Owned Enterprises, we have no choice but to come up with a more commercially driven policy for this Station. As you would have read in the letter that Mr Dunkell delivered to you, what that means is that the Station has now been rezoned as a commercial area only. Unfortunately, that means you are unable to remain in your flat. Obviously due to your long service, I'm sure we could accommodate you, if you need a little more time to vacate the premises..."

Clearing his throat, Koro begins, "Mr Harrop... Ah Paul, how much would the commercial rent for our flat actually be?"

Checking the papers in front of him, Paul replies,

"About half as much again as what you are currently paying. We are working on the basis that we would have to gut your flat and rebuild it as office space at a substantial cost that we would hope to recover over a few years."

"So, what if you could collect the new rent from this week and not have to spend any of that money to rebuild this office space?" Koro asks.

"That would be a real bonus for us at Kiwirail, but I'm sorry, you can't continue to stay in the flat and just pay a higher rent. The City Council won't allow that in a commercially zoned area."

Opening the file in front of him, Koro pulls out a copy of the Council bylaws, points to the highlighted text and asks, "Could you please read this sir?"

Paul takes the paper and scans the text, then sits back in his chair and reads it again more slowly. "Well, that's certainly interesting, but you couldn't possibly have a new business that could pay its way. I know Mr Dunkell has the builders booked to start work next week."

"I think that's a bit premature sir, as my grandson is running a successful business right now, Tom..." Koro slides the folder over to him.

"Thanks Koro." Tom opens the file and pulls out the Companies Office document showing the official incorporation date, "Here's a copy for you, Paul. White Rabbit Investigations is my new business. We are currently working on a few cases and I have a team of six, which includes both Koro and myself. I have copies in here for you. Tax records, City Council registration... the lot."

Wide-eyed, Paul is thinking fast, "Ah, that's very impressive... Ah... well... I guess that means you would comply with that bylaw."

"Of course, we'll have to sign a new commercial lease

with you and set up automatic payments for the rent," Tom adds hoping to sweeten the deal.

"Yes, yes of course. Hang on, what about signage. Isn't there something in those bylaws about…" Paul begins.

"It just arrived this morning," Koro beams, "In fact, the boys are installing it this afternoon."

Shaking his head a little, Paul makes his decision, "In that case, you are the first official business for our project. Welcome to the Kiwirail business hub."

\*\*\*

*Monday Afternoon*

Frankie wedges his shoe against the base of the ladder, and stands to one side, waiting as Connor scrambles up with the cordless drill. Devon pushes the new sign up above the front door frame and holds it in place, asking Tom, "Is it straight?"

"Looks good from back here," Tom replies. "Go for it, Connor."

"Damn, I should've brought my level in from home," Frankie curses. "We don't want it crooked. That would send the wrong message."

A few commuters slow their progress towards their trains and look at the activity before speeding up, desperate not to miss their connection.

Tom allows himself a moment of pride. The signage crowns the front door, framing some of his team who have really taken to their new roles with a passion. He starts to feel comfortable, thinking to himself, 'I just might pull this off.'

Devon turns, and starts to speak, "Heads up…"

A venomous voice hisses in Tom's ear, "I don't know how you pulled that swift one off, war hero, but you'll pay, I'll make sure of it."

Startled, Tom nearly loses his balance, wildly planting his single crutch down hard to brace himself, "Shit Dunkell, don't sneak up on me like that."

"Do you have any idea how much trouble you've caused me? No, you wouldn't, would you?" Dunkell shakes his head and continues, "I've had my project management plan all approved! All my building contractors nicely lined up, which now I have to cancel. All my office plans I had architects draw up at a huge cost, all to waste, just because you want to play at running a business. You bloody Yelich's are all the same, selfish, just selfish."

The front door bursts opens, Dani's blonde hair catching Tom's attention.

"Ah, guys, you're going to want to take a look at this," Dani anxiously calls out, "As in NOW!"

"Aroha mai Dunkell, I've gotta go," Tom excuses himself.

"Who's she? And what's that cop and skateboard punk doing here?" Dunkell asks.

Connor scrambles down the ladder and runs into the office, Devon helps Frankie with the ladder and they all race inside, leaving a speechless Dunkell standing there alone on the concourse, staring at the new sign bitterly as all his schemes come to naught.

*** 

Connor sharpens the footage and plays the scene again.

"That's definitely Eitan, one of the Mossad agents we

saw at the Roxy," Devon states.

"Damn, Dev that means we can't go and check what they're up to," Tom frustrated turns and asks, "Frankie and Koro, can you please get out to Weta Digital and see if you can spot them?"

"No problem," Frankie grins, "Come on, Rangi, time to show these youngsters what a couple of old hands can do, eh?"

"Too right e hoa," Koro replies as he pockets his phone, "Let's go."

"Just be careful out there. Mossad are pros," Tom warns.

As the older men leave the office, Connor asks, "Could Dani and I take the other car?" Seeing Tom hesitate, Connor presses, "I mean I don't have a license, but Dani can drive right? And, and we have our vests too."

Looking across at Devon, Tom sees his friend shake his head, "Probably not a good idea."

Her hackles rising, Dani stands and stares daggers at Devon, "What? Don't you think a girl can do this job, Devon Matipo?" Turning to face Tom squarely, both hands on her hips, she demands, "You're the boss Tom. Am I just here to be a glorified receptionist, or what?"

Tom admires her spunky attitude. He hesitates momentarily then following his gut instincts, gives in, "Okay. Dev, it looks like we're minding the shop. Connor, take your board with you just in case."

Dani swivels back to Devon all smiles, with her right hand held out palm up, "Keys please."

Connor scrambles out from behind his desk, scooping up his skateboard. He checks his pockets to make sure he has his phone and he beams, "Come on Dani, let's rock and roll!"

"HEY!" Tom raises his voice, "Just be REAL careful out there, and keep in touch. And if I say 'Abort', I mean it. Get straight back here. Okay?"

Dani turns as they leave the office and replies a touch suggestively, "Roger that Big Boy."

Stunned, Tom and Devon look at each other for a moment. The front door clicks shut and Devon asks, "Did I really just hear that?"

Tom shakes his head. "Whoever taught her Radio Procedure words needs a lesson or two."

\*\*\*

The big screen blinks different coloured lights marking the progress of the two cars crossing the Wellington street grid.

Tom lounges back in Connor's chair, "Come on Dev, what's going on in that head of yours?"

Devon paces back and forth in the office, glancing occasionally at the screen, "I'm worried brother... its Mossad, you know what they can be like."

"Yeah, but then we're not in Syria, so they will have to mind their manners."

"Ha, you're probably right. Still, I might just text George and let him know what we're up to." Devon uses both thumbs to tap the message on his phone.

Checking his own phone, Tom notices the battery is getting low, so searches the desk for a USB cord and plugs his phone in. He taps the screen to place a call on speaker.

The disembodied sound of the phone ringing fills the office before being abruptly cut off, "Keep your hair on Frankie, I think I've got it... Hello?"

"Koro, good to hear you're getting the hang of your

phone," Tom begins.

"Is that sarcasm I hear, you cheeky little tow-rag?"

"Looks like you're getting close. What's your plan?" Tom asks.

"I'll drive up Camperdown, then Weka and then Manuka and see if we can spot anything first," Frankie yells.

"Did you hear that boy?" Koro asks.

"Yes, thanks Koro. Okay, I'll get the others to find a park on Camperdown and get ready," Tom replies, "Call me if you see anything."

Devon's phone chirps. He glances at the message and looks up, "George wants to know if we want an official team out there to run interference with Mossad."

Tom thinks a moment, drumming his fingers absently on the office desk. "Maybe… but then that might tip them off that we're onto them… what do you think Dev?"

"It's a tough call, brother. A bit of extra safety, or possible compromise of the team."

"I know right," Tom thinks a moment longer, "Better to be safe than sorry, message George affirmative."

\*\*\*

The Alfa cruises slowly down Camperdown Road, the throaty sound of its engine just above idle, bubbling from the twin exhaust pipes.

The car turns into Weka Street. "Nothing yet Frankie, what about your side?" Koro asks.

"Hard to tell yet, Rangi. A grey jacket, wasn't it?"

"Yeah, it's a bit warm for a jacket, none of the locals are wearing one."

"The jacket will mean it's likely he's armed then,"

Frankie warns.

"It still blows me away," Koro bemoans, "that all these people are walking around my city carrying guns."

"I know, it was a bone of contention when I was on the Force, too... Hey, check out that green Toyota, two guys," Frankie nods, "We'll do a U turn up here then head back to Manuka and see if we can find a park."

Dialling the office, "I wonder where... Tom, is that you?"

"What's happening Koro?"

"We think we saw two of them in a green Toyota, parked outside a white stucco house on Weka Street, just about opposite Manuka Street."

"Good work. So, there's more than Eitan?"

"Aroha mai, yeah there's two sitting in the car. Couldn't see them clearly, so we're going to find a park on Manuka Street and take it from there. Where are the kids?"

"Looks like they are only a couple of minutes away. I'll update them and get back to you. Oh, and George is sending us some help," Tom adds before ending the call.

"What the hell does that mean?" Koro demands.

"Hang on Rangi, I'll just turn in here..." Frankie deflects, thinking while he manoeuvres his car into a driveway, then checking the road, reverses back out, "We might be getting a visit from a team of spooks."

Bristling, Koro replies indignantly, "What, we're not good enough?"

"Put it this way Rangi, if we get spotted by Mossad and they get a photo of us, we are... I believe the parlance is... 'burned'."

"So what?"

"So that means 'we' are identified as agents and our cover is blown, and not just for this operation," Frankie patiently explains.

"Oh… That would be a real shame, I'm having a bit of fun and well… it's nice to talk to someone from my own age group," Koro admits.

"I'm hearing you, Rangi, I didn't know wc would get along so well. Hey, and I feel like I'm finally getting my mojo back."

\*\*\*

"Are you sure you're going to be okay?" Dani asks, with genuine concern.

Taking a swallow, Connor notices her sincerity and answers nervously, "Just keep an eye out for me. I'll try not to stuff this up."

"You just have to confirm it is that Mossad agent in the car and then signal me… oh what's the signal?" Dani asks anxiously.

"I'll be just skating and popping an ollie every so often," Connor starts, gaining confidence as he talks about his skateboard techniques.

"What's an 'ollie'?"

"Oh, I'll just be kicking my board under my feet and landing back on the board, kinda like jumping my board. If I spot the Mossad dude, I'll do a frontside 180, which means I'll jump my board again and then while I'm in the air, I'll flip my board 180 degrees, a totally different move, got it?"

"Got it. Now, are you ready? And don't get all extra on me I'll see your sweet move," Dani replies curtly.

Connor turns his baseball cap around backwards, hops on his board and pushes off up Camperdown Road, popping his board into the air regularly. Dani walks behind him to the corner of Weka and pulls out her phone, to take some photos of the Giant Ogre at the entrance to Weta Workshop, while keeping an eye on Connor's progress.

Tapping her earbud, she calls the office, "Tom, he's approaching the car soon."

The trepidation in his voice apparent, Tom replies, "I hope he's okay."

"He's got a healthy sense of worry Tom, so I think he'll be fine," Dani responds, then anxiously, "He's getting close to the Toyota now... there it is! He's done his move! It's them, it's them!"

"Confirmed Dev!" Tom announces.

A split second later, a white SUV races past Dani and she sees another speeding past Connor coming south on Weka.

"Geez, they're quick!" a surprised Dani declares.

The two SUV's converge on the green Toyota, blocking it from moving. The passenger's door of the Toyota flies open as Eitan tries to make a run for it. Six men leap from the SUV's, pistols trained on the Mossad agents. Eitan sees his options are limited and slowly raises his hands in surrender.

Connor picks up his board and crosses the road to hide behind a tree.

The SIS agents cuff the Mossad agents and shuffle them into the rear of one of the SUV's. One SIS agent hops in behind the wheel of the Toyota and all three vehicles drive off.

"That was so quick!" Dani replies excitedly, "They've gone already."

"Did any public see what happened?" Devon asks.

"Just us."

"That's fantastic work. Let's get you all back here,"

Tom sounds pleased.

"I can't believe what we just saw," Dani shakes her head in wonder. "Okay, I'll get Connor."

\*\*\*

"It was all over in, I don't know, maybe a minute? Definitely less than two minutes," Dani retells her version of the events to the team.

"It was so fire. I knew it was him from the photo when I skated past the car, so I pulled my rad signal and then watched from behind a tree. Those spooks were so quick I nearly missed them."

"Did you recognise the driver?" Tom asks.

"No dude. He was a different guy."

"That's Mossad dealt with, now who's next... the French, Turks or bloody Albanians?" Koro wisecracks.

Tom laughs, "Hopefully just the Iranian's Koro." Thinking a moment, he walks over to the screen and points to the map of Miramar. "What if we move these two cameras, one to here, watching Manuka Street and the other opposite the Roxy?"

Devon nods, "Good thinking. We cover the targets last known meeting place and their work. Okay, I'll organise the van again."

"That should be the last job for the day for us. Koro, are you and Frankie up for another beer?" Tom asks.

"Is a frog's arse watertight?" Koro grins. "Come on Frankie, we've earned a couple today."

\*\*\*

The weights from the Lat Pull Down machine clack in

rhythm with each of Tom's pull on the handles. Perspiration runs in rivulets down his forehead. He shakes his head to clear the sweat from his eyes, easing the handles to the rest position above his head.

"Here brother," Devon offers him a hand towel.

Grateful, Tom wipes his brow and reaches for his water bottle, panting, "Thanks Dev."

"Are you up for another few sets on the Leg Extension machine?" Taylor asks.

"Sure, sure," Tom pants, "I think I'll be sleeping well tonight."

"Come on bro, you're hogging all the good equipment," Devon chides.

Water bottle in one hand and crutch in the other, Tom makes his way over to the next piece of modern torture. He takes another good drink of water before seating himself, mentally preparing for the ensuing workout.

"Okay Tom, how many reps tonight?" Taylor asks.

"Shall we try three sets of twelve for starters?"

"I'll add a couple of extra kilos," Taylor advises.

"Roger that."

"Okay, off you go," Taylor begins mentally counting the repetitions.

The sound of weights from Devon's machine echo around the gym. Taylor calls the first set, "Time, rest. Hey, I had a great night on Friday. It was a lot of fun."

"Sure was Taylor," Tom answers, "Okay here's the next set."

"Oh, those comedians were good. I liked the big Samoan guy, he had such a cute laugh," Taylor recalls.

Thinking back, Tom grunts between repetitions, "He had… a different… take on… the church."

"And the starched clothes, that line had me in fits,"

Taylor laughs.

Finishing his set, Tom relaxes a little and before he can second guess himself, asks, "So would you like to go again sometime?"

Hearing something in his tone, Taylor coyly replies, "Thomas Yelich, are you asking me out on a date? Devon did you know about this?"

Realising how he sounded, Tom's face turns red, "Ah, no, but, well, yes, but…"

"Sorry Tom, I'm just teasing," Taylor smiles, "Come on, last set, go."

Redoubling his effort, Tom tries to hide his embarrassment in the exercise.

Devon wipes down his machine and makes his way over to the couple. "I thought you were keen on Dani, bro?" Devon adds fuel to the conversation.

"Oh, what's this?" Taylor pricks her ears up.

"Oh yeah, did you not see the way he kept looking at her on Friday night?"

"My radar must be on the blink. I thought Dani was hot for you, Devon," Taylor taunts. "Especially when I saw how you two were dancing."

Finishing his set, Tom inserts, "Was that before or after the shots?"

"I don't dance," Devon looks bewildered.

"Must have been after the shots, then," Tom fires back.

"Yes, it was after the Tequila round, we were all getting a bit loose then," Taylor muses.

"Did I really dance with Dani?" Devon asks incredulously.

"Yes, you did and might I add, you have some moves," Taylor replies admiringly. "You can ask me for a dance next time."

"So there will be a next time then?" Tom quickly asks.

"If Dani comes along we can chaperone each other from you two randy guys," Taylor states.

"I can't believe I was dancing," Devon says again.

"You sure were groover. Now have you got one more set in you Tom?" Taylor pushes.

"I'll give it a go."

\*\*\*

# Chapter Fifteen – Party With Marty

*Tuesday Morning*

WATCHING THE FRANTIC tapping and clicking of the keyboard and mouse with a sense of awe, Tom comments appreciatively, "You really are quite good at this stuff, aren't you Connor?"

"What... Oh, not that good or I wouldn't have got caught... I've upped my root kit since then... nearly there..."

"I think a root kit is his hacking tools that keep him undetected," Devon relays.

"You learn something new every day," Frankie replies sagely.

"Must have been another good one last night, I've let Koro sleep in. How did you two get on?" Tom asks Frankie.

"Well, if he insists on whisky chasers, we might need a larger expense allowance," Frankie quips, "But seriously, that container crane driver let slip about a special shipment coming in from the States in a couple of days."

"What's so special about this shipment?" Dani asks.

"That, we couldn't find out. Well not yet."

"Yes, I'm in!" Connor exclaims, "They've got some crufty old software and I used an old zero-day attack to bypass their security. Give me a few minutes and I'll see what I can dig up."

"O-kay," Tom responds slowly, "I think I followed

that."

A fierce banging on the front door interrupts their conversation. Eyes swivel to the screen, to see who is at the front door.

"Not that prick again," Devon mutters darkly.

"I've got it." Tom pushes himself up from his chair, sliding his left arm into the crutch sleeve and heads to the door.

"You've the patience of a saint, brother," Devon retorts.

Another round of thumping begins as Tom reaches the door. He opens it quickly and challenges, "All right, all right. I heard you the first time Dunkell. What's the emergency?"

Dunkell puffs his chest out and thrusts a clipboard under Tom's nose. "Property Inspection. Right now! Move aside war hero."

Tom stands his ground and takes the clipboard from his nemesis. "I'm not going anywhere until I've seen the paperwork Dunkell. So cool your heels and let me read this, eh?"

"You'll find it all in order. Now out of my way," Dunkell insists.

Dani comes up behind Tom. "Excuse me sir, but I think you'll find that all tenants have to be given notice of an inspection."

"And just who are you, missy?" Dunkell demands.

"Oh Hi, I'm Dani, I work here sir," She sports a winning smile.

"Yes, look Dunkell," Tom points to the fine print. "Just down here it says a property inspection can occur with forty-eight hours' notice and at an agreed time that won't unnecessarily affect the business operation."

"What?" Dunkell rhetorically asks disbelievingly, snatching the clipboard from Tom, "Give me that."

"Shall we say Thursday morning at eight? You can meet the whole team then," Tom offers.

"This place better be spick and span by then, Yelich. If I find anything out of place then you're out on your ear," Dunkell growls, then turns and storms off.

Tom closes the door behind him. "Thanks Dani, I'm sure you softened him up."

"Nothing like a pretty girl's smile, eh?" Frankie chuckles.

"Hey, you should see this." Devon calls. "Connor's worked out who Marty is."

"Geez, you have been busy Connor," Tom exclaims seeing the many windows open on the big screen.

Everyone gathers back in the office expectantly and Devon points to the screen. "Check this out. Marty is Martin Schofield who is the IT Systems Manager, and he oversees the installation and maintenance of the entire computer system at Weta Digital."

"Yeah dude, and they have some serious hardware."

"Connor, can you please explain serious hardware to an old codger like me?" Frankie asks.

Thinking a moment, Connor clarifies, "Serious as in I didn't think we had hardware this powerful in the country. You see it running major global corporations in the States or the EU. But it does make sense when I think about it."

"But why would Weta Digital have computers that powerful?" Frankie asks.

"Have you not seen Lord of the Rings?" Connor asks. "All those hundreds of thousands of computer-generated Orcs and Elves in the battle scenes can't be generated on a PC like this." He pat's his hard drive next to him.

"Oh shit," Tom speculates, "follow the trail. High-tech computers and disgruntled employees talking to an Iranian spy."

"Iran is under UN sanctions for its nuclear programme," Devon picks up Tom's line of thinking. "And they can't import tech like this."

"So, if Iran gets one of these computers, then what? They can finish their nuclear bomb programme?" Frankie is incredulous.

"Easy as. With this tech, they could probably launch a rocket to Mars at the same time," Connor adds.

"Dev, contact George. We need to update him on this, like now," Tom instructs soberly.

Silence envelopes the room as Devon taps a message on his phone. Each of the occupants consider the ramifications of what they have discovered, deep in their own thoughts.

"Well if an Iranian gets to walk on Mars before the Yanks do, that would piss them right off," Dani tries to lighten the mood.

***

Devon stirs some sugar into his long black coffee. The spoon makes a soft ding as it hits the side of the cup.

Tom takes a sip through the frothy top, taking care not to damage the white fern design etched into the brown surface. "What?" he asks seeing his friend shake his head smiling.

"Where do I start?" Devon teases.

"What have I done now?" Tom holds his hands up in surrender.

"You and your coffee designs," Devon jokes.

"Well, they're a work of art." He notes his friend's look of disbelief. "Seriously Dev, it must take a barista hundreds of hours to get this good. I know I couldn't do it!"

"Okay. I concede the point, but your coffee will get cold if you admire it too long."

"And what else? Come on out with it," Tom demands.

"You should see the way you look at Dani, down tiger, down," Devon ribs.

Tom turns a light shade of red. "I can't go there bro. George will have my balls."

"Wouldn't you rather Dani had them?" Devon taunts.

Tom takes another drink of his coffee to avoid the question. "Is it really that obvious? Geez Dev, I don't know what I want. I mean, I thought I wanted a break."

Glad to see his friend start to get real with himself, Devon coaxes, "To be fair, it's not that obvious. It's just that I know you well enough and it looks that way to me. But if you aren't ready for a relationship, perhaps back off a little, eh? Maybe you just need to take some time out and really think about what you want."

"Yeah. Maybe you're right."

Devon glances at his phone, picks up his cup and finishes his coffee. "Come on brother. Get that pretty-looking liquid lightning down ya. We're meeting George in fifteen."

***

*Tuesday Morning - Office*

Pouring the plunger coffee into a mug and passing it to Frankie, Tom sighs, "Come on you lot, snap out of it! It feels like the headmaster is coming to tell the class off in here. Have we done anything wrong to be worried about?"

Looking bashful, Connor admits, "Well, I did hack into Weta's systems…"

"On my instructions, Connor," Tom states. "It was my call, even though Devon was hesitant."

"To be fair, look at the result," Frankie starts, "I mean, the ends don't always necessarily justify the means, but we have confirmed the likely target."

The intercom buzzer sounds and Devon races for the door, determined not to waste any time.

A flustered looking George enters the office, placing his attaché case on the oval table. "Sorry I'm late I've just been losing a tail on the way here." Then taking a deep breath to centre himself, he begins, "Good work on identifying the Mossad agents. We didn't get a lot out of them, but that is two less spooks in town."

"What happened to them Unc… ah, George," Dani stumbles with the unfamiliarity of using his first name.

"Officially, one secretary and one cultural attaché have been recalled to Tel Aviv from the Israeli Embassy for administrative reasons," George explains.

"Don't they get charged by the police or you guys for carrying weapons or something?" Connor asks.

"Unfortunately, Connor they don't. They have Diplomatic Immunity. That was some brave work on ID-ing them Connor. They were completely taken by surprise when our collection teams swooped." George chuckles. "Eitan wanted to know how they slipped up. Of course, we didn't tell them. So you lot are all still under the radar."

Tom makes his way to one of the cork boards and points at the photos of the Israeli spies, "We only recognised Eitan, so this other one is still active?"

"Affirmative Tom, although they are two spooks down, I suspect the Israelis have at least two or three more at the embassy, so keep your eyes peeled," George warns.

"Coffee George? It's still pretty hot," Koro offers.

"Yes please, Rangiwahia, I didn't get a chance before I went into an urgent meeting." George pauses and gratefully takes a large mouthful of coffee, "Ahh, that's better. Now Devon gave me the heads up on your computer theory and the Iranian spy. The timing couldn't have been better."

"We thought you'd want to know ASAP. What do you think of our analysis?" Tom asks.

"You're all on the money. That urgent meeting I was called into was with our friend Kendrick, the Director-General, the Senior Operations Manager and two of my colleagues. Kendrick was at his usual ball-breaking best, trying to tell us how useless we were missing this Iranian operation and he demanded that we place all our resources at his disposal so he can catch them in the act."

"I'm not working for that bastard!" Koro vows vehemently.

Tom and Devon exchange a look of mutual concern, as Dani joins in, "Neither am I!"

"Don't worry," George says. "He hates me even more now." He takes another drink before continuing, "When he'd finished his tirade, the DG asked if any of us would care to shed some light on this. I informed them that we already had a team covering the Iranians and that I would have thought a fellow Five Eyes partner would have, as a matter of courtesy, informed us that they were working with the Israelis on an operation in our capital. We had to of course, remove the Israelis so they wouldn't interfere with our ongoing operation."

"I bet that put him in his place," Frankie interrupts.

"Momentarily. Now he wants access to all our operational data, and how come we hadn't informed the CIA about this operation."

"Tell him to come and get it," Koro brandishes his tokotoko as a weapon.

"I said I will keep him up-to-date on a weekly basis," George soothes. "But, of course, the report will be mislaid. I'm not compromising any of you."

"So, what do you want us to do now George?" Tom asks.

"The Iranians have to get the computer out of the country somehow, probably by ship. Rangiwahia, do you have any contacts on the wharf?"

"Āe, Frankie and I have been working that angle and there is something dodgy happening with a US ship coming in this week."

A look of respect crosses George's face, "Well done, I'm not sure how that relates yet."

Connor pipes up, "Excuse me, I've just checked the CentrePort Shipping Arrivals schedule, an American container ship is due in today, around the same time as a Chinese log carrier, but a Greek container ship arrived yesterday and is leaving Thursday."

"That lines up with the Iranian meeting with the Greek Captain last week," an excited Dani exclaims.

"Connor, when are the departure dates and times for the Greek and Chinese ships?" Tom asks.

"Ah," Connor clicks through a few screens, "They both head out the same day, Thursday, the Greek ship heads out at 2:30pm and the Chinese at 3:45pm."

"So potentially it's either ship. The Chinese and Iranians have an alliance," George theorises, "We have to get this right as the diplomatic fallout will be unbearable if we fail."

"Kendrick will have a field day," Devon notes.

"And you can kiss goodbye to any independent New Zealand Intelligence Service as the Yanks will just take over," George reasons.

"This is a tad serious then," Frankie observes.

George looks at his watch. "Tom, draw up a plan and call me at nineteen-hundred with details. I'll run interference until then. Apologies team, I've got another meeting with Kendrick and the DG."

"Thanks George," Tom sees him out, then returns to his team, "Koro, what sort of access can we get to the wharf?"

*\*\**

Two stony-faced CIA men stand either side of Kendrick's chair, almost daring someone to make a provocative move. The Director-General places both hands on the table, leans forward slightly and states coolly, "With all due respect Kendrick, you are not taking over the NZSIS to score brownie points for your boss. We know what we are doing and I have full confidence in my Operations Officers."

"You never disclosed that you were running this operation to us! How are we to trust you if we don't know what our supposed allies are up to?" Kendrick demands.

"That's the pot calling the kettle black, YOU never disclosed that you were taking over the CIA operation in Wellington," George accuses.

A cold smile crosses Kendrick's face. He turns from George to the Director-General, "If you want a full blown diplomatic incident with your strongest ally, then just keep trying to play hardball, Ma'am."

With the tension rising in the room, the Director-General leans back in her chair. "Kendrick, we know you have at least four teams at your disposal, and one team currently on R and R in the Coromandel." Seeing the surprise on his face, she presses her advantage, "Yes we do keep tabs on your 'unofficial' presence in our country. Just as you do on our teams in the States."

"Your point?" Kendrick insists.

"You don't need any of our teams for manpower, so what do you really want?" the Director-General asks.

Pointing at George, Kendrick demands, "I want what he knows and I want to know who his team is."

Bristling George fires back, "After how you ran Operation Crimson Sky, I wouldn't trust you with the lives of any Kiwi."

"Gentlemen! Just calm the fuck down. There's enough testosterone in this room to give me a hairy chest," The Director-General intervenes.

George and Kendrick pause gobsmacked, looking at the Director-General. Even one of the CIA goon's icy façade cracks, a slight smile curls from the corner of one of their mouths.

"Now that I have your attention... Kendrick, in the spirit of closer co-operation, how about I put one of my teams at your disposal on the condition that you liaise with me before any 'intervention' takes place, so that you don't compromise any of our other ongoing operations?"

Mollified, Kendrick replies, "I think I can live with that Ma'am. May I call you Virginia?"

"No, you may not!" She snaps. "George, you still have full autonomy and I'll detail another team for your operation. However, you will keep me in the loop daily."

"Yes Ma'am," George answers smartly, already mentally planning the new team's tasks.

***

The corporate colour scheme extends to the black carpet, green painted walls and green chairs that Devon and Tom sit in, patiently waiting admittance by the indifferent platinum blonde secretary.

Tom feels the irritation slowly rising within him. The grating sound emanating from the oblivious secretary's nail file as she shapes her perfectly manicured talons. Each quick stroke adds to the internalised frustration growing within his chest.

Sensing the tension in his friend, Devon taps Tom on the arm, "So are you going to ask Dani out on Friday night again."

"Wha… Oh you… you're having a laugh, aren't you," Tom replies, thankful for the distraction.

"Nah man, is that what's eating you at the moment?" Devon asks.

"No it's…" Tom nods towards the secretary.

"She looks a bit young for you bro. More Connor's type wouldn't you think?" Devon asks.

"Ha! No, I reckon Connor's type would have blue hair, half her body covered in ink and probably dressed Cosplay style like her favourite Anime character."

Looking at Tom quizzically, "Have you met her already? I thought he was single?"

"No, just a guess."

"That's one heck of a description," Thinking a moment, "That's not one of your kinks is it?"

"What? No, no, of course not," Tom dismisses.

"I can't say I've seen you reading much Anime, but you never know what Dani might be into," Devon ponders.

"You seem to be thinking a bit about Dani yourself, Dev. I mean you two were dancing together on Friday. Are you sure it's not you who is interested?"

The office door opens, disrupting their conversation, a bespectacled ginger haired man of average height comes out and scuttles away down the corridor, leaving the door open.

"Mr Schofield will see you now," the secretary states without looking up from her nails.

Standing together, Devon leads the way into the office and closes the door once Tom had entered the room.

"Good morning gentlemen, this meeting is highly inconvenient," Mr Schofield complains.

"Good morning, Mr Schofield. This is Investigator Matipo and I'm Tom Yelich," Tom begins, while Devon flashes Mr Schofield his NZSIS warrant card. "We have a delicate matter of national importance that we need to discuss."

Having taken in the warrant card, Mr Schofield sits up straight, "The SIS… national importance… what's this all about?"

"In a nutshell, your supercomputer. Just how secure is it?" Devon asks.

"What? Old Betsy? Well… since we've moved to cloud-based computing over the last year, we actually don't have much use for her," Mr Schofield admits. "In fact, we disconnected her last week with a view to moving her to one of our sister studios later this week. She's currently sitting in a container out the back."

Exchanging a concerned look between them, Tom turns back to Mr Schofield, "Can we take a look at it, please?"

"Well, we have an urgent project due for completion this week, so I can't spare much time…"

"Mr Schofield, I don't believe you have grasped the urgency of the situation…" Tom starts.

Glancing at his watch, Mr Schofield decides, "You're not going to leave me alone until you've seen this computer, are you?"

"We have a job to do sir," Devon responds.

Mr Schofield stands and runs a hand through his hair, then picks up a swipe card attached to a green and black lanyard, "Sorry, I'm being rude, it's just we're getting a lot of pressure from the Hollywood accountants about the deadline. Call me Marty. Come on I'll show you."

\*\*\*

Pushing off with his left foot, Connor describes, "First up Dani, you have to learn to Ride Switch, which is skating with your right foot forward on the board like this, pushing with your left foot and then swapping over like this."

Connor stops and swaps his foot placement, pushing off with his right foot.

"O-kay," Dani replies slowly, carefully placing her right foot on the front of Connor's spare skateboard and gently pushing off with her left, slowly gaining confidence as she reaches the wall by the stairs.

"Good work Dani!"

The front door rattles as Tom and Devon enter reception, "We're back," Tom calls, making his way to the office.

Embarrassed, Dani picks up her board quickly. "Sorry, we were…"

Eying them both with skateboards in hand, Tom laughs, "Having some fun? Well, why not?"

"So you're not angry?" Connor asks.

"Put it this way," Devon interrupts, "In the army it's always hurry up and wait."

"Yeah," Tom agrees. "It's not action twenty-four-seven, so you have to find ways to keep sane, or you die of boredom."

"Oh, that's rad dude, I just thought I'd teach Dani a few moves when we get a bit quiet."

"Knock yourselves out, Tom takes a seat at the office table.

"Good point," Connor misinterprets, "Dani I'll bring in my old knee pads and a helmet for you tomorrow."

"I like your dedication to Health and Safety," Devon jokes.

"So how was your party with Marty?" Dani asks as she slides her board alongside Connor's, behind his chair.

"He took a bit of persuasion, but he's going to play ball," Tom smiles in reply.

"Yeah, they are working to a deadline this week for one of the new comic movies," Devon adds.

"Not the new Marvel one? Doctor Strange or Spiderman?" Connor asks eagerly.

"Not sure. We saw some of the artwork. Some guy with a billowy robe," Devon explains, seeing the look of disappointment on Connor's face, "Aroha mai Connor, I didn't grow up with comics so I don't know who it was. But, I've got a surprise for you."

"So, Connor, we saw the size of the supercomputer Ms Betsy," Tom interrupts. "It's huge! And it's already in a container, but what else could Ray and Theo do to help the Iranians?"

"If it's in a container already, then it's easy to put on the Greek ship as is," Connor thinks out loud, "But I suppose… yeah dude, if they had access for an hour or two, they could remove all the semiconductor chips."

"How big are these semiconductor chips?" Devon wants to know.

"It depends dude, from an inch to twelve inches."

"What if we put a couple of cameras around this computer?" Dani asks, "That way we would know when they were there."

"That's your surprise, Connor. You and I are heading back there at five to meet Marty after Ray and Theo have left for the day, to install some cameras," Devon grins.

"Dude!" Connor cries, "That is so rad! Do you think I could see some of that artwork?"

"Computers and comic book heroes Connor, could your job get any better?" Tom chuckles.

\*\*\*

# Chapter Sixteen – Missing Persons

*Wednesday Morning*

KORO CONCENTRATES AS he pours plunger coffee into the assorted cups and mugs, then peering closer, picks one up growling, "Hey, who owns this fancy new mug? Are mine not good enough?"

"Ah, that's my one," Connor sheepishly claims, "Mum was so proud of my certificate and that I'm staying out of trouble that she insisted on getting me a present from the mall last night."

"Oh, that's so sweet," Dani smiles, passing the cups around the team, "What a lovely mum."

Frankie takes a sip from his cup. "Great coffee Rangi, just hits the spot."

"You were saying that about the whisky last night too," Koro grunts.

"How did you two get on last night?" Tom enquires.

Frankie shakes his head. "The place was packed."

"They have signed on a stack of temps this week to get through the workload with both the Chinese log carrier and the Yank container ship," Koro explains. "Some old faces I haven't seen in a while and heaps I've never seen before."

"And, of course, everyone has to have a beer after the shift," Frankie adds with a big grin.

"I can see this assignment is doing wonders for your social life," Devon chips in sarcastically.

"Us old dogs know how to mix business and pleasure, something you have yet to learn, you cheeky little tow-rag," Koro growls.

"And the business side...?" Tom queries.

"Yeah, on that," Frankie begins, "There's something on the U.S. ship that is going to go 'missing' according to our new crane driver buddy, Darryl."

"But we couldn't find out what it was," Koro adds, "We'll have to go back tonight and see what else we can pick up."

Thinking a moment, Tom asks, "Devon is there anyway George can get information on what the American ship is carrying?"

While Devon considers Tom's question, Dani pipes up, "Wouldn't that be on the ship's manifest?"

"I could have a crack at getting that off the CentrePort system," Connor offers.

"Okay, Connor you try that and Dani can you help decipher the manifest." Tom directs. "Devon, let George know what we are up to, and Koro and Frankie see what you can find out this afternoon. In fact, I think Dev and I might pop in after the gym and see what you've found out."

"I've been thinking about the timeline." Dani walks over to the white board and starts marking up her thoughts, "The Greek ship arrived two days ago, the U.S. and Chinese ships arrived yesterday. The Greek and Chinese ships leave tomorrow so we've got about thirty-six hours to catch the Iranian spy in the act."

"Yes, you're right. Where are you going with this Dani?" Tom wonders.

"I think we should all be prepared to put in some long hours. Maybe even staying here overnight. What do you think?"

"You only live up the road, Dani, but Connor... Frankie what do you think?" Tom weighs up.

"Dude, I can crash anywhere. If you've got a couch even better, but I better let mum know, or she'll worry."

"Good call Dani, Tom I don't think I can sleep on a couch, but..." Frankie starts.

"Frankie, you can have my bed," Tom offers. "Koro have we still got those old moth-eaten camp stretchers in the back of the storage cupboard?"

"I haven't thrown them out, so they should still be there," Koro informs him.

"Dev, can you get a good car from Rent-a-Dent for the next couple of days, and I've got my first proper meeting with the shrink in a half hour so I'd better get going."

"When you get back, we will have the place set up for a... well... sleep over?" Dani ponders the right word.

"Oh damn, I just remembered," Tom smacks his hand onto his forehead, "We've got Dunkell doing a property inspection at eight tomorrow morning!"

"I think we'll have our work cut out for us today then," Koro observes.

*** 

"Fancy a cup of peppermint tea before we start Tom?" Sandra asks.

"Yes please. It might be a nice balance to the black coffee I had an hour ago."

"I would recommend you limit your caffeine intake to before lunch, or it may increase your anxiety and interrupt your circadian rhythm."

"Thanks, I'll keep that in mind," Tom takes a seat in the comfy chair. Taking a moment to review the week since he was last in this office, he realises he has been on the go and hasn't really stopped. The investigation pushes its way back to the front of his mind, 'That extra team of Georges will come in handy, if we have to watch all three ships.'

His thoughts are broken by Sandra as she enters the room, offering a steaming cup of tea "Here you go. Watch out it's hot."

"Thanks," Tom takes the cup and rests it on the arm of the chair.

Sandra closes the door and takes her seat. She looks at the notes in front of her. "So, Tom, how did you get on with the sleep hygiene handout I gave you?"

"Ah, well… to be honest, I'm finding it hard to get to bed at the same time."

Sandra makes a note and asks her next question, "Any flashbacks?"

"Thankfully none," Tom realises.

"How's the memory? Forgetting much at the moment?"

"The sleep hygiene for one… Ah…" Tom tries to recall.

"So how are you coping?"

"By keeping busy."

Sensing something is up, Sandra tries another tack, "Okay, how about you tell me what your week has been like."

"Well, maybe you can help me with something that's been troubling me all week," Tom responds, "See there's this girl…"

\*\*\*

Closing the door behind him, Tom swings his crutch in time with his good leg and makes his way into the office, looking around at the changes.

"Wow, you guys have been busy!" Tom exclaims, noting the paperwork tidied into trays, large sheets of art paper rolled above the white board and corkboards in readiness to cover the information.

"Yeah, Dani has been working us like a slave driver," Frankie retorts, sweeping the stairs with a brush and dustpan.

"I think those wooden stair rails would look better if we buffed them with some furniture polish," Dani decides brightly.

"I'm in the CentrePort system dude. This one has some serious encryption, but I should have that manifest soon."

"We got a call from George," Devon adds. "He's being shadowed by the CIA and couldn't slip them this morning, so he's asked that we only contact him from my phone until he advises."

"I must say team, I'm seriously impressed," Tom answers.

"I'm just heading up to help Koro with the camp beds," Devon heads for the stairs.

"I better come up and see how much work we need to do on the flat," Tom decides.

Climbing up the stairs, Tom hears Connor call out, "Dani, I'm in."

Tom leaves his team to get on with their tasks. He looks around the orderly living area. Even the cushions on the chairs are evenly spaced. "Hey, have you guys done up here too?"

"We thought if Dunkell gets up the stairs and sees

how tidy this is, he might not look much further."

"What are you driving at Dev?" Tom asks.

"Brother, if anything is going to get us kicked out of here, it's the state of your room," Devon retorts.

"But...," Tom begins.

"No buts bro. Where's all your army training gone eh?"

Tom climbs the stairs to the next level and opens his bedroom door to survey his unmade bed, piles of washing not put away and a collection of half-empty glasses of water. "Fair call, I suppose."

"Shall I leave you here to get this shipshape? Or do you need a hand?"

"No, no, you go help Koro," Tom waves Devon off.

Tom checks the time, mentally gives himself fifteen minutes to get his room to barrack-room inspection standard and gets stuck in.

A few minutes later Devon pokes his head in and nods with approval. "Much better. I like the military corner folds on the bed. Hey, George has just sent through a stack of photos for Connor's facial recognition programme."

Straightening the books on his bedside table, Tom looks up, "Who are they of Dev?"

"Looks like one Mossad and nine CIA spooks. Could be helpful if we know where they are," Devon answers.

"Have we had any more hits?"

"Just Ray and Theo heading to work this morning, nothing else."

Tom puts the last of his clothes away in the drawers. "Nearly finished here. How are the camp beds?"

"Serviceable. Let's hope we don't need them," and Devon heads off downstairs.

One last look around his room, and Tom smiles,

satisfied. He picks up the three now empty glasses and heads for the stairs, nearly bumping into Koro who is carrying a small pile of sheets.

"Hey, watch out there boy," Koro growls.

"Aroha mai, Koro."

"Here, take a set of these and change your bed. You can't have Frankie sleeping in your old sheets. Then you can help make up the camp beds for you and Devon."

Sighing, Tom puts the glassware down, takes a set of sheets and remakes his bed.

\*\*\*

Tom flicks through his phone's gallery, finding the photo of the CIA agent holding the door for Kendrick as he was leaving the BS ministry last week. He leans over to show Connor, pointing at his screen, "Is this guy one of the agents in George's batch?"

Connor takes a close look and considers, "No, I don't think so. Send it to me and I'll scan it into the programme."

Their conversation is interrupted by the front door buzzer. The screen reveals an elderly lady. "Poor dear has probably mistaken us for the public toilets," Frankie observes.

"Don't all you men get off your bums to answer the door, I'll get it," an irritated Dani says, stalking off.

Bewildered, Frankie asks, "Was it something I said?"

"I'll get the kettle on," Koro offers. "I might even break out the biscuit tin as a peace offering. Dani has really taken ownership here."

Tapping away at his keyboard, Connor pronounces, "Definitely a new spook, Tom."

"Thanks Connor," Tom replies as he slips his crutch

on and stands.

Dani can be heard greeting the old lady and having a short conversation. Turning to the office, Dani calls, "Tom, can you please help." Then turning back to the lady, invites, "Please come in and take a seat, Mrs..."

"It's Mrs Talbot, Dorothy Talbot and what's your name?"

"It's Dani, Mrs Talbot and this is the owner, Tom Yelich." Dani turns to Tom.

"Good afternoon, Mrs Talbot," Tom makes his way over to offer his hand.

Dorothy shakes his hand and asks, "Yelich, that's one of those Dali names isn't it? Aren't you lot from up North?"

"A few generations back, yes we were," Tom replies, "Now how may we help you Mrs Talbot?"

"It said on the sign that you are private investigators and my Percy is missing," Dorothy breaks down crying.

Dani grabs a box of tissues from the front desk and offers them to Dorothy, "Oh, that's awful."

"It is, he's normally so reliable," Dorothy sobs, "He... he leaves in the morning after breakfast and is always home in time for his tea, but he hasn't come home. Can you please help me?"

Thinking on his feet, Tom asks, "A missing person... have you tried the police Mrs Talbot?"

"That bunch of hopeless idiots," Dorothy wipes her nose, "They said to go away and come back tomorrow. Something about forty-eight hours."

"Now you just wait here a moment, Mrs Talbot," Dani suggests. "I'll just get the form from back here and get some details,"

Tom looks at Dani questioning, "We have a form?"

"What do you think I've been doing when you've

been out detective-ing?" Dani races around to the front desk and pulls out a clipboard, pen and her paperwork.

"Do I have to fill out more forms? Those idiot policemen gave me lots to fill out too, I couldn't make head or tail of them," Dorothy grumbles.

"No, no Mrs Talbot, I'll fill it out for you," Dani offers.

"You're a good girl Dani, please call me Dorothy."

"Okay Dorothy. I've got your name and Percy's, but I just need some contact details, oh and here's our rates of engagement," Dani begins and efficiently collects the information.

"Thank you, Dorothy," Tom starts, "Now you say Percy left home yesterday morning and hasn't been home since."

"Yes that's right."

"So where does he go during the day? Is he still working?" Tom asks thinking about an accident at work.

"No. He's never worked a day in his life. He's a lazy old bugger but I love him dearly," Dorothy replies.

"Has he ever done this before?" Tom asks.

"No, he's always at home bang on five to six for tea and then we curl up on the sofa and watch the news."

"That doesn't sound normal behaviour then, where is he…" Tom wonders.

"It's not, and I want him back! Won't you help me find dear Percy?" Dorothy breaks down again.

"Of course we will, won't we Tom?" Dani soothes handing more tissues to Dorothy.

"Yes, yes of course," Tom rapidly answers. "Ah, Dorothy, would you have a photo of Percy on you?"

Reaching into her handbag, Dorothy pulls out a golden framed photo and hands it over, "Here he is, asleep on the sofa after a big day out. Isn't he adorable."

Dani takes the offered photo and looks at it wide eyed and shows Tom, "Oh, look he is adorable."

Surprised Tom does a double take, then plays along with Dani, replying in a decisive tone, "Well I guess we should take a look. Do you mind if I take a copy of this photo Dorothy?"

"I'll do that Tom," Dani offers taking the photo frame and setting it on the reception desk. She snaps a few photos with her phone.

"So will you help? I don't care how much it costs." Dorothy pleads.

Wondering how he will fit this in to today, Tom confirms, "Of course we'll help Dorothy, in fact I'll get some of our team to call in and see you today."

"Well, I'd best get home and put on a batch of scones if I'm going to have visitors," Dorothy brightly decides and stands up spritely.

"Oh, you don't need to go to any trouble…"

"It's no trouble young man. I'll see you soon," Dorothy heads for the door.

"Dorothy, don't forget your photo," Dani rushes over and helps her with the door.

"Thank you dear, thank you both," Dorothy replies heading out into the concourse.

Back in the office, Tom instructs, "Dani can you print off a dozen copies of Percy's photo and maybe a note 'Missing, please phone us with any information'. We can pin them up in the neighbourhood."

"What's this?" Koro asks.

"Well team, we have our first 'Missing Person' case to solve," Tom announces grabbing everyone's attention.

"Do we have capacity at the moment with this Iranian operation?" Devon sounds doubtful.

"I don't think it will take too long. Especially if we all head out shortly."

"The first forty-eight hours of a missing person's case are the most important," Frankie chips in.

"Connor can you access the alert system on the laptop?"

"Sure can Tom. There'll be a bit of lag, but it's doable. Give me five." Connor plugs the laptop into the hard drive and gets to work.

"Great, Dani can you send the photo to everyone's phone and let's get on the road," Tom directs.

A series of chirps resound in the office as their phones receive the photo. Devon the first to swipe open, looks in disbelief, "Wait... What? You gotta be joking me."

Tom grins. "That's right Dev, our first missing persons' case is a ginger tom."

"Seriously?"

Dani bristles, "This is a frantic little old lady who is missing the most important person in her life. It's serious enough for her to go to the police and then to find us, I mean are we investigators or what?"

"How hard can it be? We put up a few posters and knock on the neighbours' doors. Maybe an hour and a half, tops and if we get a hit on the alert system, we manage it from there," Tom insists.

Getting a few dubious looks from Devon and Frankie, Dani adds, "Dorothy is also making scones."

"Scones? Well, what are we waiting for?" Koro asks, pulling on his jacket. "Where are we headed?"

"Barton Terrace, up off Tinakori Road. Connor bring your board please," Tom instructs.

\*\*\*

Piling out of the cars onto the footpath, Tom looks at the letter box, then pointing to an old weatherboard villa, "Okay, Dorothy lives up there, I'll pop up and see her. Connor can you please skate around the neighbourhood and put up the posters then get back to the car and watch the laptop. Dani and Devon can you take the even numbers on the other side of the street, Koro and Frankie on this side."

Everyone disperses with their own tasks, and Tom climbs the short steep footpath to Dorothy's front door. Raising his hand to knock, he is surprised as the door swings open.

Smiling, Dorothy exclaims, "You've come! My, my young man, you didn't tell me you have such a big team."

"Mrs Talbot, Percy may be a cat, but he is clearly very dear to you."

With tears in her eyes, Dorothy reveals, "Percy was given to me by my late husband Neil to keep me company. Neil passed away twelve years ago. He knew the heart surgery was risky, but followed the doctor's advice."

"I'm so sorry to hear that, Dorothy." Tom replies sympathetically, "All the more reason to pull out all the stops. Do you mind if I take a look in your back yard?"

"Thank you. The back door is down here, will you be alright with your crutch?" Dorothy turns and leads the way.

"I'm fine, lead on." Looking around Tom notices the close smell of an unaired house, observing the old wall paper lining the passage way, starting to lift along the seams. Dorothy automatically taps the old barometer which hangs on the wall to one side of the door to the kitchen as she passes, glancing at the result, "Looks like the rain is coming, probably by Friday."

"Nice place you have here," Tom remarks as they

walk into the kitchen. The warm smell of baking wafts from the oven.

"You are too polite Tom. Since Neil passed, I find it hard to keep up with everything. Now Percy eats his meals over there," Dorothy points out at the large water bowl and cat dish half-filled with dry cat biscuits, "He came and went as he pleased through the cat door."

"I see," Tom glances through the kitchen window. "It doesn't look like you have much of a back yard."

"That was the only drawback about the property when we bought it as newlyweds. Not much room to dry the washing," Dorothy comments as she unlocks the back door.

"Thanks," Tom says as he opens the back door and manoeuvres with his crutch down the two steps to the concreted area. There is a new wooden fence on the north side, a concrete block retaining wall to the west and a dilapidated wooden rail and wire fence to the south. A small potters shed is backed into the south west corner, sporting a cracked window pane and some broken pieces of fibrelite siding. An old clothes line anchored to the side of the shed stretches across the entire section with a long pole in the centre to support the wire.

Turning back to the house, Tom lowers himself onto the back step and inspects the cat door, "Hmm, looks like this has jammed Dorothy." Checking again, Tom sees the latch has been moved to the lock position. "That's strange, it's locked." Freeing the lock latch, Tom tests the door to ensure it is working properly.

"Oh really? I didn't lock it. Poor Percy wouldn't have been able to get in."

"Well, it's working now. Do you mind if I look in the shed?" Tom thinks he'd better check it just in case.

"Go ahead. It's not locked. I'd best rescue these scones."

At the shed, Tom tries the pitted chrome door handle, which makes the obligatory screech of protest from disuse. Inside is a cardboard box by the window, with a pair of old blue overalls on it. 'A well-used nesting spot,' Tom decides. 'Now where did Percy get in?' Bracing himself on his crutch, Tom crouches down and sees a cat-sized hole in the broken fibrelite with some tell-tale orange cat fur around the edges.

As he heads back to the house, his phone chirps. He stops to read a message from Dani, Success! C U in 5. Smiling, Tom steps up to the back door.

"Good news Dorothy, Dani has found Percy, he is on his way home," Tom smiles while reveals the good news.

"Oh, that's wonderful!" Dorothy replies joyfully as tears come unbidden to her eyes.

"I'd better let the rest of the team know," Tom thinks out loud as he taps a message to the team.

"Do you think there will be enough scones?" Dorothy asks fretfully as she wipes her eyes on her apron before collecting a tray of steaming hot scones from the oven and placing them on the stainless steel benchtop.

Tom eyes up the mouth-watering mounds of doughy perfection, "There is only six of us so that looks plenty Dorothy. Do you need a hand?"

Dorothy spreads a pile of side plates on the counter top and pulls a butter knife from the cutlery drawer. "Can you please get the butter and jam from the pantry cupboard... yes that one to your left."

While Tom is at the cupboard there is a knock at the front door. He places the butter and jam on the counter. "Come on Dorothy, the scones can wait."

Throwing a tea towel over the scones, Dorothy heads for the front door with Tom not far behind. The door swings open to reveal Dani holding a large cardboard box, with two children who have a close resemblance to the woman standing behind them. Devon and Frankie gather at the front gate waiting for the others.

"Hi Dorothy, this is Tiffany, David and their mum Steph. They've been looking after Percy at their place. He showed up last night and meowed until they let him in." Dani puts the cardboard box down on the front step and opens the lid.

An indignant Percy pops his head up, hisses at Dani then leaps out of the box in one stride and races to Dorothy. He rubs his chin against her legs, purring loudly.

"Oh Percy! You're home!" Dorothy wells up and compulsively leans in and hugs Dani. "Bless you, Dani." Then standing back and wiping the tears from her eyes, she acknowledges Steph and the children, "Thank you very much for looking after Percy. I was so worried."

Surveying the scene, Tom's heart fills with delight and his eyes get a little glassy. Swallowing hard, he sees Steph about to speak.

"We didn't know his name was Percy, so we called him Garfield. He was very good with the children, they loved to pat him. I'm glad Dani came knocking as I was about to phone the SPCA to see if there were any missing cats reported in the area," Steph explains.

"Percy is such a good boy, I'm sure he lapped up the attention," Dorothy replies, "I don't think I've seen you around here?"

"We only moved in a couple of weeks ago, haven't had time to get out much. We're still unpacking." Steph apologises.

Little Tiffany plucks up her courage, "'Cuse me Missus, but can we come and see Garfield sometimes?"

"Of course, you can Tiffany, that's if it's alright with your mum," Dorothy offers, "Would you all like to come in for a scone and a cup of tea.

"If you kids promise to be on your best manners, then yes Dorothy we would love to," Steph replies.

Devon, runs up the short path, "Sorry to break this up, but we've just got an alert."

Tom turns to Dorothy, "Sorry Dorothy, but we have to pass on those lovely scones. But I'm sure your new neighbours will help."

"Thank you Tom and you too Dani," Dorothy beams.

Making their way back to the others, Dani turns to Tom, "Thanks Tom for taking Dorothy seriously. I know it's been a distraction."

"You know what Dani? I could get used to helping people like Dorothy. It's a nicer world to live in than the one I've been in for years."

Re-joining the team, Devon explains, "Connor's got a hit on one of the Langley lot heading into the Emporium Café. I've sent Frankie off for…"

Devon is drowned out by the throaty roar of Frankie's Alfa reversing up Barton Terrace at speed, screeching to a halt, Frankie yells, "Come on! Get in!"

Tom decides, "Dev, Koro you go with Frankie, Dani can get us there in the Rent-a-Dent. Don't look at me like that, Go! Go!"

\*\*\*

"We're on the motorway, ETA two minutes. Where are you Dev?" Tom asks.

"Pulling into Kensington Street now. I'm heading for the Café. Is he still there?"

Connor refreshes his screen, "Yeah dude!"

"You hear that? Affirmative, can you ask Koro to head to the footpath by the highway at the end of Kensington. That's where the French agent disappeared last time," Tom asks.

Dani swings the Subaru right into Victoria Street and floors the accelerator, speeding up towards the Abel Smith Street intersection.

"Lights Dani, Lights!" Connor warns, desperately hanging onto his laptop.

"Damn, they've gone red," Dani curses, braking hard then smacking the steering wheel with one hand when she comes to a stop.

"Have you been taking driving lessons from Frankie?" Tom queries.

"Funny, Ha, Ha," Dani replies sarcastically.

"So, what do we do when we get there?" Connor asks eagerly.

"First we find a park. Connor, I want you in the car watching the laptop." Seeing Connor's face drop, Tom adds, "What if something goes down at Miramar? But keep your board handy, I might need you in a hurry."

Dani accelerates around the corner into Abel Smith Street, "And me?"

Anxiously hanging onto the door arm rest with one hand and his crutch in the other, Tom replies through gritted teeth, "Geez, slow down Dani! We don't want to attract attention." His phone buzzes. "What's happening?"

Devon whispers, "He's on the move, I'm getting a coffee."

"Roger that." Tom ends the call. "Okay, CIA is coming

out. There he is!"

The American walks towards Cuba Street. Dani passes him, indicates and pulls into a car park easily, "What now Tom?"

"We wait until he walks past us, but I want to know where the French agent is," Tom says with a touch of frustration. Buzzing again, Tom answers while glancing at his phone's screen, "Frankie?"

"Yeah, Tom. It's Henri the Frenchman. He's walking towards the café, coming from Victoria Street heading east. I got a good photo too."

"Excellent Frankie. Stand by in case he uses the same exit route. Can you phone Koro if he's heading that way?"

"Sure can," Frankie ends the call.

Tom watches the American approach through his side mirror. "Right, everyone, stay cool. I want to see where he goes. Dani, can you get out once he's passed us and go and put some money in the parking metre?"

Dani snatches her shoulder bag from the back seat beside Connor. She rummages for her purse to look for some small change. Tom turns away from the agent as he passes and talks to Connor, "Keep looking at your laptop, and don't look at him. Good, okay Dani you're on."

Opening the driver's door, Dani gets out of the car and walks casually to the parking metre, nonchalantly glancing towards the American as he walks onwards.

Tom raises his phone and snaps a couple of photos, then seeing a large black SUV emerge from Cuba Street, "You've got to be kidding." He continues taking photos.

"What? Oh, he's getting into the back of the black Chevy," Connor observes. "Do we follow them now?"

Watching the American vehicle tear off down Abel Smith away from them, Tom zooms into his last photo.

"No need, I'm sure those are diplomatic plates."

Dani races back to the car, jumping into the driver's seat she breathlessly asks, "Do we go?"

"No, no that's an embassy car for sure. Let's see what Henri does," Tom replies as his phone chirps, glancing at the message from Devon, He's taken the sugar, stay alert.

Connor echoes excitedly, "Looks like he's swiped all the sugar again. Here he comes."

"Good, now Connor get your board ready, just in case."

Tom watches the café entrance from the side mirror. The Frenchman crosses the road and walks west towards Kensington Street. "Connor have you got a map up on the laptop?"

Tapping a couple of keys, Connor turns the screen towards Tom, "Here."

"Okay," Tom scans the roads, pointing, "See how Footscray Ave curves here, do you reckon you could get through to the carpark by the footpath there?"

"No probs." Connor grabs his board.

"Good, just practice your tricks and keep an eye out for him. Stay in the car park and phone me with an update, okay?"

"Okay," Connor echoes as he opens the car door.

"And Connor… just be real careful," Tom warns.

Swallowing hard, Connor answers sincerely, "I will."

The tension is broken by Tom's phone chirping. He reads out loud, "From Dev, turning into Kensington."

"Tom, where do we go?" Dani asks.

Tom pulls the laptop into the front and points out, "Look, we've got Frankie here in Kensington, Koro here and soon Connor here, with Devon following him up Kensington. We know he went up Kensington and disappeared last time, but now we have eyes we can see where he goes. With Frankie there and us here on Abel Smith, we can go out onto Cuba and Frankie can cover Victoria. So, it's a waiting game right now. Just get ready."

Buzzing sounds in the car, Tom hits the speaker, "Frankie, you okay?"

"Yeah, he walked straight past me. Devon is just coming up now. I gave Rangi a heads up," Frankie reports.

"Great, get ready to move if I call."

"Ten Three, sorry yeah I'm available," Frankie explains the police call sign then ends the call.

Tom's phone buzzes immediately, "Koro!"

"Hey boy, he didn't even look at me! Can you believe it?" Koro asks incredulously.

"That's good. Are you okay, what's happening?"

"He's walking towards the Cuba Street intersection, no wait… what's the fool doing?" Koro asks rhetorically.

"What? What?" Dani asks excitedly.

"He's running across the motorway, bloody idiot will get himself killed… no, he's made it," Koro answers with a hint of disbelief.

Tom glances at the map. "Keep talking Koro. Dani lets head here to the Cuba Street intersection."

"He's gone into the carpark on the other side of the motorway… and he's getting into a white car. Here's Devon," Koro reports.

"Koro, can you ask Devon to head to the corner of Victoria Street please."

Dani turns into Cuba Street, narrowly missing a courier van, The Indian driver shakes his fist at them.

"It looks like the white car is pulling out into Victoria Street, I can't see anything from here," Koro growls.

"Okay, wait there," Tom ends the call, then taps

another contact.

"Damn it! The lights are red," Dani complains.

"Frankie, it's a white car heading up Victoria Street. Go. Go." Tom instructs then cuts the call and taps his friend's name on the screen.

The lights change and Dani speeds out onto the motorway.

"Dev, see anything?" Tom asks.

"Yeah, the white car has headed for Willis Street not Webb Street."

"Can you call Frankie and relay that. Cheers." Tom taps another contact. "Connor, he's crossed the motorway. Sorry bud, but can you head back to Koro and Devon."

"I thought it was him, but wasn't sure, so I stayed here like you said," Connor replies.

"Good on you, talk soon," Tom ends the call.

"AHH!! What's with these damn delays today?" Dani demands as she pulls up behind an orange Mazda waiting at the pedestrian crossing, with a window washer rapidly cleaning the Mazda's windscreen.

The lights change and Frankie roars past them, heading up Victoria Street, pulling into the right-hand turning lane.

Tom checks the map on the laptop screen. "Looks like Frankie is going north down Willis. We should take the left hand turn just in case." Tom taps the screen again and puts it on speaker. They listen to the ring tone.

"Tom," Frankie answers, "I can't see that car on Willis so I'm on Aro Street, but still no sign of it."

"Damn, we'll head up Willis. Can you circle back to pick up the team please?"

Dani waves the window washer away and accelerates into the left turning lane. She comes to a halt at the red lights, "Seriously?"

"Well, I think that's it for this time, Dani. Let's head back." Tom sighs knowing the chase is over.

"I can't believe how many red lights we got today. If only we had a bit more luck," Dani muses at what might have been.

"Hey, on the upside," Tom starts.

"There's an upside?" Dani quickly fires back.

"Oh yeah. I've seen how good you are in the driver's seat."

"I got heaps of practise on the farm with my brother's old Anglia. We used to do lots of donuts," Dani explains.

"Now, that I'd like to see," Tom replies enthusiastically.

"Well let's see…"

\*\*\*

The contrasting smells of pizza and Koro's fry bread, along with the laughter and chatter from the occupants, colour the living area with a sense of joy and purpose not seen in the apartment for many years.

Koro and Frankie are telling improbably tall tales of the afternoon's feline escapades to Devon and Sheila at the table. Connor is perched close by on the edge of an armchair, a piece of pizza in one hand and half an eye on the laptop.

Tom feels his shoulder muscles tighten from this afternoon's gym workout as he lifts the full jug and pours the hot water into the teapot and fills it right up. Dani sidles up beside him. "Do you need some help with that?"

"I've got this, but can you get some cups from that cupboard please?"

"Sure, sure," Dani eagerly helps, setting cups and saucers on the table.

"Any more fry bread left, brother?" Devon asks as Tom approaches the table with the teapot.

"No you greedy beggar. Looks like you've scoffed the lot," Tom ribs.

"Not even ow!" Devon defends himself.

Sheila elbows Devon in the ribs, scolding, "Speak properly boy, you know better English than that!"

"Yes Aunty, aroha mai," Devon apologises like a schoolboy who has been soundly told off. He turns to Tom and speaking in his best Queen's English says, "No Thomas you are quite incorrect. I did not indeed scoff the lot, but partook in my own fair share of said fry bread."

The room erupts with laughter and Tom answers back, "I'll consider myself rightly put in my place then. Now who wants a cuppa?"

While pouring the tea, Connor hesitantly interrupts, "Ah dude, the Miramar camera has been triggered. Looks like Ray and Theo are on the move."

"Aroha mai Sheila. It looks like our little party has ended and we have to go to work," Koro apologises.

Devon stands, "Excuse me, I'll get the car." Frankie follows suit.

Tom asks, "Connor, which camera?" He takes a quick sip of tea.

"It looks like they've left home and are walking back to work. Are we coming too?"

Making a snap decision, "I think if you and Dani mind the shop, we'll take both the cars and we'll see what happens."

"My, my, this job of yours sounds very exciting, but Rangiwahia, you aren't wriggling out of that drink you promised me," Sheila stands and picks up her handbag.

"We might get back in time for a beer at the Thistle."

"Good, then you can pick me up from my place," Sheila instructs.

"You don't have to go right now Sheila. Stay and finish your tea," Dani offers.

"Hmm, I might just do that. It would be a shame for this pot of tea to go to waste." Sheila sits back down reaching for the green biscuit tin as the four men race for the stairs.

\*\*\*

A buzz from Tom's phone breaks the silence in the car. He hits the speaker icon. "Connor, what's happening?"

"Theo and Ray have just passed the Camperdown camera, so it won't be long until they get to work. Also, I've checked the other cameras and there is no activity from the Iranian Embassy."

"Good work! We're about five minutes away, so Frankie should just about be there."

"Yeah, he's on Tauhinu Road already. About two minutes,"

"Roger that, Connor, message me when they get there." Tom ends the call.

Turning to Devon, Tom explains, "This doesn't feel right, no Iranian activity, no truck. It doesn't add up."

"Unless they are just going for the semi-conductors," Devon suggests.

"I suppose," Tom answers unconvinced, and the silence stretches between them.

They swerve around the roundabout. "I thought you were laying off Dani," Devon says.

"What do you mean?" Tom asks defensively.

"You two serving the tea tonight. What's that about?"

"Hey bro, I was just making the tea and she offered to help. Nothing going on."

"Hmm, I dunno, brother. Maybe she is sweet on you after all."

"I think you're seeing more into this than there is, Dev." Tom's phone chirps. "Okay they've arrived at Weta Digital. Frankie and Koro are pulling up now on Weka Street."

"You still wanna go up Manuka?"

"Yeah, I think we need to scope the street in case the Iranian has a truck parked there," Tom theorises.

"Have you given much thought to the French and the CIA working together?" Devon asks.

"Makes no sense to me. Just why would the CIA be using a dead drop to pass information to the French?"

"So there's no electronic signature?" Devon thinks aloud. "Maybe, it's more deniable that way?"

"But what could be that important? Hey, what if we intercepted the message next time?"

"Then what? Try and crack one of their codes?" Devon throws cold water on the idea. "Connor might be good, but we'd need the entire resources of the GCSB and I doubt if even George could swing that with the DG."

"You're probably right, still… might be worth a crack."

"Okay, look there's Frankie's car," Devon comments as he turns into Manuka Street.

Tom's phone buzzes and he rapidly taps the speaker icon, "Connor, we're here."

"Yeah, I can see that on the map. Hey Theo and Ray have accessed the storage room that leads to the container with Marty's card. This could be it, Tom," Connor excitedly predicts.

"Thanks. Stay on the line and let me know anything that they get up to."

Devon leans over and asks, "Connor, where's Dani? She's unusually quiet."

"Dani is walking Sheila home after her cuppa." Connor checks her location on the screen. "She's... by the pub, must be on her way back now."

"No sign of a truck or anyone sitting in a car out here," Tom notes.

Devon pulls the car up to the curb twenty metres from Weta Digital on the opposite side of the road. He stops exactly between two lamp posts to take advantage of the ambient darkness.

"Now we wait," Devon yawns, leans back in his seat and shuts his eyes. "Wake me when they come out."

"Okay dudes, it looks like they're coming back out," Connor informs them.

"What? That's strange. What has it been? Five minutes Dev?"

"Yeah, hey Connor," Devon asks, "how many of those chips could they have got in five minutes?"

"If they had the right tools, maybe a couple each," Connor guesses.

"Looks like it's a false alarm."

"Yeah, Tom. They are definitely leaving. They've just gone past the first camera," Connor informs them.

"Okay Connor, thanks, I guess we follow them home and call it a night," Tom decides, ending the call, "I'll phone Frankie and we'll leapfrog each other to make sure these two get home safe, eh?"

"Yeah, good call brother," Devon replies.

\*\*\*

They stand quietly waiting for the pedestrian light to change, both deep in their own thoughts about a woman, wondering if their best friend secretly desires the same one and if they could guide him to another equally attractive woman, or if they should just wait and see what naturally happens.

The atonal drone announcing their passage across Thorndon Quay, breaks their reverie.

"How's Sheila's form, eh? Leading young Dani astray," Devon starts.

"Don't you think Dani can handle herself?" Tom asks, as they step onto the small traffic island.

"Well, to be fair, I don't really know," Devon contemplates, "We need to organise some self-defence sessions at the gym."

"So, are you going to ask Taylor about it? She might like that," Tom ribs.

"I thought you were the boss?" Devon counters.

"But it's you she wants to dance with bro," Tom pushes.

"Okay, I'll ask her," Devon exaggeratedly sighs, "We should also run a training session on those pepper spray devices."

"Not a bad idea Dev. We should get Connor in on this. It would boost his confidence. Maybe even Frankie and Koro too," Tom expands, waiting at the next crossing.

"Ha, I don't know if we could teach those two old dogs any new tricks," Devon laughs.

Glancing towards the front door of the Thistle Inn, a familiar figure exits and heads up Kate Sheppard Place, Tom quietly comments, "Look there's Darryl leaving."

"Seems a bit early," Devon notes, the pedestrian lights turning green announced by a discordant drone.

They make their way across Mulgrave Street, and walk quickly to the corner. In Kate Sheppard Place they see Darryl crossing the road towards a parking lot.

Thinking on his feet, Tom quietly observes, "Look there's a couple of smokers opposite the car park. Let's go over there and see what Darryl's up to."

They cross the road and walk up Kate Sheppard Place approaching the two smokers. Devon asks, "Hey fellers, could I pinch a smoke off ya?"

The shorter of the two men grumbles, but reaches inside his puffer vest withdrawing a generic green packet of cigarettes adorned with its obligatory gory photo of a cancer victim. "Bloody expensive habit these days man, you got a couple of bucks?"

"Sure, sure, I'll need a light too mate," Devon pulls his wallet from his rear jeans pocket and hands over an orange note.

Taking the lighter from the man's nicotine-stained fingers, Devon sparks up his cigarette, inhales deeply and replies tightly in a cloud of smoke, "Thanks man."

Devon moves a bit further up the street with Tom following, to get a better view.

Tom leans his back against the red brick wall and surveys the parking lot. "He's talking to someone."

Devon blows the smoke out of the corner of his mouth away from their line of sight, "Yeah, you're right, I can't make out who it is. Try your voice recorder brother, we might just pick something up."

Tom pulls his phone out, taps the ringtone to silent and activates the recorder, angling towards the car park couple. They both inch closer to the curb.

Devon moves one foot onto the road and faces Tom side on, so he can still see their targets. He whispers,

"Damn, I still can't make out the other bloke."

Tom puts his finger to his lips. Devon nods and takes another drag on the cigarette.

Keeping his phone angled on the two figures, Tom studies them from his position. His sniper's instincts take over. He breathes slowly with his mouth slightly open, mentally calculating the distance… eleven metres, wind speed and direction… slight southerly fluctuating between five and ten knots, humidity… about seventy-five percent. The cigarette smoke causes his breath to gradually get shorter and faster and his mind drifts back to the village. The carpark scene becomes overlaid with images of villagers screaming, running for their lives. Tom's heart races, sweat breaks out on his forehead and he starts to feel dizzy, croaking, "Dev…" as he puts a hand out to steady himself.

Devon throws his cigarette into the gutter and grabs Tom's arm, "Tom, are you okay? Silly question. Come, try and walk."

Tom shakes his head to clear the memory, plants his crutch onto the footpath and swings forward a couple of steps.

"Deep breaths brother. Come on, big deep breaths," Devon encourages as he leads Tom to the red brick wall.

Following his friend's instructions, Tom inhales slowly filling his lungs. The slight breeze cools his damp forehead.

"Can you walk further? Come on let's get you moving," Devon instructs.

"But, Darryl…" Tom starts.

"Hey, is he alright?" the smoker asks as they walk past.

"Yeah, thanks… Tom, let's worry about him later.

Come on man let's go. We might get spotted," Devon encourages making their way back towards the pub's front door, "Let's go around the corner."

"I'm…, no, not too good," Tom stutters as they pass the steps leading up to the entrance and round the corner. The movement helps to centre him back in the present. "I went back to the village," Tom admits.

"Damn… so how are you feeling now, bro?"

Stopping to lean against the window of a closed takeaway shop, Tom takes stock, "I'm a little rattled to be fair. I was just running through my sniper assessment, trying to get a line on the other guy Darryl was talking to and then I'm back in the village."

"Shit brother. What do we do? How can I help?" Devon asks feeling powerless.

"I guess, just what you did." Tom pauses. "Maybe I do need some of that medication Sandra offered."

"Hmm, have you talked to Sheila about some rongoā? Might be quicker."

"You know what? You're right. Come on let's go see her," Tom decides.

"You sure you wanna go right now?"

"Let's do it," Tom decides.

They make their way to the side door and step inside the packed, noisy bar. Devon commenting, "Follow me."

Devon leads the way, plunging into the crowd with a series of "Excuse me, thanks mate," making space for Tom to follow on his crutch close behind.

"Look what the cat's dragged in," Sheila cries in a loud happy voice, nearly spilling her glass of Barcardi and coke.

"Hi Aunty. Are you leading young Dani here astray?" Devon asks with a smile on his face.

"Are you smoking again?" Sheila growls. "Naughty boy!"

"Hey guys, any news?" Dani asks as she takes a sip on a tall Pilsner glass of light amber.

"Aunty, I've got a problem I need some help with," Tom comes straight to the point.

Casting a studious eye on Tom, Sheila notes the matted hair on his forehead and the slightly flushed features, "Hmm, panic attack?"

"Yeah, I think so," Tom confesses.

Dani looks on, concerned at the exchange.

"Devon, mind Dani and my drink. We'll be back soon," Sheila instructs, climbing off her bar stool. "Come with me young man."

"Don't worry, brother, I'll look after Dani," Devon smiles.

Playfully punching Devon on the bicep, Dani indignantly says, "I can look after my own self thank you very much!"

*** 

"So what concoction did Sheila put in here?" Devon asks hefting up the two litre bottle and shaking it from side to side.

"That's between her and Papatūānuku, but it doesn't taste too bad," Tom confesses as he closes the front door behind them.

"That's Mother Earth, isn't it?" Dani asks.

Devon nods, "Yeah, you're picking this up fast, aren't you?"

Noting his friend's familiarity with Dani, Tom jealously thinks, 'Yep, I knew he was keen on her.'

"Hey, how was the pub?" Connor asks.

"A bit of fun, but we left Sheila with Frankie and Koro," Dani replies.

"Anything happening here?" Tom enquires.

"Nothing yet. I still can't work out what Theo and Ray were up to. I've played the recordings over and over," Connor sounds frustrated.

Remembering the recording he took earlier Tom pulls his phone out and opens up the screen. "Connor, can you please have a crack at cleaning up this recording and see if we can hear what Darryl was saying in the carpark?"

"Sure can dude," Connor pulls on a pair of over-ear headphones and plugs them into the hard drive.

Devon smacks his head. "Of course, sorry bro I completely forgot."

"Don't beat yourself up Dev, my panic attack, if that's what it was, kinda took priority for the both of us," Tom reasons.

"I don't mean to sound condescending, but is this type of work really what you need at the moment Tom?" Dani gently probes.

"That's just what Sheila said earlier," Tom admits, adding, "But, I think if I sat on my arse doing nothing, it would be worse."

"Okay, I guess you know best," Dani acknowledges.

"I'm putting the jug on. Who's up for a cuppa?" Devon heads up the stairs to a chorus of "Yes".

Connor interrupts, "Hey Tom, who's on this tape with Darryl?"

"We don't know. He had his back to us. Why?"

"I think this is pretty big. Have a listen to this," Connor offers his headphones.

Nestling the pads over his ears and adjusting the size,

Tom nods to Connor who starts the recording, "…easy as… swapping a container out… cost extra… Yanks won't like… ten 'K' up front… tomorrow… DEV… TOM ARE YOU OKAY?"

"Geez-us!" Tom exclaims, removing the headphones, "That last part was loud. Excellent work man! Can you clean it up any more?"

"I'll try with another programme. It might take a bit of time though." Connor is already clicking on his mouse.

"Thanks Connor, you're an invaluable member of this team," Tom replies appreciatively.

"What's on the recording?" Dani asks.

"Hopefully Connor can pull some more out of it, but Darryl is in it up to his eyeballs. Something about a container swap with the American ship."

Moving over to her computer, Dani says, "Then there must be something of real value in the manifest. But I've only found normal trade goods so far."

\*\*\*

# Chapter Seventeen – Portside Shenanigans

*Thursday 7:30am*

THE FLAT AND office are a hive of activity. Frankie is on the end of the vacuum cleaner in the bedrooms, Tom is at the kitchen sink with Connor drying the dishes, Devon and Koro have packed up the camp beds and are putting them away upstairs and Dani is giving the office and reception a once-over.

Sensing some hesitancy from his washing-up partner, Tom invites, "I can see you're trying to say something Connor. So come on out with it. I promise I won't bite."

"Well… um… okay then," Connor finally finds his voice. "When do we get paid? Only there's this real extra set of trucks that I wanna get for my board."

"Oh, of course," Tom thinks embarrassed, "I hadn't really thought about it. Ah… let me have a look at that after Dunkell has finished here, okay?"

"Sure, sure," Connor replies, "Hey, I'm gonna have another go at that manifest. I got in only so far, but I've had an idea."

"Thanks, I'd appreciate that, it would be good to get an indication of which container Darryl's going to swipe." Tom wipes the bench down with the dishcloth. "That's the last pot, I'll start putting them away."

The whine of the vacuum cleaner stops and a murmur of male voices can be heard above them as they descend the stairs.

"Haven't you boys finished those dishes yet?" Koro grumbles.

"Just about. Can you give Dani a hand, please?" Tom asks while stacking some plates in the cupboard.

Connor hangs his tea towel over the oven handle and follows the other men downstairs to start his work. With the last pot in the cupboard, Tom looks around at the flat's transformation noting the little feminine touches of Dani's. A vase of flowers, cushions set nicely on the armchairs, the wooden dining table oiled and polished.

He makes his way down the stairs, thinking, 'That girl is transforming our lives.'

His heart fills with a mix of pride and delight watching his team all working together. Frankie and Devon are standing by the corkboard pointing at some of the agents they have identified, while Koro leans back in his chair nodding as he follows their line of discussion. Dani leans over Connor's shoulder asking questions and watching in fascination as Connor's hand flies over the keyboard. Tom looks at his watch. "Five minutes, team," he calls. Let's cover those boards now. Connor can you put the screen saver up please?"

Koro asks, "How do you want to play this Tāmati?"

"Ah… how about Dani and I greet him and lead him through here so we can introduce Dunkell to the team?"

"Should I hide or something? He really has it in for me," Connor asks.

"No, let's try being straight up with him," Tom suggests. "Well… to a point."

The buzzer sounds, followed by a frantic pounding

on the door. Dani and Tom make their way through to Reception. Dani opens the door, brightly inviting with her trademark smile, "Good morning, Mr Dunkell. Please come in."

Slightly disarmed, Dunkell replies, "Ah... yes... Miss?"

"It's Dani, Mr Dunkell," smiling Dani offers her hand, "Danielle Franklin."

"Oh, pleased to meet you, Dani." Dunkell shakes her hand, caught completely off guard.

"Please come on through Mr Dunkell and meet the team," Tom takes over. "This is our reception area and the office is through here."

Taking in the clean new desks, the lush sprawling potted tree and new sofa, Dunkell comments, "Well this is very neat and orderly. Not what I expected from you Yelich's. Through here, eh?"

Tom leads them through to the office. Dunkell bristles as he sees the occupants, "What's that skateboard punk doing here? And the cop too?"

Tom takes a deep breath. "Mr Dunkell, this is Connor O'Neill. He's our IT expert, and here's Francesco Vettori, retired Detective Inspector NZ police and Devon Matipo, retired Sergeant NZ Defence Force. And, of course, you know my grandfather. We are White Rabbit Investigations."

Dunkell looks at each of them in turn, before turning back to Connor demanding, "Hmm, IT eh? Well don't let me catch you skating on my concourse again. Got it?"

"No sir," Connor replies respectfully.

"Well, this looks all very impressive on the surface, but what's behind these sheets of paper?" Dunkell steps over to one of the corkboards.

Devon intercepts him placing a hand firmly on the

sheet of paper, "Sorry Mr Dunkell, but we can't compromise our ongoing investigation, I'm sure you can appreciate our client's privacy."

"Hmm, I suppose so," Dunkell grunts, "So you're another war hero, eh?" He turns to Tom. "So, what 'investigation' are you working on?"

"We have to protect our client's confidentiality of course, but we successfully handled a missing person case yesterday.

"Hmm, so this ground floor looks acceptable and complies with the commercial premises standards. But what about your squalid living area? Let's see that," Dunkell demands.

"Perhaps I'll show you around upstairs, eh Dunkell?" Koro replies and leads the way to the stairs.

"If you must, Yelich," Dunkell spits, "I can only imagine what fetid, sordid mess awaits."

Once they are out of earshot, Devon comments, "Geez he is hard work, but I promised Koro."

"I know right," Tom agrees, "Hey thanks Dani, your smile seems to works wonders with him."

"You know, I think underneath all that bluster is a very sad man," Dani intuits.

"What's his background, Tom?" Frankie asks.

"I have no idea, I've asked Koro countless times what his problem is, but he tells me to always mind my manners, and not be nosey."

"Koro has always asked me to be kind to him too," Devon adds.

"So Rangi knows. I'll see what I can find out over a couple of drinks," Frankie offers.

"Being the kind man that I am, I'll pop up and put the kettle on," Devon winks.

"No spitting in his cup!" Tom fires back as Devon slips up the stairs sporting his cheeky grin.

Connor slides back into his chair and gets back to work on the manifest.

"Hey Tom, the camera covering the Iranian Embassy is up the road isn't it?" Frankie queries.

"Yeah, right up the top by the intersection, why?"

"Well, what if he took a taxi? Or another car we don't have the rego number for? We'd miss him entirely, wouldn't we?" Frankie theorises.

"Damn, you're right," Tom groans.

"But we have the super computer covered, right? And that's the target," Dani reminds them.

"Whoa, apart from this," Connor pipes up, "I've just got into the manifest details. Check this out."

Dani races over, "What, where?"

Connor points at the screen. Tom leans over his other shoulder, "Oh Geez-us!" The pieces of the puzzle start to fall into place, but are interrupted by three men descending the stairs, led by Devon with the tea tray.

"You know that's a health and safety hazard Yelich?" Dunkell mutters.

"What's a hazard?" Koro asks, almost drowned out by the front door buzzer.

"I'll get that," Dani races through to reception.

"Having to walk up and down these stairs with a hot pot of tea, what if he fell over eh? Bloody third degree burns on top of a broken neck, a bloody big hazard," Dunkell explains a hint of pain in his voice.

"You know what Dunkell, you're right," Koro replies gently.

Frankie walks over and suggests, "Mr Dunkell, Would you approve of a small kitchen bench sink, maybe under the stairs? That would solve that hazard, wouldn't it?"

Looking a bit unhappy, Dunkell agrees, "Hmm, yes you could get away with that, I do have the contractors on call. I thought I might have had you then Yelich."

"We have a visitor bearing gifts!" Dani announces.

"Good morning everyone," Dorothy declares, "I've brought you some scones to make up for the ones you missed out on yesterday."

"Isn't she sweet?" Dani asks as the warm smell of the scones fills the office.

Dunkell takes a sharp intake of breath, before moaning, "Not scones on top of the stairs..." His legs go jelly like and he starts to collapse.

Koro grabs him quickly and supports Dunkell to a chair, "It's okay Cyril. Take a deep breath."

Sobbing, Dunkell fishes a handkerchief from his pocket, "S-she made... the best scones before..."

Koro pulls a chair up beside Dunkell. "I know she did Cyril," he consoles him. Margaret was one of a kind."

Devon mouths to Tom, 'Who's Margaret?'

Tom shrugs his shoulders, and turns to a stunned Dorothy, "Thank you for the scones, Dorothy, ah... I'm not sure..."

Koro pipes up, as he pats Dunkell on the back, "Dorothy, they will be perfect. Devon pour the tea, Dani would you be a dear and pop up and get some butter and jam from the fridge. Connor can you please bring some plates."

Emerging from his misery, Dunkell weeps. "I don't think that's a good idea Rangi. She fell..."

"Cyril, I know how Margaret... look, grief is damn hard, and you know I've been where you've been. Some wounds never heal and others take a hell of a long time, but perhaps we can start by helping to celebrate Margaret's talents, eh?" Koro replies compassionately.

Blowing his nose, Dunkell looks into Koro's eyes and sees only kind-hearted empathy, "Maybe you're right, Rangi."

\*\*\*

"I feel like I'm climbing the walls in here, Rangi," Frankie states, the tension in the room palpable, radiating from everyone as they try to be useful.

"Dev, better contact George and see if he can get in for an update," Tom advises.

"Tom, how about Rangi and I drive out to Miramar now and scout around," Frankie proposes. "Maybe we can drive past the Iranian Embassy on the way?"

"Good idea. Dani can you please go and get another car, just in case we need you and Connor," Tom instructs.

"My Dude! Now you're talking!" Connor is excited.

"Keep us in the loop," Frankie remarks as he and Koro take their coats and head for the door.

Dani saunters over to Devon and clicks her fingers, "Credit card please."

Devon takes his wallet out of his jeans' back pocket. He grins as he extracts the card and hands it over. His call connecting, he discloses, "George, Tom wants a word."

Taking the phone from Devon, Tom starts, "George can you get in for a briefing? We have some new Intel... Okay... ah huh... Okay, I'll write that down." Tom grabs a pen from the desk and writes on his hand, "Go ahead... Roger that." Tom ends the call and waves to Dani as she leaves.

"Is he going to make it?" Devon asks.

"No, he's still got a couple of agency goons on his tail," Tom transfers the number on his hand to the white board, "Okay, listen up, this is the number for the SIS team that is on call for us, the code word is 'Trekka' and their response should be 'Skoda'. Got it?"

"Why are you writing it down?" Connor asks.

"Because, you might have to step in Connor, especially if we are tied up and can't talk, I'll text you to make that call, got it?" Tom coaches.

Swallowing hard, Connor's voice rises to a question, "Ah, roger that?"

"Good. Now get that laptop ready in case you go mobile with Dani."

"Come on, brother. Let's get out to Miramar too," Devon encourages.

"Yeah, I've got itchy feet too, let's go," Tom snatches his crutch and jacket.

*** 

The Subaru hums along Cobham Drive, Tom's attention wanders to the three multi-coloured towers of cubes, slowly rotating on their axis helped by the near-constant breeze coming from nearby Cook Strait. His reverie is broken by the sound of his phone. He swipes the screen and taps the speaker icon, "Hey Koro."

"Talk about timing, boy. We were driving past the embassy and saw the Iranian spy in a green Nissan car leaving at the same time, so we're following at a distance," Koro updates them.

"No wonder we haven't picked up his movements," Tom replies, "Good work, let me know any news."

"Will do boy," Koro excitedly acknowledges, then

quieter, "How do you turn this off again Frankie?"

Tom ends the call smiling, "He swore he'd never own a mobile phone."

"He's picking it up well," Devon replies, then adds, "Poor old Dunkell, eh?"

"I know right," Tom shakes his head, "I never saw that coming. He's always been such a prick."

"Grief plays out differently for some people," Devon is wistful.

Suspecting something has subtly perturbed his friend's normally rock-solid sense of calm, Tom probes, "Are you thinking of something similar, bro?"

Devon thinks of an answer, "It's…"

Tom's ringing phone interrupts the conversation, "Connor?"

"The shit's hit the fan!" Connor yells.

"What shit? Slow down," Tom focuses on the urgent tone in Connor's voice.

"The fire alarm has gone off at Weta Digital, and Ray is in the storage room. It looks like he's heading outside to the container!" Connor's excitement is contagious.

Devon accelerates around the roundabout, bypassing the airport traffic heading for Miramar.

"Okay, take a breath and tell me what's happened," Tom instructs.

Dani interrupts, "Hey Tom, I've just got off the phone with Marty. He said both Ray and Theo are missing from the head count, but there are still people coming out from the buildings."

"Yeah, I noticed a stack of people running around inside as they passed one of the cameras, and I checked that both Ray and Theo arrived at work at their normal time," Connor relays.

"A fire alarm is a great distraction. They are clearly making their move, okay. I'll call for back up," Tom decides.

"Do you want us to head out too?" Dani asks.

"Not yet, but get ready. You might have to back up Frankie and Koro. Is the microphone working on the camera outside the container?" Tom asks as he ends the call.

Connor replies, "Why?"

"I've had an idea for the backup team. I'll let them know."

The Subaru's tyres screech as Devon corners the roundabout into Tauhinu Road.

Dialling the number on the back of his hand, he only has to wait for one ring before the call connects, "Trekka" Tom starts.

"Skoda," comes the deep bass reply.

"Great, are you near Miramar?" Tom asks.

"We're in Byron Street watching the flat," the baritone voice answers.

Tom fills them in with the information and they speed onwards to their destination.

*** 

The battered blue container truck backs down the alleyway behind Weta Workshops. Ray swipes the access card through the lock receptacle and swings the yard gate open, signalling to guide the driver into the best position.

Leaping from his cab, the dark-skinned driver grunts at Ray and manipulates the remote control in his hands, expertly lining up the hydraulic arms and bracing feet, in less than two minutes. Then releasing the chains from the overhead arm, he efficiently hooks the chains onto the base of the container and activating the remote, lifts the container swiftly onto the truck bed. Then withdrawing the hydraulic feet and locking the container in place, the driver waves to Ray and jumps back into the truck cab. The entire operation taking less than five minutes.

Theo runs out of the back door with his back pack, yelling, "Hey, when do we get paid?"

"The money is with your tickets at the airport information desk," the man replies in a thick Persian accent, then reverses out the way he came.

Ray joins Theo and they walk back to the rear door of the storage warehouse, "So what happens now?"

"We head home for our bags and get to the airport, come on Ray, move it!" Theo orders.

***

The Alfa Romeo idles into the carpark and Frankie manoeuvres it in beside the Subaru, the passenger door springs open and Koro climbs out greeting the team, "Kia ora kōtou, good we're all here."

"Where's the Iranian?" Devon asks.

"He parked on Ballance Street and started walking towards the wharf," Frankie replies as he locks his car.

"Good, then it's definitely going down soon. Are we ready team?" Tom asks encouragingly.

"Koro are you sure these Hi-Viz vests and helmets will be enough to get in?" Dani asks, handing a set to both Koro and Frankie.

"Hamish said we would fit in well. We'd better get a wriggle on." Koro starts walking towards the pedestrian crossing.

"You heard the man," Tom affirms and obediently follows his grandfather.

Connor scoops his laptop from the bonnet of the Subaru and stows it into his shoulder bag. Devon taps a quick text and joins the rest of the group.

"So how does it feel to be out in the field Connor?" Dani asks as they cross Waterloo Quay.

"This undercover stuff is just so rad," Connor nods trying to be serious.

Smiling, Tom notices a slightly stooped old man with wild long grey hair waving in the breeze, emerge from the Portacabin planted by the gated port entrance.

"Kia ora Hamish," Koro hails as the two men meet at the side gate, vigorously shaking hands.

"Rangi, you old bastard, you'll owe me a few drams tonight," Hamish replies, then turns and addresses the group, "Okay you lot. If anyone asks, you're all middle management and trainees doing a snap Health and Safety inspection. I can get you close to a small shed by the Greek ship and there's a Portacabin near the American ship, and here's a bunch of 'Visitor' badges for your Hi-Viz, now follow me."

The team pin the badges on their Hi-Viz vests and follow the grizzled old Scotsman to the back of the Portacabin. He points to two oversized yellow golf carts, "They're easy to drive, jump in."

Devon takes the driver's seat of the rear cart, Tom decides, "Connor you're with us, Dani can you go with Koro and Frankie please."

Hamish takes off at speed and Devon follows the lead cart as it tears off through the truck park, heading for the container yard.

Weaving their way around a large fork hoist, Tom

shudders as he remembers his doctor's reference to an old patient getting run over by a fork hoist, crushing his legs, but recovering to run a marathon. He thinks to himself, 'I guess I'm doing okay.' Focussing back on the task in hand, he leans over his seat to Connor, "Now don't play at being a hero okay? We don't know if these guys are armed or not."

Gulping a breath of air, Connor replies seriously, "I've got butterflies, dude."

Smiling, Tom offers kindly, "So have I. It's normal Connor. Listen to your gut. It's our caveman instincts keeping us safe."

Tom's phone goes, he taps his ear bud, "Hi George, yeah we're getting into position... That's good news... Thanks."

A fork hoist suddenly backs out from a row of containers narrowly missing Hamish's cart, Devon slams on the brake pedal and swerves to miss the lumbering giant.

The driver angrily yells out at Devon, "What are you fuckwits doing here?"

Tom waves a clipboard. "Health and Safety audit. What's your name?"

"Ah piss off! I've got real work to do!" The driver drives quickly back into the row of containers.

"Wow, it worked!" Connor comments disbelievingly.

Devon floors the accelerator and slowly gains on Hamish who abruptly turns left between a row of containers, "Hang onto your hats," Devon warns as he corners at speed and closes the distance.

"I hope we don't have another fork hoist show up," Connor worries.

Hamish slows and turns right then stops by a container next to a small shed. Devon pulls up alongside the lead cart. Hamish points, "There's your shed where you can monitor the Greek ship. Who's going there?"

"We will," Tom dismounts from the cart with his crutch supporting him.

"Well, that cart is going to stick out like dog's balls," Hamish states.

"I'll drive it," Frankie offers getting out of his rear seat.

"Good." Hamish says. "It won't look out of place at the next Portacabin."

"Thanks Hamish." Tom looks around the area, noting the distance to the Greek ship. Containers were being loaded and moved around by straddle carriers and gantry cranes.

Devon and Connor grab their shoulder bags and move towards the shed as the carts drive off.

Connor peers inside. "It's a bit sus, dude."

Devon walks in. "What are you complaining about, bro. It's a palace."

Tom enters the gloomy space, cobwebs thick in the corners and roof space. Four filthy white plastic chairs surround a table constructed of two forty-four gallon drums and a splintered sheet of plywood, with dark coffee cup ring stains.

"Excellent. You've got a table to work from Connor. Get set up."

Devon wipes some cobwebs from the small window facing the ship, and pulls a small pair of powerful binoculars from his shoulder bag. "A good view from here. What did George say?"

Tom steps up beside Devon and peers through the cobwebs. "He said he finally shook off Kendrick's guys and has linked up with the SIS team. They will be moving into position soon."

"Okay, I've got the map up. It looks like the others are stationary by the Portacabin. What do we do now?" Connor asks from the makeshift table.

Smiling Devon turns and explains, "We call this 'hurry up and wait' in the army, remember?"

"Oh, right," Connor recalls.

Tom's phone buzzes. He answers it. "Yes? Okay, good… so where's Darryl? Got it."

"Wassup?" Devon asks.

"The others are in place and have a good view of the American containers. And Darryl is driving a green Straddle carrier."

"Touch wood," Devon taps the wall framing timber, "It's all going according to plan."

"Famous last words!" Tom adds sceptically.

\*\*\*

Sipping his coffee, George savours the bitter sweet flavour of a local roaster. He surveys the area looking for his targets. Smiling slightly he notes his men's positions, surreptitiously stationed at random spots near the information desk.

Nearly choking on his coffee at the sight of the garish yellow and green Hawaiian shirt Theo is wearing, George coughs slightly and then drains his brew. He watches both men approach the information desk, dragging a wheeled suitcase behind each of them.

He places his cup on the saucer, stands and walks casually to the counter. He nods to two of his men to close in.

Ray is showing his driver's license. "I believe you

have our tickets and maybe an envelope in our names Ray Donald and Theo Scott?"

The grey-haired kiosk attendant responds, "Just a moment… Ah, here it is." She pulls out a large white A5 envelope and hands it to Ray, smiling, "Have a nice trip."

"We will now," Ray turns to leave.

"Ray Donald and Theo Scott, can you please accompany us," George interrupts, flashing them his warrant card as two of his men each take one of their arms.

"Wait! What? Who are…" Ray splutters.

"New Zealand SIS. You are both under arrest for espionage," George explains quietly, pointing to the exit, "This way. We have a car waiting."

"Oh no, nothing ever goes our way," Theo moans despondently dragging his heels towards the exit.

\*\*\*

The sun beats down mercilessly on the shed's tin roof, stifling heat radiating downwards causing the occupants to perspire freely.

Tom's phone chirps, swiping the message screen open, he dashes a bead of sweat from his eye and reads aloud, "From Dani, Darryl has left his crane, looks like he's taking a break."

"So, we could be here a while then?" Connor asks.

"More than likely mate," Devon replies wistfully.

Wiping the moisture from his brow, Connor comments, "Sure is hot. I wish I'd bought a drink."

"Well as they say, you can't beat Wellington on a fine day," Tom quips.

Devon groans as Connor looks at Tom with confusion.

The roar of the container crane has become a consistent

background noise, along with the metallic clatter of the chains tensioning around the containers as the Greek ship is being loaded.

"Incoming," Tom comments. He points out a dark blue container truck carrying a red container. It drives into view and parks near the loading area in front of them.

"Amazing that wreck of a truck can still get a warrant of fitness," Devon comments. "Damn, I can't see the driver... Tom, what do you reckon?"

"Yeah, I reckon... we just need Darryl to turn up... What's this?"

A straddle carrier rumbles along the wharf. Clutched beneath it, a forty-foot almond-coloured container with a distinctive brown and yellow badge emblazoned on its side.

Devon looks through his binoculars. "Isn't UPS an American company?"

Connor taps a search engine query. "Yeah dude, United Parcel Service. Why? Oh, right! The manifest!"

Tom swipes open his phone and taps a contact, waiting for it to connect, "I bet that's the... George, I think we're go. Just need to sight the truck driver and the wharfie... Roger that."

A mix of fear and excitement crosses Connor's face, "What do we do now?"

Tom turns and puts a restraining hand on Connor's shoulder, "Chill dude. I need you to stay here and keep your head in the game, okay?"

Taking a deep breath, Connor replies a little uneasy, "Okay, I guess it's just like the other day."

"You got it my man. Now phone the others and ask them to confirm Darryl is there and if he isn't, to get here ASAP. Got it?"

"Got it," Connor answers, picking up his phone.

Surveying the scene with his binoculars, Devon adds, "And look who's stepping out of the passenger's door of the truck."

Tom takes a quick look outside and sees the Iranian agent walk to the front of the truck waving to the straddle carrier driver. He smiles and taps a number on his phone, "Trekka... Good... yes, confirmed, all go!"

"How do you want to play this, brother?" Devon asks.

Picking up his clipboard and putting his white hard hat on, Tom grins, "I believe I can see some Health and Safety non-compliance out there, can't you bro?"

Scooping his helmet up on to his head in one fluid movement, Devon laughs, "A major hazard if I ever saw one, brother."

\*\*\*

Dani bursts into the cafeteria, swinging the door open quickly, nearly hitting a surprised stevedore about to exit.

"So sorry, have you seen Darryl?" Dani apologises.

"Watch it miss. Darryl who?" The bearded man asks.

"Darryl Bigham, ah... what about Hamish?"

"Oh, Hamish is out the side, having a gasper," he points to the side door.

"Thanks," Dani races for the side door, scanning the room's occupants.

She steps outside, back into the bright sun and interrupts the social smokers' conversation, "Excuse me, Hamish, have you seen Darryl?"

"No, he's not due for a break for another hour," Hamish answers.

"Damn, I know I saw him leave his crane thingee

about fifteen minutes ago," Dani states.

One of the smokers laughs, "Did you hear that boys, crane thingee!"

"Darryl drives the green straddle carrier miss, unless…" Hamish thinks.

"He's pinched someone else's," Dani finishes, then urgently asserts, "We've got to get over to the shed!"

Hamish throws his cigarette on the ground and crushes it beneath his old abused work boots. "This way then Miss." He leads her out the side gate towards his cart.

\*\*\*

"I'm sorry Kendrick, but you can't move your teams portside just yet, or you will compromise one of our ongoing operations," Virginia explains.

"Now wait just a goddamn minute! You promised full cooperation Ma'am," Kendrick explodes his face beet red.

"On the proviso that you won't compromise…" Virginia patiently attempts to clarify, before being rudely cut off.

"I don't care what peewee little operation you may be running. There's an American vessel sitting at the port with sensitive cargo waiting for my team to escort it, and it's critical that I make sure it gets delivered safely and on time!"

"Oh, so you're a glorified courier driver now, are you Kendrick?" Virginia baits.

His face flushes an even deeper shade of red. "I'll have you know Ma'am, that particular package is an ultra-secret state of the art CIA spy satellite that is to be launched by your Space Agency! And I intend to make sure it gets there safely!"

"And just why wasn't our Government informed of this? You do realise that launching a spy satellite is illegal in New Zealand." Virginia asks coolly.

"It's on a strict need-to-know basis and my boss obviously didn't think you needed to know," Kendrick replies in a low tone.

"Under our Five Eyes agreement, this should have been disclosed to me so I could have informed our Prime Minister. He needs to know this!" Virginia objects.

"Well, consider yourself informed," Kendrick says through gritted teeth.

Glancing at her watch, Virginia asks, "Are we ever going to be able to work together like equals Kendrick? Or is your tactless bulldozer style just something I'm going to have to put up with?"

Taken aback at being called out, Kendrick smirks, "May I remind you that your country is a very junior member in our Intelligence partnership and we have long memories of you breaking up our ANZUS military alliance."

"Check your facts Kendrick, it was you Americans that abandoned the ANZUS agreement and shut us out," Virginia presses.

"We have the largest naval fleet in the world, and you Kiwis started chucking your weight around and had the audacity to question our nuclear status!" Kendrick snaps.

"Unlike your government, WE never quit our responsibilities in the South Pacific. And guess who's filled the vacuum since you left eh? Ensnaring our neighbours with debt entrapment, and guess who's been bailing them out eh?" Virginia asks rhetorically.

"We... we were fighting the war on Terrorism," Kendrick flounders.

"And our Special Forces have been fighting right alongside you, as you well know. And look how that's going for you...," Virginia counters, then sighing with resignation, "How soon before your men are ready?"

"They are lined up outside already. So as soon as I'm finished here," Kendrick replies soberly.

"You'll need an escort into the Port as it's a restricted area. I'll just make a couple of calls and will join you shortly," Virginia determines.

"Thank you Ma'am," Kendrick smiles like the cat who has got the cream.

***

Walking confidently across the asphalt surface toward the straddle carrier, Devon waves his hands above his head to attract the driver's attention. Tom joins in by exaggeratedly pointing to his clipboard.

The driver appears not to see them. He moves his vehicle towards the stacks of containers being loaded onto the Greek ship and lowering the almond coloured container before reversing out into the port area.

The driver moves towards the blue container truck. Tom notes that the driver is about to unload the red container. "Change of plan Dev. Head for the truck!"

Devon turns and walks briskly towards the truck. He keeps clear of the yellow monster as it drives past them. He waves his arms at the crane driver. It is Darryl driving.

Pointedly ignoring them, Darryl lines up to collect the red container as the Iranians unload their truck.

Tom races towards the truck. He stretches his gait with the crutch to try and keep up with Devon. "Go ahead Dev, we've got to stop that truck from leaving!"

Catching a glimpse of a flashing orange light out of the corner of his eye. Tom sees Hamish and Dani speeding between two rows of containers towards them. Dani is pointing and yelling, "Stop the truck!"

Hamish nods steering toward the vehicles, while Dani points with one hand. She grips the safety bar in front of her with the other hand.

The Iranian truck driver panics. He fumbles with the remote, and the container stops halfway. It swings wildly as the driver hesitates. Should he carry on, or put the container back on the truck? His companion gesticulates and fires a rapid stream of Dari at him.

Devon reaches the truck first, yelling, "Hold it, Health and Safety!"

Hamish and Dani arrive next. They pull the cart up in front of the truck. "Do you need any help?" Dani asks.

The Iranian agent, reaches inside his jacket. He pulls a pistol out and points it at Devon, "You! Move away!"

Devon raises his hands. "All right, all right! Guns are against the Health and Safety..."

"Shut up!" the Iranian agent yells.

The truck driver finishes unloading the container and signals to Darryl. Slowly the Straddle carrier moves over the red container.

"You!" The Iranian agent demands of Hamish, "Move your cart away."

"Do it please Hamish." Devon instructs. "Don't make any sudden moves."

Darryl is now over his target. He lowers the lifting assembly onto the red container.

Obscured by the crane, Tom watches the machine. He makes his way to the side and edges along the outside of the wheels. Towards the centre, there is a set of steps and a cover panel.

Hamish drives forward out of the truck's way. "Stay real calm guys," Devon says. "This guy is a bit upset."

"You! Shut up I said!" The Iranian shouts, then he speaks in Dari to the truck driver.

Darryl engages the telescopic spreader to lock the container into the lifting assembly.

Unseen, Tom pulls the cover panel open. Inside, is a mass of hydraulic hosing. 'Here goes nothing,' he thinks. He pulls on the hoses ineffectually. No damage done. He leans back and jams his crutch in amongst the hoses. Leveraging against the side of the case, he pushes hard. Some of the hoses prise loose, and Tom sprays the front of his Hi-Viz with hot hydraulic fluid.

The Iranian agent moves to the passenger's door. With his gun still pointed at Devon, he climbs into the truck. The driver starts the engine and waits for the Straddle carrier.

Darryl lifts the red container. He drives forward and turns towards the Greek ship, leaving a trail of hydraulic fluid behind him.

The blue truck is making a turn, when three white SUV's appear. Two pull up in front of the truck, the other pulls in behind it. Men in black, wearing body armour and wielding assault rifles, leap from the running boards of the vehicles. They surround the truck. George emerges from the passenger's door with a loud hailer, "Drop your weapons and give yourselves up." Then he repeats the message in Dari.

The Iranian agent puts the pistol on the windscreen's dash. He raises his hands. "Don't shoot, we have diplomatic immunity!"

Frankie and Koro pull up next to an oil-stained Tom. "You alright? Need a lift boy?" Koro asks.

"I'm okay, that oil was hot, but we need to get Darryl."
Tom climbs into the rear seat of the cart with his mangled
crutch.

The straddle carrier is getting closer to the Greek
ship's containers. Suddenly, the left-hand wheels seize.
The crane lurches over to the left. It is threatening to tip
over. Darryl tries in vain to move it before abandoning the
cab. He starts to scramble down the access ladder.

Frankie speeds towards the stranded beast. He pulls
up alongside Darryl as he leaps from the crane. Darryl runs
towards a stack of containers. "Going somewhere Darryl?"
Koro asks.

Tom leans forward and jams his crutch between
Darryl's legs causing him to trip and keel over headfirst
onto the asphalt.

"Maybe not."

***

The police cars' red and blue flashing lights reflect
off the shaded mirror windows of the black Chevy SUV's.
There are five of them and one large empty container
truck. Burly dark-suited men with crew-cut hair and dark
sunglasses search around the containers stacked next to the
American container ship.

A short port official in a Hi-Viz jacket is remonstrating,
"I don't care who the hell you are, you and your men must
wear safety hard hats and Hi-Viz jackets, if they are in the
Port area!"

"I don't give a goddamn rat's arse about your health
and safety mister. Just where the hell is my container?!"
Kendrick spits in the port official's face.

Calmly pulling on her Hi-Viz vest and nodding

thanks to her aide, Virginia strolls over. She interrupts the confrontation, flashing her warrant card. "Excuse me sir, I will ask our American friends to comply with your request. However, can you explain where the container in question actually is?"

Hearing her soothing authoritative voice, the port official calms down. "Well Miss, as I was about to say. We had one of our men disappear with another man's Straddle carrier and I've tracked him to here. But... well... both him and one of the American containers are gone."

"Gone! GONE!" Kendrick fumes. "Just what in the Sam Hill kind of operation are you running here? Containers don't just disappear!"

Two police officers walk over to the growing group. Virginia intervenes, "Now can we all discuss this like mature adults? Or do I have to insist you leave the Port Kendrick and leave the grown-ups to tidy up your mess?"

"I didn't lose a valuable container..." Kendrick protests.

A yellow cart pulls up beside the arguing group. Its orange flashing light adds to the colourful lights dancing over the assembled vehicle's windscreens.

"Need some help?" George asks, as he steps out of the cart.

"And just what the hell are you doing here?" Kendrick demands.

"Kendrick, settle!" Virginia commands, then turning to George, "How did your operation go Captain Gillies?"

"Successfully Ma'am," George replies, unconsciously bringing himself to attention, "I'll have to head off shortly to debrief the team."

"I might have known you'd have something to do with this Gillies," Kendrick spits.

"I'm warning you, Kendrick. Now call your men back," Virginia cautions. She turns back to George, "Captain, can you shed any light on Kendrick's missing container?"

"We caught it before it was loaded onto a foreign vessel," George explains.

"A foreign ship?" Kendrick pales, picturing the end of his career, "Where is it now?"

A large yellow straddle carrier rumbles into view from behind a stack of containers, an almond UPS branded container hugged tightly in its clutches. "Here it is. I know where I'd like to stick it… but would you like it loaded on to your truck Kendrick?" George asks.

\*\*\*

Leaning back against the wall, one arm resting on top of the filing cabinet, Tom is finding a renewed strength in his leg. He evaluates his odd-ball team as they laugh and joke amongst themselves.

Devon sidles up, "I'd have loved to have seen the look on Kendrick's face when George and Hamish showed up with his container. What a picture!"

"I know right!" Tom laughs, "How red do you think his face went?"

"Oh, as bright as…" Devon's reply is cut off by the front door buzzer.

Dani glances at the big screen, then races to get the door, breathlessly she trips over her words, "Unc… erm, George, come in, come in."

"Thanks Dani." George walks through into the office with his trademark attaché case. "Kia ora tatou! Hey, well done everyone! Top effort!"

"Hey George!" Devon calls out cheekily, "How was Kendrick?"

"A right picture! I swear he's going to have a heart attack one of these days if he doesn't stop getting so uptight." He takes a couple of bottles of sparkling wine from his briefcase and hands them to Devon. "Get these on ice Sergeant and we'll enjoy them after the debrief."

Devon looks at the labels approvingly. "The good stuff, eh? We must have done well."

"Your expenses account is going to take a hit tonight, George," Koro warns.

George laughs, "Hamish has already hinted that a few drams are in order Rangiwahia."

Connor puts his hand up like a school boy, nervously asking, "Ah, Mister Gillies, now we have caught the Iranian spy… Well… does that mean our jobs are over?"

Anticipation grips the room in silence as everyone looks closely at George.

"The Director General has instructed me to pass on her thanks and to enquire whether you are all up for another assignment? We want to know why the Americans are passing information to the French. Who's interested?"

Tom looks around the room, "No pressure guys, but if you're up for it, I'm keen."

"I'm in!" Connor bursts out.

"Me too! Dani adds, enthusiastically clapping her hands together under her chin.

"Well… it does keep me from moping about the house," Frankie hesitantly replies.

"Of course, I'm where you assign me sir, but I'd like to stay on," Devon answers.

George nods, "I'll speak to Robin," Looking around to a quiet Koro, "Rangiwahia?"

"Hmm, I suppose someone needs to keep an eye on these kids," Koro grunts gruffly, "Now what's this debrief thing all about?"

**The End**

*To be continued...*

# Characters

| | |
|---|---|
| Tom (Tāmati) Yelich | SAS Sniper (Medically Retired) |
| Koro (Rangiwahia) Yelich | Tom's Grandfather |
| Devon Matipo | SAS Sergeant, SIS Operative |
| Danielle Franklin | George's Niece |
| Connor O'Neill | IT/Hacker |
| Frankie (Francesco) Vettori | Detective Inspector (Retired) |
| Sheila Ellison | Rongoā Nurse |
| Taylor Leblanc | Gym Instructor |
| George Gillies | SAS Captain, SIS Case Officer |
| Virginia | SIS Director General |
| Robin | SIS Case Officer |
| General Frank Adams | US Commander Special Forces |
| Theodore Kendrick | CIA |
| Eitan Freidman | Mossad |
| Henri Chevalier | DGSE |
| Cyril Dunkell | Kiwirail Official |
| Bert | Kiwirail employee |
| Paul Harrop | Kiwirail Manager |
| Theo Scott | IT Contractor |
| Ray Donald | IT Contractor |
| Martin (Marty) Schofield | IT Manager, Weta Digital |
| Hamish MacRanald | Stevedore |
| Darryl Bigham | Stevedore |
| Dorothy Talbot | Scone Maker Extraordinaire |
| Megan Donovan | Veterans Affairs Case Officer |
| Ceit | V.A. receptionist |

| | |
|---|---|
| Dave | Security BS Ministry |
| Sally | Reception BS Ministry |
| Dr Peter Cleeland | GP |
| Dr Sandra Williams | Clinical Psychologist |
| Stefanos | Greek Embassy Official |
| Erasmos | Greek Ship Captain |
| Trang | Taxi Driver |

## Military Terms

| | |
|---|---|
| Clicks | Kilometres |
| CO | Commanding Officer |
| Comms | Military Communications |
| Dustoff | Helicopter Medical Evac. team |
| Helo insert | Helicopter insertion |
| Medevac | Medical Evacuation |
| Recon | Reconnaissance |
| SAS | Special Air Service (Special Forces) |
| Tango | Enemy |
| TARFU | Totally and Royally Fucked Up |
| Troop | SAS Squad of four soldiers |
| X-ray | Unknown Target |

# General Terms, Acronyms and Slang

| | |
|---|---|
| 401(k) | American pension account |
| ACC | Accident Compensation Corporation |
| BS | Bull Shit |
| Brummie | Person from Birmingham |
| Burned | When an agent is compromised |
| DG | Director General |
| PPE | Personal Protective Equipment |
| SIS | Secret Intelligence Service |
| Spook | Spy |
| VA | Veterans Affairs |

# Connor's Slang

| | |
|---|---|
| Anime | Japanese Animation (Comic, TV) |
| Cosplay | Dressing up as a character from a Book, Film, TV Show, Video Game |
| Crufty | Poorly built |
| Dank | Excellent |
| Extra | Over the top, exaggerating |
| Fire | Cool or Amazing |
| Rad | Radical |

| | |
|---|---|
| Root kit | The programmes a hacker uses to stay undetected |
| Skux | A Lady's Man |
| Spill the tea | What's the gossip |
| Zero day attack | Cyber-attack that exploits a programme vulnerability |

## Māori Dictionary

| | |
|---|---|
| Āe | Yes |
| Āe e hoa | Yes my friend |
| Aotearoa | New Zealand |
| Aroha mai | Apologies, sorry |
| Ata Mārie | Good Morning |
| E hoa | Friend |
| He toa taumata rau | Bravery has many resting places |
| Hīanga | Naughty, prankster |
| Hongi | To press noses in greeting |
| Kai karakia | Blessing for food |
| Kaimoana | Seafood |
| Karakia | Ritual chant or prayer |
| Kia ora | Welcome, Hi, Good health |
| Kia ora rā kōrua | Greetings, Hello: to two people |
| Kia ora kōtou | Hi to three or more people |
| Kia ora tatou | Hello everyone |
| Kia ora ehoa | Hello my friend |
| Kia tere | Hurry up |
| Kaumātua | Elders |
| Kōrero | Conversation, discussion, speech |
| Kuia | Female elder |

| | |
|---|---|
| Mana | Status, Prestige, Authority |
| Manaakitanga | Hospitality |
| Manuhiri | Guests |
| Marae | Formal: Courtyard |
| | Informal: Meeting house |
| Moko | Grandchild |
| Nau mai | Welcome |
| Pākehā | European, foreigner |
| Papatūānuku | Earth Mother, Wife of Rangi-nui |
| Rangatahi | Youth, younger generation |
| Rongoā | Traditional medicine |
| Tahi rā koe | Cheeky |
| Taihoa | Wait, later, Don't yet |
| Tangi | Funeral |
| Taonga | Treasure, property |
| Tauparapara | Incantation (type of Karakia) |
| Tēnā koe i tēnei ahiahi | Good afternoon (to one person) |
| Tēnā rawa atu koe | Thank you very much |
| Te Reo | Māori language |
| Tīpuna | Ancestors, grandparents |
| Tokotoko | Traditional carved walking stick |
| Tūrangawaewae | Home, place to stand |
| Wahine/Wāhine | Woman/Women |
| Whakawaiwai | Delicious, mouth watering |
| Whānau | Family |
| Whare | House |

# Acknowledgements

Amazing work from our wonderful copy-editor Joan Rosier-Jones, thanks for the insightful questions. This book wouldn't be the standard it is without your input.

Huge thanks also to Michael Harris for use of the magnificent cover photo, please check him out at michaelstevenharris.com

And a big thank you to the numerous other people who passed on their comments and suggestions that makes this work of fiction almost believable and loads of fun.

Awesome work from Mark Innes-Jones for his work on the cover and formatting tuition.

Thanks again to all the crew at Bach Doctor Press, keep leading the way, you do make a positive difference.

# About the Author

After assisting many other authors, Darin decided it was time for him to write his own stories and share his unique humour.

When he is not hunting down "out of print" books in charity shops and other odd places to add to his own extensive library, you can find Darin coaxing vegetables to grow, working out the best way to mix a cocktail or doting on a stray cat.

*Also available from the Bach Doctor Press:*

**Sharks With Lipstick**
Book 1 – Trinity Trilogy
Hinemura Ellison and Ted D Hughes

Freshly back from Europe with a new job, Samantha Svensson (Sven) reconnects with her old friends while managing a new role within the Big Super Ministry – where everyone is busy playing their own internal political games. After the HR Director ends up dead on the same train that Sven was on, suspicions abound, not least from the chief investigating police officer, Charlie Rogers, who happens to be her ex and is still incredibly damned hot! With Wellington still reeling after a recent big earthquake, Sven must use all her canny resourcefulness to clear her name and identify the killer within their midst.

Available via:
www.bachdoctorpress.com/books/sharks-with-lipstick

**Snakes In Suits**
Book 2 – Trinity Trilogy
Hinemura Ellison and Ted D Hughes

Freya returns to Wellington to restore her inheritance, 'Portobello', an Art Deco building in Petone, to her former glory. Only to find dubious dealings with various Snakes in Suits, Lawyers, Bankers, the Council and an unscrupulous property developer who will stop at nothing, even murder, to get what he wants - 'Portobello'.

Freya fights back with the help of her childhood friend Zac - who just happens to be drop dead gorgeous, and Simon her cute Bank manager who is also competing for her attention. Reuniting with her besties Sven and Clara, together they navigate their chaotic lives, a massive earthquake and help each other to find love and to solve the murders that plague them.

Available via:

www.bachdoctorpress.com/books/snakes-in-suits

## Scorpions In Stilettos

Book 3 – Trinity Trilogy

Hinemura Ellison and Ted D Hughes

Caught in a compromising position, Clara AKA Flat White, the classy, conservative career girl of the Trinity Trio, struggles as her carefully constructed life comes crashing down around her.

Juggling a complicated love life, a career, a domineering mother and her own demons from the past, may be just a little too much even for her.

How can Clara recover and navigate her way back?

The exciting finale for the Trinity Trio.

Available via:

www.bachdoctorpress.com/books/scorpions-in-stilettos

## Concealment
M.W. Innes-Jones

Our genes: will they be our hope or our undoing? Three centuries from now humanity has made its last stand – a city high in the Swiss Alps, a place of safety and security from a deadly past. This is the reality of Nathanial Paquette's life and it has been this way for the whole of his sheltered twenty-three years. But with a knock at the family's apartment door everything changes. Now he must face an uncertain future and unexpected truth – he is genetically altered, and what really matters is what lies hidden within his blood. Together with eleven others, Paquette finds not only does he have to navigate the competing agendas of the city's ruling council and a corrupt man of science, but survive the rigorous training he and his fellow recruits find themselves faced with. It's a world where friendships are forged, enemies are made, and death awaits – ever wanting to become everyone's new best friend.
Concealment – book one of a six part series which follows Nathanial and his fellow internees through a world of deception and lies. Where the dark underbelly of power and science meet, threatening at every turn.

Available via:
www.bachdoctorpress.com/books/concealment


## Revelation
M.W. Innes-Jones

Nathanial and those left of the original twelve may have made it to the end of phase one of their training, but will they all make it to the start of the second, let alone finish it? Book Two, the chess board becomes deadlier; Professor Redmond sharpens his game and the council's fractious nature starts to unravel. Against this, Nathanial must act to survive Chris' retribution while treading carefully not to become a statistic for the mystery informant who is killing the remaining eight, one by one. And what has this all to do with the cryptic question Commander Reed gave Nathanial to figure out? In the end the real question is; of those who are left standing, which side will they be on? Revelation is where lines are drawn, death knocks, and deception awaits to strike from the most unlikely of places.

Book Two in M.W. Innes-Jones' sweeping epic six book saga, the Engelberg Records, set in the Swiss Alps, which follows Nathanial and his friends fight for survival.

Available via:
www.bachdoctorpress.com/books/revelation

### The Dark Side of Paradise
Anna Winton

The devastating telephone call in the night, leaves Catherine reeling at the news of her beloved sister's suspicious death in Samoa. Searching her sister's belongings and her memory for clues to the events that lead up to the tragedy, Catherine uncovers a sinister plot, and with the help of David Harris, the New Zealand police detective, will they uncover the truth?

Available via:
www.bachdoctorpress.com/books/the-dark-side-of-paradise

**Fabulous Faerie Folk – Discovering a Hidden World**
Virginia Innes-Jones

This uniquely illustrated collection of Faerie Folk stories for children and adults, will inspire and transport you into other parallel worlds. As they say you CAN have the best of both worlds!
The secret is 'to be' and to live in the now to enjoy and capture a slice of this uplifting and captivating other world allowing this to live on inside of you.
So come with me and travel to this world that lies so very close to you and within us all.

Available via:
www.bachdoctorpress.com/books/fabulous-faerie-folk-discovering-a-hidden-world

Check out more information about our authors and their latest projects at:
www.bachdoctorpress.com